The Claiming:
Book Three of
The Circle of Ceridwen Saga

Also by Octavia Randolph

The Circle of Ceridwen

Ceridwen of Kilton

The Hall of Tyr

Tindr

Light, Descending

The Tale of Melkorka: A Novella

Ride: A Novella

The Claiming

Octavia Randolph

The Claiming is the third book in The Circle of Ceridwen Saga by Octavia Randolph

Copyright 2005 Octavia Randolph This print version 2014

ISBN 978-0-9854582-6-3

Pyewacket Press

Bookcover design: DesignForBooks.com

Photo credits: Viking Drakkar, iStockphoto©Isamass. Textures, graphics, photo manipulation, and map by Michael Rohani.

The Circle of Ceridwen Saga employs British spellings, alternate spellings, archaic words, and oftentimes unusual verb to subject placement. This is intentional. A Glossary of Terms will be found at the end of the novel.

For you

List of Characters

Ceridwen, a lady of Kilton in the Kingdom of Wessex

Godwin, Lord of Kilton

Sidroc, a Dane

Ælfwyn, a lady of Wessex, wed to Sidroc

The Saxon

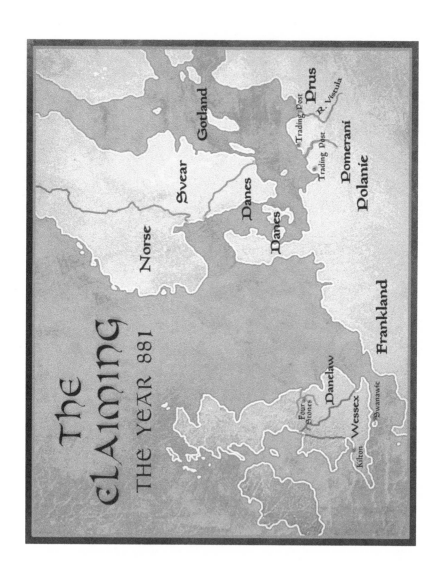

The CLAIMING

THE YEAR 881

Norse

Svear

Gorland

Danes

Danes

Trading Post

Prus

R. Vistula

Trading Post

Trading Post

Pomerani

Polanie

Frankland

Four Stones

Danelaw

Wessex

Kilton

Swanawic

Contents

The Claiming

The Claiming

Preface

There is peace now in the kingdom of Wessex, and a stay from the war and waste which too long ravaged our lands.

This is the Peace that our good Ælfred wrought with Guthrum, King of the Danes. Ælfred shared out the land of Angle-land, so that the Saxons kept some of it and the Danish warriors took and settled the kingdoms they had conquered.

At Kilton, my home for near these ten years, three Yules have passed since the battle at which so many of our folk fell to Danish iron. Burnt timber has been renewed, and the mark of spear and sword sanded away.

Yet our losses have been great, and tho' others have filled the empty spaces at the tables massed in the timber hall, the ghosts of those gone be ever amongst us. And the wheel of life, like the wheel of the year, has turned, exacting its toll, war or no.

I am a woman, my name is Ceridwen, and this Summer I shall have twenty-six years.

Chapter the First: Leavetaking

The Year 881

THE merchant ship to carry me to Four Stones lay at anchor off the spindly pier. I had travelled overland to Swanawic with my son Ceric to meet it, and the thegns were even now carrying aboard our hide packs and food baskets. I stood with Godwin as he eyed the ship.

"I do not trust him," Godwin said of a sudden, and I did not have to ask who it was he spoke of.

I took breath and said, "He has kept the Peace. Ælfwyn has written me about all the good works he has done in Lindisse; even to building up the nunnery at Oundle. He has been quick to adopt our ways and been just in all his dealings."

He did not answer any of this, but turned his gold-flecked eyes to me. "You must promise me that you will be - cautious with him," he asked.

I did not want to follow his path, and simply said, "I am Ælfwyn's guest, not his. It is her company, and comfort, I seek."

Ceric was just at my side and I did not want his uncle's unease to make him fearful of the Dane to whose stronghold we journeyed. I made a little gesture to him, and Godwin nodded.

The Claiming

"The ship to bring you back will be at Saltfleet on St Mary's Day," he said again, naming the point on the coast of Lindisse at which we would be picked up. This was a full three months, all the best of Summer, that Ceric and I would have with Ælfwyn at Four Stones. "Make sure you are there before the tide is full. I will have upon it as your escort these four thegns and a serving woman."

This was the final time he could repeat this to me, for the thegns had finished their lading and were even now approaching us. "I thank you, Godwin," I said. He looked from the thegns to me, and I added, "For everything. And for allowing me to go."

I had to say this, for he did not want me to make this trip, and yet let me do so, and even paid out of his own silver for my passage. He rode with me across Wessex to the sea port of Swanawic, bringing with him four of his best thegns and a serving woman, who would sail with me to Lindisse. Once there Ceric and I would be met by Ælfwyn's party, and the thegns and woman return by the same ship to Swanawic and the ride home to Kilton.

He gazed on me now and said, "Be well and strong. Take joy in your friend." He moved his hand as if to encircle my wrist, and stopped himself.

A tear was forming in my eye, and I blinked it away. I did not trust my words, and only nodded.

He looked down for a moment, and then back to my face. His voice was very low. "Do not concern yourself with other matters."

I nodded again, and he turned now to the saddle bag of his horse. He drew forth from it a carved scabbard that held an angled-bladed weapon with a silver wrapped hilt.

"Chirp," he said to Ceric, using the name he had given the boy as a babe. Ceric turned to him as he held out the shining weapon.

"You know what this is," Godwin asked of him.

Ceric nodded, his green eyes wide in his round face. "My father's seax."

"Yes, and it is the best in all Kilton, finer than my own. Now it is yours, and you must wear it with pride. One day you will be my pledged man, and offer the acts of this weapon to my service. For now I want you to stay alert, and obey your Lady Mother."

Godwin squatted down and undid the leathern belt that cinched Ceric's belly, and slid the scabbard upon it. Looking into the boy's eyes he buckled it around him. Ceric was speechless with awe, and finally looked up at me.

"This is a sacred trust, from the Lord of Kilton," I said to him quietly.

Ceric nodded in quick bobs of his coppery curls. He found words. "I thank you, my lord," he said in a wavering voice.

For answer his uncle grinned and tousled Ceric's hair.

It was time for us to take ship; the serving woman already aboard, the thegns waiting. Godwin lifted his arms and embraced me, his right arm strong against my back, the

4

left so light against my wool mantle that I scarce felt it. I turned my face from his, but his lips just brushed my cheek.

"Fare you well," I told him, and meant it truly; be well in everything.

"And you, Ceridwen," he breathed, and released me.

We had never before taken ship, but before we were even settled in the bow Ceric was racing up and down the broad deck, climbing over lashed chests and casks of goods, petting two great coursing hounds that were on board, prodding the rowing men with questions. One of the thegns finally pulled him aside and brought him to me as the rowers took their oars. Godwin sat upon his chestnut horse at the end of the pier, and lifted his hand to us, and we lifted ours in salute. Then the merchant-steersman called out, and the ship was heaved away from the pier by the burly men upon it, and the dry oars dipped into the dark May waters.

It was mid-day, and the steersman ordered the woven sail lifted to the freshening wind. The ship lurched when it was unfurled, and my belly followed. I sat down at once upon a bench near our piled possessions. The serving woman was busy on her hands and knees, ordering our bedding and food hampers, and the thegns had joined Ceric in the stern with the steersman and merchant whose ship it was.

I took deep breaths. Gyric and Godwin had taken me many times in the little sailing boats out into the swift channel that Kilton was built above, and the brothers had laughed at my weak belly but always obliged and taken me in when the water got too rough for me. But no pleasure sailing had I done for over a year, and now the ship I was in was owned by a wealthy merchant, eager to make his next landfall. I had hoped that the great size of the ship would mean that I would feel the sea's movement less strongly. In this I was wrong, for the deck rose and fell with every roll of the white-tipped waves. I could hear Ceric's delighted whooping, and saw him jump into the air to have the deck meet him half way down, and I closed my eyes and thought of the unmoving red rock upon which Kilton lay.

The ship would be coasting, which meant that each night it would land and we would camp on shore; and it was this thought which lent me the little comfort I could take that first day. To be sea-sick is an odd misery, for those about you can be as hale and strong as they are on land, and you so weak and wretched that nothing save dry land allay your suffering. I tried with all the force I could summon to stay strong, but my weakening belly weakened too my resolve; and before the afternoon was out I was clinging to the smooth railing with my fingernails as I retched over the side of it.

Githa the serving woman wiped my brow, and gave me fresh water to rinse out my mouth, and wrapped me warmly in a wool blanket. Tho' my head ached my belly was now empty, and I sat again and leant back upon our piled packs and closed my eyes.

I felt shamed to be sick, and more shame that no one else aboard was, tho' this infirmity I would wish on no one. Githa looked a bit green at times, and I feared she too would be sick, but she swallowed it back and was not. Once while I sat there drowsing I heard Ceric swoop near and call me, and as I opened my eyes Githa caught him around the waist and sent him back again to the thegns.

Before dusk we neared the land we had never left sight of, and the ship furled its single sail and dropped anchor. The rowing men left their oar well and some of them took up a small boat that lay upon the deck, and heaved it overboard. Into this we climbed down by a rope ladder. I almost thought I would not have strength for this, tho' a thegn go before me and behind to keep me from falling, and only the knowledge that land was but a few oar strokes away bid me go on.

On shore I was well again almost at once, and walked up and down the empty sandy beach in the fading Sun light. Ceric was full of high spirits, and when the merchant called him to run the hounds with him, left me at once to join the man. The thegns set up the sleeping tent in which Githa and I and Ceric would rest, and Githa laid and struck the fire for our meal. Beside the merchant and his rowing men there were four other men of Wessex aboard, one the reeve of Hamtun, taking ship as we were, and we clustered about our respective camps, with Ceric running between all three of them.

Githa boiled up a thick browis of barley and peas, flavoured with roast fowl, and we had still several flasks of Modwynn's fine ale from Kilton. Her face came before me as I sipped her ale, which neither her other daughter-in-law Edgyth nor I had ever been able to equal in our brewing, try as we might. I recalled that which Gyric had told me of his mother so long ago, when we travelled in danger from Four Stones to Kilton. "All she does, she does well," he said of Modwynn, and in my ten years at Kilton I had seen this myself, and loved her for it, as she loved me as daughter. She had blest my coming, and now blest too this journey I had

7

wished to make; and I knew her open heartedness to me to be one of the great gifts in my life. The Sun was set, and I thought of what she and Edgyth and little Edwin would be doing at Kilton, as I sat upon this sandy southern shore.

After we had supped I felt so weary that I knew I must soon sleep. I called Ceric to me, who was again playing with the coursing hounds, but he wanted to spread his sheepskin bed roll upon the sand alongside those of the thegns, and so I let him. The tent they had set for me was of linen, waxed against any damp; and upon the sandy floor were laid cow hides as ground cloths, and upon these sheepskins and linen sheets and soft woollen blankets from my own bed. I crawled inside even before Githa had finished her washing up, and pulled off my gown and felt the sand firm beneath me in gratitude.

We were up at dawn, and drank the broth that Githa had boiled the night before, and the thegns and Ceric ate too of wheaten loaves we had, but I did not for fear of soon losing them. We were rowed off to the waiting ship. A few of the merchant's men had spent their night aboard, and they steadied the rope ladder as I clambered up it, and hoisted me over the side for our day's journey.

I was sick again, but without the violence of the first day, for I had but little in me. Mostly I sat upon the bench, my back against the straked hull of the ship, and listened to the skirling sea birds as they called out in mockery, it seemed, to me. I was able to take a bit of bread, and a few gulps of water, and when I could I stood and looked across the blue seas to the green shores we skirted. We passed a burh, for I was standing then and saw its high timber buildings rising within its palisade walls, and would have asked one of the thegns which it was if I had felt steady enough to walk to them. Our

King Ælfred had done much in these three years of peace with the Danes to build up the defences of Wessex, lest that peace not hold; and this burh looked to me of timbers newly hewn.

Once we sighted a ship, coming the other way, a broad beamed merchant vessel such as our own, its creamy sail bulging with the weight of the wind as its keel ploughed up the foaming seas. The men aboard ours were watchful, tho' they hailed out cheerily their greeting, and I saw the merchant at the stern unlash a chest which might hold weapons; and saw too the fresh alertness of Godwin's thegns, who made haste to pull on their ring-shirts. Then they stood, their spears gathered before them, and placed their hands on the hilts of their ready swords. But the greeting was returned, and the other ship, so laden with bales of goods that it seemed hardly a deck plank remained uncovered, passed by and was soon lost to view.

When the Sun was lowering we headed in to land, and glided by wooded shores until we reached a settlement. This was the town of Limenemutha, for it was at the mouth of the River Limen, a place large enough to have its own pier at which the ship rowed to, and where we would spend this night. The day was a fine one, and there were still folk out and about who came and looked upon us as we walked down the wooden pier. It was a place of no great size, but the river mouth gave a harbour both sheltered and deep; and here the merchant had a store-house, in which we were welcomed to pass our night. Here too the reeve of Hamtun and his three men took their leave of us.

There was a washing shed behind the storehouse, with much fresh water to wash with, which I welcomed, tho' Ceric lamented the sight of it. We spent the night bedded down within the stout timber walls which sheltered the merchant's wares, and I knew some of the small casks near me held beeswax, as the sweet odour lulled me to sleep.

Set aside in a small room into which the merchant showed us next morning were tall pottery pots of wine from Frankland. One he unstoppered, and drew forth wine as red as thinned blood, and bid me taste from bronze cups. It was delicious, with a fragrance that swirled to the nose as I lifted my cup; and was both sweet and warm in the mouth. I readily parted with some silver to carry a pot of it to Four Stones with me as gift.

The weather stayed fair, and to my relief I was not sick the next day, nor the next, only queasy, and began to feel, as Githa had told me, that one could grow used to the sea and so overcome its sickness. But the fifth day the skies were grey and the winds high, and I was sicker than I had been the first. We camped that night upon a pebbled beach, and in the dark the rain lashed at my tent so that drops formed on the inside of the waxed linen, but we women were mostly free from wet. It was crowded in the little tent with the restless Ceric between us, and he was unhappy that the hounds had been left behind at Limenemutha, but at last we slept.

We awoke to the day of our arrival, and tho' it did not rain upon us the Sun was not as warm and bright as I had hoped, for the thegns, sleeping out as they had, were wet through. Githa went to work hotting broth as Ceric ran about upon the beach. I sat cross-legged in my linen shift upon my soft bedding, combing smooth my hair with my pear-wood comb, and tried to think which gown today to wear.

I pulled my smallest hide pack toward me. It was of leather dyed dark green, and upon its oiled surface I had with a small poker burnt designs of running plaits. Within were my two finest gowns, one of yellow silk, and one of green, both given me long ago by Ælfwyn; now gone unworn for over a year. I had brought them so I might honour her, and my visit to Four Stones, by wearing them; but chose today a wool gown of dark russet hue, for should I sicken on this last day's sailing I would rather be in wool than silk. But it was a fine gown, for not only did the russet colour rest well against my hair, but I had lavished many days of effort upon it, drawing in coloured thread-work patterns of linked spirals in brown and red.

We set out. The Sun struggled all morning to shine, without winning, but neither did more rain fall. We were coasting past East Anglia, a Kingdom now ruled by Danes, and ruled too by the chiefest of them all, for Guthrum they called their King. This whole side of Angle-land was now theirs, and as we headed North I stood and saw how the thegns of Godwin studied the shores we passed. With the great Peace signed between Ælfred and Guthrum sea travel was once again possible, for all merchant ships were to sail unimpeded from Kingdom to Kingdom. But the wariness of Kilton's thegns and the merchant-steersman, and of his rowing men at work at the oars, made me know that they feared sudden attack from renegade Danes who did not take this Peace as their own. Then too, other Danes ranged up and down along the coasts of Frankland, plundering what they could; and any of them could cross the Channel between lands and strike a merchant ship laden with fine goods.

But we saw no other ship, save a small fishing vessel, well ahead of us and sailing on. The shores looked a mix of marsh and forest, and a few times we spotted burhs with palisades high and strong; and I knew that these had once

11

been those of dead lords of Anglia, now taken by the Danes to be their own strongholds.

Ceric was quiet now; the unease of the thegns and soberness of the rowing men made him so. He came and sat by me and I wondered if Godwin had taken him aside and warned him against the man we were soon to meet. I could not hope he would have any memory of Ælfwyn; he had been a babe of less than two Summers when he had seen her. I put my arm about his shoulder and spoke anyway.

"I am thinking of how you and Ashild played together when her mother brought her to Kilton. She is just your age, and you two clung together and could not be parted."

He made a face, as boys of nine Summers will do when reminded of any affection they once bore for a girl.

I smiled and gave him a little squeeze. "And you know it was Ashild who brought us the Browny," I told him, for this tiny tortoiseshell cat was still a favourite with Ceric.

At this he nodded. "I recollect her," he said in a small voice.

"And Lady Ælfwyn has a son, too, a little younger than you, so you all can play together."

He nodded again, but the way he thrust out his lower lip told me he was fearful.

"I want my seax," he demanded of a sudden. He had been allowed these past two years to wear a small knife on his belt, but now I knew it was Gyric's weapon he called for.

"Of course," I told him, and pulled at the hide pack in which I had laid it for safekeeping. "It is yours."

He took it from my hands, and himself slid it upon his belt. It was so large on him to look almost a sword across his belly. Godwin had taken the precaution of wrapping a leathern cord about the guard, and tying it tightly around the scabbard, so the blade could not be drawn without stopping to untie it. He plucked at the cord now, but I stilled his hand.

"You know that is a Peace Band," I said. "Your Lord put it there. You must not untie it unless you feel yourself to be in true danger."

He gave a little sigh, and I added, "We are going as guests to the hall of another lord, and you must show him that the warriors of Kilton can keep the Peace."

He considered this, and thought on the fact that his mother numbered him amongst the warriors of that great burh, and nodded his head.

The morning went on, and the waves were flat enough that I did not sicken. Ceric went and stood by the thegns as they watched the green shores slipping by, and if they spoke of these lost Kingdoms to the boy I did not hear it. Githa had straightened up our hide packs and now sat with hands folded in her lap; she and the thegns would return tomorrow on this same ship and this I knew she welcomed.

When the Sun had just passed its highest point I knew we must be near, for the steersman turned his ship closer in. The shores of Lindisse were well-timbered, but we saw not one burh nor other settlement; it was an empty land upon this eastern coast. We passed a small cove, with a tall and rocky bluff ringed by shrubby growth fast by it, and rounding this came upon another cove, and the steersman cried out.

His hail was answered at once from shore, and our eyes were fixed on it as the rowing men oared in. Three or four buildings, all of timber newly cut, stood there, and a cluster of men at work upon the pebbly beach stopped in their labours and looked up at us. This was Saltfleet. A pier, half-built, rose from the lapping sea water, and around the men lay a store of fresh peeled timbers and piles of sawn planks. Further back, near the buildings, were groups of men awaiting the ship and its cargo with waggons and ox-pulled wains. In one of these groups were several horseman who clustered about a small horse-drawn waggon. These men were heavily armed, wearing in this time of Peace ring tunics on which the dull Sun shone, and carrying spears. One of them reined his horse forward, and I saw the animal to be a bay stallion, and the man upon it, Sidroc, Jarl of South Lindisse.

The sail was furled and wrapped, the oarsmen lifted their oars, and we came to rest in the shallow water. The merchant-steersman's voice rang out over our heads as the stone anchor dropped, and the small boat was heaved up from the deck and overboard. Ceric was at my side, one hand clutching at my skirt, the other upon the tied hilt of his seax. I bent down to him and kissed his round cheek. I smoothed my skirt and took a breath. We made our way to the merchant, standing by the stilled steering beam, and I thanked him for the safe passage he had given us. Then one of the thegns scaled the rail of the ship and another helped me grasp the hempen ladder. I climbed down into the little boat and Ceric scampered down the ladder after me, and the thegns lowered our hide packs and the big pot of wine. When the four of them were aboard the boatsmen took up oars and stroked the short distance to the narrow beach, running the boat ashore with a little plashing bump.

A thegn helped me out, and I took Ceric by the hand and walked towards the group of horseman. No woman sat on the waggon board or stood with them. I lifted my face and my eyes were met by Sidroc. He swung from his horse and walked to me.

"I will kill a piglet in thanks for your safe journeying," is what he said. His flint blue eyes were fastened upon me, and the scar upon his cheek, not quite covered by his dark beard, went crooked as he smiled.

Sudden water came into my eyes, and I blinked it away. Ceric was squeezing my hand, and I bent down and said, "Ceric, this is Jarl Sidroc, the Lord of this land. My friend."

Ceric knew what a friend was; knew this term was reserved for a person not kin who had earned one's utter trust, and who had proved himself deserving of the same. Playmates could be many, but friends were few, and this he had already learnt.

Sidroc looked down at him. "I recall you from your hall; tho' you have grown so much," he told Ceric in a mild tone. Sidroc turned back a moment to the group of horseman, and gestured with his hand. Upon the wrist glittered his silver disk bracelet. A child mounted upon a fat black pony came forward.

"This is my boy, Hrald," said Sidroc, and then looked to his son. "This is Ceric, a friend of the great warrior King Ælfred of Wessex."

Ceric's eyes, wide with his own wariness of this big man, now blinked in surprise. He looked at Hrald and added in his piping voice, "And the King is my god-father, too."

Hrald, straddling his fat pony, blinked his own surprise and grinned down at Ceric. He had his father's dark hair, but the little pointed chin spoke clearly of his mother Ælfwyn, and I laughed as I saw his eyebrows lift just as hers so often did.

"I am happy to meet you, Hrald," I told him, and my heart moved at the sweetness of his ready smile. He bobbed his head as his cheek coloured, and then looked back at his father.

"Hrald has brought you a horse to ride," Sidroc told Ceric, "or you can sit in the waggon." Hrald had turned his pony and now came back leading another, just as fat as his own, with a dappled grey coat.

At once Ceric's hand was out of my own as he moved towards the little beast. Tho' small for his age he was an expert rider, fearless and smart, and I saw nothing would please him more. He held out his hand at the grey pony's head, just as Worr, the young horse-thegn at Kilton, had taught him, so that the beast might sniff of him and learn his smell. He patted the shaggy neck, and with a grin reached up for the reins that Hrald offered.

Sidroc watched him swing up upon the saddle, and then turned back to me. "I have a mare for you," he offered, and gestured to a bay mare, much like my own, which was tied at the waggon board. "Or perhaps you wish to sit," he said, and lifted his hand to the waggon seat. The driver was a grizzled older man, a Dane from the look of him, who bobbed his head.

"I think I will choose the waggon," I told him, for in truth I did not know if I was fit enough to truly ride.

The thegns were just behind me, my packs in their arms. I turned to them. "I thank you for your fine service to me," I said, and the chiefest of them nodded. One of Sidroc's men had dismounted and stood at the rear of the small waggon, having unlaced the hide tarpaulin covering the cargo space. The thegns did not move, and Sidroc himself walked with the men to the back of the waggon. I watched them, eyeing each other, and the wordless way in which the thegns surrendered my goods. Sidroc's men still on horseback looked down upon all this, their fingers gripping their spears, but their faces unmoved. I walked to the waggon as the pot was lifted in.

"Frankish wine," I said, in what I hoped was a light tone.

Sidroc's smile grew across his face, and he nodded, but said nothing.

Across the beach the merchant was busy unlading his ship, and now stood with the well-dressed men who met him there, and I saw his rowing men carry aboard chests of goods these men had brought in their ox carts. I turned now to the thegns for my final Fare-well.

"Lady, we will return for you on St Mary's Day," said the chiefest of them, and tho' it was me he addressed it was Sidroc who his eyes held.

"You will see us," Sidroc answered, not taking his gaze from the thegn's.

"Yes," I added in a firm voice, that they would not doubt it. "I will be here."

We turned away from the men and Sidroc gave me a little boost onto the waggon seat. He swung upon the bay horse. He called out, and the driver snapped the reins and the waggon rolled forward as I lifted my hand a final time to the thegns.

Sidroc turned too to look back. "When the ship comes again the pier will be finished," he told me. I did not know he was building up this port, and thought of his wisdom in doing so to advance trade. And too, he would gain in riches, rightfully claiming tribute of landing rights of those merchants who put into shore there.

Now he looked ahead down the pounded road. "We will go for some hours, and stop tonight at Ælfwyn's nunnery. In the morning we will reach Four Stones."

"At Oundle?" I asked, tho' I jolted a bit at hearing him name it so, as if she herself were consecrated there. This was the foundation that ten years ago, finding herself widowed and with child, she wished to flee to.

"Yes, Oundle," he answered, and smiled down at me. "She wants you to see it, and would have come herself, but she is much occupied making all as she wants it for your visit." He kept looking at me so that I glanced a little away. He looked up the road. "Also Ælfwyn's mother is there now."

"So she has left the world, as she had wished," I answered. I thought some little time about this; she would not have taken the veil unless she knew Ælfwyn and her sisters to be well and truly fixed at Four Stones. Still, it must

18

be hard to lose a woman so skilled at the running of a hall as the old mistress of Cirenceaster would be.

Finally I spoke again. "Ælfwyn will have even more to occupy her then, without her mother's help."

"There is always much to do at a place like Four Stones. But her sister, and Jari's wife too, help her." His eyes swept the few trees about us. "Also in two days begins the gathering-time, what she calls the hall-moot; and so folk from all over my lands are coming to Four Stones, and she must provide for them too."

"I am sorry to come at such a busy time," I began. Hall-moots at Kilton were held once or sometimes twice a year, and were always times of strain, both of tempers and resources. Each shire lord served as judge, and all grievances brought between his people would he listen to and rule upon. Only those few cases he could not resolve were sent to the King.

He only laughed. "All times are busy," he said. "What is important is that you are here. Gathering-time is only worse because I know however I decide I will anger someone."

I nodded my understanding. Hrald and Ceric were jogging along before us, and I could see their heads turning as they rode side by side and spoke to each other.

"It was kind of you to bring that pony for Ceric," I said to Sidroc, seeing his eyes followed them too.

"It was Hrald who made it so; he asked that it be brought for him," Sidroc answered, and I was again moved by the sweetness of this child.

I looked over to the bay stallion that Sidroc rode. It was a big horse, well-muscled under the glossy red coat, and now showing a frost of white hairs on the dark muzzle. "That is your same bay," I recalled aloud.

He patted the thick arched neck. "Yes. I have many of his sons and daughters," and here his head tilted to the mare tied at the back of the waggon, "but he is still my favourite, tho' he grows older. As we all do," he added, stroking his own beard with a laugh.

In truth, Sidroc looked not a day changed from the last time I had stood before him, three years ago at Kilton. The single lock of grey at his left temple was no lighter, and he stood and moved with all the power of his thirty-three Summers. He was now, as then, richly dressed, and today wore a green linen tunic under his dark leathern one. Over this glinted a ring-shirt of linked steel. He wore dark wool leggings strapped with brown leather, and his weapon belt bore two blades, the larger a sword with a shining silver pommel wrapped with gold wire. Out of the tail of my eye I looked again at his belt. Instead of the straight knives favoured by the Danes, I saw he now carried a short angle-bladed seax, the weapon of my own people.

I wore no jewels, knew my cheek was pale, my eyes dull. The three years felt to be an hundred. I smoothed my skirt and looked ahead along the road. Meadow land was here, newly cut, for stumps of trees ready for Fall burning pocked the fresh green grass, and I thought that all this land, a full day's ride and more, was what Sidroc ruled.

It was hard for me to speak to him. I was weakened and shaky from the sail, but a weariness greater than this stilled my tongue. I was grateful for his ease in my silence as he walked his big horse steadily alongside the slow waggon. We rolled down the pounded clay road, and came upon a Cæsar's road, made of closely cut stone, and the waggon's iron rimmed wheels rang out against the grained rock.

We were not upon it long, which gladdened the boys upon their ponies, for we turned once again upon a clay road and they cantered ahead a little ways with the kinder smoothness of it under their mounts' small hooves.

Sidroc had not spoken for some time, his men behind him riding silent, the old Dane next me fixed upon the manes of his team. I think I closed my eyes and let the steady motion of the waggon lull me.

"Your letter came," Sidroc said, and I turned my face to him, "brought by a priest stopping at Oundle. He rode to Four Stones with it, gave it to Ælfwyn. Now that she reads she takes such things alone. I heard her scream, went to the treasure room and found her upon the floor, holding the parchment. She was sobbing and would not talk to me. I took it from her. I saw at the bottom the word that is your name; knew you had inked the letter and still lived. But she would not stop crying. I got the priest, and ordered him to read it to me."

His words were calm and slow, recalling all of this; and now as he finished he saw the tears streaking my cheek. He did not expect an answer, and only nodded at me, and I wiped my face and thought of the letter bearing the single line which Ælfwyn had sent in return: I implore you to bring your son and come to me.

Chapter the Second: The Telling

WE reached Oundle as dusk was falling. The convent was encircled by tall palisade walls of timber, and the gates were still open as we rolled in. Within was an oaken hall of good size, a barn for beasts, and the same outbuildings that any settlement will have, fowl-houses and grain stores and workman's sheds. Set to one side of the hall was a small timber church, marked by its wooden cross above the gable peak, and before this rose a half-built church of stone. Sidroc was already off his horse, and came to help me down from the waggon board. He saw my eyes rest upon the costly new building, and smiled.

"Ælfwyn's church," he told me, and looked at the rising walls of finely fitted stone. He lifted his hand. "It is all Ælfwyn's; she has spent much of her silver on these holy women."

When she had come to Lindisse to wed the Dane Yrling she had carried with her great stores of treasure as her dowry, and grown richer I knew beyond compare, from all the war booty Sidroc had won. Now she gave it away to honour her God, and from his tone I knew he grudged her none of it. She was very good, and he so good to her that I wished I might say such a thing, tho' I did not.

Serving folk had come forward in a familiar way to greet Sidroc and his men, and were taking off the horses for the night. From around one of the buildings came two women, dressed in the way of Benedictine nuns, in dark gowns and dark head wraps.

One was young, clearly in attendance on the older, a tall woman of mayhap forty Summers. She was solidly built, but moved with the quickness of a younger and much slighter woman. Her brow was broad and calm, her mouth and chin so firm as to be almost manly; but above that stern mouth sparkled eyes filled with warmth.

She stopped just before us, the fine ivory cross on her breast still moving against the dark wool.

Sidroc inclined his head to her, and she spoke.

"My lord," she smiled, and looked to me. "You are Lady Ceridwen, beloved of our patroness-sister Ælfwyn. I am Sigewif, abbess here. I welcome you to Oundle, and to God's love."

This was so simply said, and with a gesture of her large hands which seemed to press me to her, tho' she had scarce moved, that I was touched. Looking on her steady face I recalled in her the strength of Modwynn and Edgyth, and of every good woman who had ever suffered and then found strength to be kind.

"I thank you, Abbess Sigewif," I murmured.

Ceric and Hrald hung back behind us, and now she bent down and a smile creased her face. She extended her arms and Hrald came to her as if to his own mother, and she clasped him to her bosom and kissed the dark head. "And you have brought a brother with you," she smiled.

Hrald's eyebrows rose, and his lip twisted. "He is Ceric, not my brother," he answered.

"Indeed he is your brother, in our Saviour's eyes, and thus you must treat him so, for in God's love we are all brothers and sisters."

Hrald had heard this talk before; his face showed it, and now he nodded. Ceric made the little bow he had been taught to make with priests and nuns, and found himself swept up in the arms of the Abbess for a moment.

She straightened. "You will want washing, and ale, and food. All is ready for you, here in our hall," and led us to the oak door as if she be the lady of any burh in any Saxon kingdom.

We dined that night at the high table with the abbess, and tho' rich food and plenty filled the table, it was Sidroc and I and the boys and his men who partook of it, for Sigewif herself ate of the plainest fare, a browis of wheat meal and simmered dried pease. She took a single cup of ivy ale with us, smoky and bitter and full in the mouth, and laughed off my praises of it. Oundle now had fully a score of nuns, and as it was chartered a Double House by the bishop, a few men had begun to join, and Sigewif ruled them all. Most of the women consecrated here were young, with faces that shone with the ardency of their calling; but of the men, few were youthful, and as my eye travelled over their worn faces I thought most of them to have been once battle-weary thegns, seeking now in this time of Peace a greater peace still.

I slept in an alcove in the main hall, and was glad to see no fear in Ceric's face as Sigewif bid him join Hrald and the Danes for a night in the men's hall. The long ride on the mismatched ponies had shown Ceric and Hrald to be ready playmates, and they sported and jested with each other with ease.

The Claiming

I lay upon a feather bed, with linen sheets, and knew as I breathed in the scent of lavender that the sisters around me slept on straw, for after their softly muttered prayers I heard the crunch of straw matting that these women chose to bed upon.

We took broth and bread with Sigewif in the morning. Her hall was near empty, the nuns and brothers in her care long gone to their day's labours. After this she took the boys and me to the wooden church, across the yard in which Sidroc and his men were readying the horses. At the door stood a nun of middle years, with a narrow face and small rounded cheeks. Her bright eyes made her almost bird-like, as did the quick movements of her pointed chin. Her dark gown was of a fineness of wool that belied its plainness, and as she smiled at me I knew Ælfwyn's mother stood before me. She embraced me, but spoke not, and I knew she still lived under a vow of silence that all newly consecrated women took.

Sigewif smiled upon us both and bid me enter. The Abbess crossed herself as she stepped upon the plain plank floor within, and I lifted my hand to my brow, and saw the ready way in which Hrald and Ceric crossed themselves as they passed the threshold.

It was a simple timber building, but the table that served as altar was laid with a linen covering of exquisite fineness, and the candle holders upon that altar were of silver and held tapers of pure beeswax. To the left of the altar stood another table, and upon it was a wooden statue of Mary, Mother of God. It was brightly painted, as all statues are, but it was not the brilliance of her blue cloak nor yellow hair that caught my eye. About the statue's neck hung a necklace of gold disks linked together, and each disk was set with a gem stone of a different colour, and I gasped a quick breath when I saw it.

25

This was the necklace that Yrling had placed about Ælfwyn's neck ten years ago on the morning of her Hand-Fasting to him; for that was the wedding ceremony she had of her heathen lord and husband. I had stood next her in the wretched chamber that was our own at Four Stones, and watched as he draped her slender neck with this costly treasure, and I myself had wrapped their wrists together with a length of yarn that they might be joined as man and wife.

Sigewif came up beside me and said in a low voice, "Lady Ælfwyn has ever been generous to us," and the gentleness in her words made me know that it was a service to Ælfwyn that Oundle receive this treasure and relieve the Lady of Four Stones from the memory of a day she did not wish to recall.

We made our thanks to her, moved to the waiting horses, and went on our way. As we passed out of the gates I said to Sidroc, "What a fine lady, and a gracious one."

He nodded. "She is a strong woman. Kinswoman to the King of Anglia."

I was not surprised; even her name was a noble one, Sigewif, and bore the meaning 'Victory Woman'. So she was kin to Edmund, King of Anglia, killed more than twenty years ago by Danish invaders. Now she was in another land, Lindisse, ruled by another Dane, but these Earthly boundaries meant I knew, as naught to her.

The day was a fine one, warming as mid-May ought to, and we passed small trevs where cottars looked up at us as they toiled weeding their greening barley fields.

Sidroc had five warriors with him, and they were all so heavily armed that I began to wonder at this. Each man not only wore a ring tunic, but had strapped behind his saddle an iron helmet, and the men carried spears as well as swords. Within the waggon I had seen six round wood shields, their leather faces painted in bold paint, when my goods had been lifted in. Yet there was peace, and all this land Sidroc's own, and all upon it owed him fealty.

My eye rested on the dull metal chape at the tip of Sidroc's sword sheath. His own eyes scanned the fields around us, and I watched him. All warriors who lived beyond five-and-twenty years were wary, and still lived due to that wariness; yet in time of peace and on one's own lands even such as Godwin rode out armed only with his seax.

"Do you always ride so heavily armed through Lindisse?" I asked at last.

He glanced down at me. "When I ride with treasure, yes," he said.

He picked up nothing from the merchant's ship, accepted no casks or chests from the man. Then I knew.

"Of course," I said. "Hrald is with you."

He paused a moment. "Hrald knows what to do if we are set upon, that he must spur his horse and head for Four Stones, no matter what."

"O," was all I could say, realizing I was what he spoke of. I said no more.

The Claiming

We came to the banks of the Trent. I had once clung to a horse which swam this very river, fearful I might slip off and drown. I knew I must cross it again, and did not look forward to it. But tho' the banks be gently sloping and firm we did not urge the horses into the water, but turned South and went upon the grassy greensward.

"I have built a bridge; we are not far from it," Sidroc explained.

We went on some little way and came to it, a bridge of peeled timbers set upon stone footings. I marvelled at it. I had seen small bridges, spanning creeks and streams, but none to match the length nor breadth of this, upon which the horse waggon could be driven. Sidroc made the boys get off their ponies and walk them across, lest they startle; and indeed, all the men did this, and I too was glad to walk across the planked surface on my own two feet.

Once on the other side I recalled the first time I had seen Four Stones, sitting beside Ælfwyn in her waggon as we looked out upon the desolation wrought by the man she was to wed. Now instead of bleak February it was lush May, and birds sang out over our heads as we rolled past meadows upon which new-shorn sheep grazed. I looked long on these, knowing them to be Ælfwyn's flocks which she had laboured to build, and my heart was brimful with pride in her, and the faith she had always kept that she could make Lindisse good sheep country like her own home of Cirenceaster.

Now we could see beyond us on either side of the road a few crofts, well-tended, with trim plots of growing peas and beans, and a few folk moving about outside, who lifted their hands to their lord as he rode by. Some of these folk I could see were Danes, for the women wore gowns with paired shoulder clasps, and their hair wrapped up differently from ours; but some were clearly folk of Lindisse, the remains of the cottars of the lord Merewala, dead these twelve years by Yrling's hand.

We rounded a bend, cleared a line of whitethorn trees, and before us lay Four Stones. I could see the great hall rising behind the tall palisade wall, and see too the second hall, nearly as large, which Sidroc had built to house his many men. Through the open palisade gates folk were passing.

Outside the wall was a group of women dressed in bright gowns, and I blinked back tears to try to make out Ælfwyn as she stood there with her sisters. Then I saw her, in a pale blue gown, and she was moving towards me, and I was off the waggon seat and reaching for her arms. I vowed I would not weep, not at my welcome, in front of all, but my throat was clenched so tightly that when my name left her lips and I saw the tears in her own eyes, all I could do was sob.

She wept, and I wept in her arms, and I felt the arms of some other woman about us, and heard the husky voice of Burginde cooing and chiding at the same time; and Ælfwyn's childhood nurse led us away.

Ælfwyn guided me through the crowded yard through a low withy fence. Burginde was just behind us with Ceric and Hrald, and I heard her jesting ways with the boys, and heard her order a serving girl bring ale and broth and bread.

I had calmed myself enough to speak. We passed through a pleasure-garden, carefully dug, filled with early bloom. Before us stood a round house, much like the bower house at Kilton.

"I tried to make it like yours," Ælfwyn told me. "Of course it is nothing so grand, the garden not so large, no seas crashing upon rocks to look at..."

"It is beautiful," I said, thinking on the drear of the yard of Four Stones when I had left it.

"Come in," she smiled, and led me through the bower house door. "It is to be yours alone for your stay. Ceric, I think, will want to sleep in the hall with the other boys."

Within was a carved bed piled high with feather cushions, a table and two chairs, and chests ready to receive my goods. Upon the wood floor sat several large pieces of slate, and a brass brazier rested upon them, to ward off any chill.

"I had it built three years ago. Some nights I do not like to sleep in the treasure room," she admitted. "So I come here, where I can be quiet, or with Ealhswith when she was colicky."

Fresh tears came to my eyes, but I wiped them away. Serving folk had followed us inside, bearing my hide packs. Others carried in ale ewers of beaten bronze, and plates piled with small wheaten loaves. Burginde hurried them out, and now turned to me.

"The little lords can go with me now, and you two be alone," she said.

I smiled at Ceric, who had looked by turns bewildered and troubled. "Burginde is a friend," I told him, as she beamed back at me, "and a great one. You may go with her and Hrald, or stay here with me, as you like."

From the doorway of the bower house now peeped a girl in a sky coloured gown, with a veil of thin linen wrapping her honey-hued hair.

"Ashild," I called to her, and she smiled and curtsied. Around her neck hung a gold cross, finely wrought, and I could see where she had fallen in her play and muddied her gown. Her eyes darted from my face to Ceric's, and she giggled and ran away. Hrald was off in an instant after her, and Ceric at his heels, and Burginde laughed and swayed as she followed.

Ælfwyn and I were alone, and for a moment just regarded the other. Seven summers had passed since we had looked upon the other. She seemed to grow in loveliness. Her wondrous flaxen hair poured down along the blue silk of her gown, and the blue of her eyes was like still waters. She had gained some flesh with her last child, and it lent a pleasing softness to her slender frame. Next her, I who had always been so vivid, felt drab and colourless.

"You are so pale, Ceridwen," she said, and stroked my cheek. "How grateful I am that you are here with me."

I nodded my head, my heart too full for words.

"I could not eat for days when your letter came," she recalled, and tears started in her eyes. "Gyric...dead..."

We wept again, and held each other. I found in her arms the true understanding of the depth of my loss, for she had

31

loved Gyric too, and loved him before I had ever seen him, and had once yearned with her whole being to be his wife.

"And your little daughter too..." she whispered. She was the mother of loved children, and tho' none had been taken from her, this threat was that which all mothers lived and loved under. "How many folk were lost?" she asked, a question I saw she dreaded. She was Lady of a large burh; the sorrow that had visited Kilton could have done so at Four Stones.

"At the hall, nearly two score. More than that number in the village."

She led me to the table and poured out ale into two silver cups. She pressed one of them into my hands. "Drink, and stay strong so you may tell me all, and I will drink with you that I might bear the hearing of it."

So I began.

"When the fever came, it spread quickly through Kilton. We do not know how; some merchants had stopped to sell their wares just as they always do in Fall, and grain-buyers too had been at the burh. It struck some of the serving men first. Modwynn knew it would be bad. She saw the scarlet faces of the fevered, and had them carried outside our walls to the villager's granary. But it was too late. Within seven days many were sick. Those who died, died quickly, in two or three days. Some caught fever, but not badly; their faces flamed and heads ached for a few days, but they did not lose the ability to speak or hear. Then they were better, and did not catch it again. Some never caught it at all, tho' they nursed the sick and dying day and night. Edgyth was one of these."

The Claiming

I closed my eyes, thinking of the goodness of my sister-in-law as she worked without rest to bring ease to those who tossed in frenzy upon their beds with burning flesh.

"Godwin's wife," murmured Ælfwyn.

"Yes, as you know she lived for years with the holy women at Glastonburh, and learnt their healing ways. But for some, even her arts could avail little. Godwin was ill, but not badly. Ceric was spared completely, as was little Edwin. He had only two Summers and so we feared for him."

"Your own child which you gave them, that they might have an heir," sighed Ælfwyn.

My heart ached, and I came close to telling her that which I had told only one who walked this Earth. But I stayed myself; that added grief would bring naught but further sorrow to her.

"Little Ninnoc had not reached her first year, a fair and lithesome babe, as I wrote you of her. One night she woke screaming. She was teething then and often awoke in tears, but this was different. I picked her up in the dark and felt even then the heat on her body.

"I ran to the hall in the night, woke Edgyth and begged her tell me what to do. I did not want her to come to the bower house, feared for her, but came she did. We worked all the night to ease Ninnoc; bathed her in dittany-water, laid mugwort compresses on her little body, gave her tincture of dwarf-mint; nothing helped. Her screaming stopped, and she faded away.

"Gyric was beside himself. When she was crying it was terrible for him, hearing her suffer, but when she grew quiet he was in torment. Because he could not see her he feared every moment was her last, and kept always a hand upon her to be certain she still breathed. She died in his arms, cradled to his chest."

The door opened, and Burginde came in. She pulled a stool up to the table and dropped down heavily upon it, her hands crossed over her rounded lap.

"Ceridwen has just spoken of the death of her babe," whispered Ælfwyn over my head, for she had left her chair and our arms were wrapped around the other.

Burginde shook her head. "Ach," she clucked. "It be now seven-and-twenty years since my own babe perished, and each Winter I mark the time."

Tho' my face be wet with tears I had to smile at her, this grief so common amongst women that scarce no mother lived untouched.

She looked at the platter of uneaten loaves, and our silver cups still full of ale. She pushed the platter before me. "And do you be wanting to be carried away by a breath of wind yourself?" she demanded. "You were always a fine and hearty maid, and grew to be a lady of beauty, but if you starve yourself a bit longer we can find work for you in the fields, scaring off the rooks."

We laughed then at her, we had to; and I said, "Burginde, whenever I am with you I do not know how I will live without you," which made her slap her hands upon her lap. "But I do not know if I could keep you dressed so finely, and still have a good gown myself," I ended, and her answer was a hoot of laughter.

She had suckled Ælfwyn at the breast, and tended to her ever since, and made the perilous journey to Ælfwyn's new home at Four Stones. She looked after Ælfwyn's own children, and did all with good cheer and good sense. Over all these years this serving woman had, I knew, been the only constant in Ælfwyn's life. In truth, Burginde looked no longer a serving woman, but kin; a poor cousin perhaps, and her gown of well spun brown wool was pinned with a bright bronze brooch set with cut glass, and her plump neck hung with strings of beads.

"Drink, drink," she urged us now, and her stubby fingers flicked toward the ale cups.

I lifted mine. My throat was tight from crying, and I needed ale to ease the words to come. Ælfwyn was back in her chair, and I saw from the way her white fingers gripped the stem of her drinking cup that she braced herself against what she was about to hear. I took a calming breath, let it out slowly.

"Gyric would not let go of her body. He did not believe her to be truly dead. At last Modwynn and Edgyth coaxed him, and he let them take the babe from his arms. We did not know that even then he was ill.

"By nightfall the fever had come fully upon him. He was raving, thrashing; we could not confine him." I had to stop here, recalling that night of terrors, my daughter dead, my husband sickening. I drew another breath, and dug my fingernails into my clenched hands that I might feel their pain and not the ache in my heart.

"The next day was the Sabbath. Gyric died at Sun-down."

Ælfwyn's face was covered with her hands, and her shoulders shook behind them.

"I...I moved as if in a dream. Modwynn and Edgyth helped me wash his body, dress him in all his finest linen. Around his neck was the golden cross Ælfred had sent him after Gyric returned blinded to Kilton; he had never taken it off. I kissed his hand, as he had so often done to me, and took from off his finger his golden ring, and slid it upon my own with the ring he had given me. Modwynn cut from her own loom the linen shroud she had been weaving for herself. She wrapped her son's body in it.

"He was buried in the stone chapel, by the chancel, at his father's side. Little Ninnoc we wrapped and tucked on Gyric's chest, where she had loved to be, and where she had died.

"I remember going to the statue of St Ninnoc, and looking upon that smiling face, and pulling off the two rings and laying them at the saint's feet."

Within a few days of my first coming to Kilton, I had overheard Godwin telling his younger brother that I looked like the painted statue of this saint. It was thus that Gyric had any inner image of my face, for when we had met his eyes had been already burnt out by Danish captors. When the daughter we longed for was born, it was he who chose the name Ninnoc for the babe.

"I cannot recall much else, even now. I swooned before the statue, and have only slight sense of the days Modwynn and Edgyth wiped my brow and fought the fever that had come upon me. I recall Modwynn telling me I could not die; she could not lose me too."

"Ach," nodded Burginde, sucking on her lower lip. "And so you fought to live, for the Lady's sake; you could not let her grieve alone."

I blinked the tears from my eyes. "Burginde, how wise you are. As you say it, I know you are right; as much as I wished to die I could not abandon Gyric's dear mother to her sorrow."

She waved this away with a little grunt. "You see eight-and-forty Summers, and you will have wisdom too," she answered.

Ælfwyn had mastered herself enough to speak, tho' her voice be but a whisper. "Was he...out of his head the whole time, or could he speak to you?"

I looked into my palms, where curved red marks showed the imprint of my nails.

"He could speak...at the end. He knew he...was dying. He said, Live. Live; as if an order, or a prayer. I do not know if he was asking it for himself, or meant it for me."

Now I sobbed again, and Ælfwyn did too. Once again she came to me, and knelt down at my side, and we clung together to weep for this man we had both loved.

"I did not know I could cry like this any longer," I told her, when I could speak again. "I have wept so much these eighteen months that I thought every tear had fallen; felt dried out."

"These be new tears, Lady," sniffed Burginde from her stool. "These be the tears you never before wept for him, saved up to share them with my lady here."

I nodded my head, and tears flew from my face. Burginde rose and brought over a linen towel, and a basin with some water in it. She wiped my face as if I were a child, and then did the same for Ælfwyn.

"He be in Heaven now, whole and strong again, gazing on his wee babe's face in delight," she told me, and I kissed her for this.

Chapter the Third: Two Offerings

"COME into the garden," Ælfwyn invited, and we walked out into the pale Sun of the afternoon.

It was good to stand and stretch, and restful on sore eyes to look upon the budding blooms of rose and lily. Where we now stood was once a trampled scrap of waste land fast by the ruins of the fowl coops. The pleasure-garden was not a large one, but this marked it the more as the work of a Lady such as Ælfwyn, for each bit of land was precious in a hall yard as bustling as Four Stones'. Small fruit trees grew in its corners, and pathways paved with gravel made for dry walking even in wet weather.

"I cannot believe you have done all this," I told her, and squeezed her hand.

She gave a little laugh. "I am glad it looks so changed to you; all I see when I look about is what I wish to do."

From out the hall door stepped three women, all clad in brightly hued gowns, and I saw them to be those who had stood with Ælfwyn and Burginde before the palisade gates.

"My sisters Æthelthryth and Eanflad, and Inga, Jari's wife," said Ælfwyn. "With my mother now at Oundle I am blest to have them help me run the hall."

As they looked on me I think my cheek flushed at my poor manners. At their own gate I had been overcome, and not greeted them in any way, and was a guest at their hall.

39

I smiled on Æthelthryth, who I knew was now wed to Asberg, one of Sidroc's chief men. She was a woman of three-and-twenty, comely, with waving light brown hair and a plump body. Inga was a tall hearty woman of two or three years more, I thought, with an open, freckled face, and a calm and pleasing way about her. She did not wear the doubled clasped brooches that I had seen on the Danish women of the village, but was dressed much in the way of Ælfwyn or her sisters or me.

I looked too on the third woman with them, who, tho' she had now twenty Summers, had the still face of a sleeping child. In her arms she held a girl of two years.

"Eanflad I have met before," I said, and smiled again upon her. Her blue eyes were turned towards me, but her face looked an utter blank.

Burginde now spoke up in a merry tone, and Eanflad looked to her. "Eanflad, bring Ealhswith to me," and the little girl was passed to the arms of Burginde.

"My daughter, Ealhswith," said Ælfwyn softly, and I knew she had kept this child a little back from me so that I not be pained at the sight of her.

Looking upon the little curling head my arms rose at once to her. She smiled shyly and ducked her head under Burginde's ample chins. "A beautiful child," I said, smiling at Ælfwyn with brimming eyes.

The little one now lifted her hand, and we followed its motion. At the kitchen yard gate three children were being shown out: Ceric, Hrald, and Ashild. They were clutching cakes and scampered off as the gate was fastened behind them. I looked to Ælfwyn.

"Ceric has already been shooed out of the kitchen; he is fitting in well," she laughed.

Ælfwyn walked me back to the bower house. "You must rest," she said, "and be fresh for tonight," and in truth I knew I would welcome the quiet of the little house. Ceric and Hrald were kicking at gravel in the pleasure garden, and after we stopped them I invited him to rest with me, at which he rolled his eyes. "But you must come to the bower house before dusk to wash," I warned him, for he was now covered in dust.

Alone in the little round house I pulled off my gown and sunk upon the feather cushions of the carved bed, and slept.

I awoke to a gentle tapping at the door, and rose in the dusk to see a smiling Ælfwyn holding Ceric by the hand. I reached my arms to him and he gave me a kiss with a mouth still sticky from the honey cake he had eaten.

"Hrald has his own falcon, and a scar on his arm where it pecked him, and the grey pony is to be mine for all Summer," he recited breathlessly.

Ælfwyn and I laughed with him as he told of his day's adventuring, and I got him to wash his face and change his tunic. I chose for myself the gown of yellow silk, and shook it out and pulled it on under Ælfwyn's approving eyes.

"How well you have kept these two gowns," she praised.

I smiled back. "I wear them only at festivals, high and happy days," I told her, and then added, "Once I had hoped that Ninnoc would wear them after me." I was still smiling as I said this, and she touched my cheek in answer.

I drew forth my pear wood comb and began combing out my hair.

"How beautiful it is," said Ælfwyn, and swept up a few locks in her hand. "Like oiled chestnuts, and amber, and everything good about old gold."

"Amber," I repeated, and turned to her. "I am indeed a poor guest. First I neglect to greet your sisters, then I sleep away all the afternoon, and now I need you to remind me - of this."

Here I took from a small wood casket my gift to her. Three years ago, at the signing of the great Peace, the King and lords of Wessex had given rich gifts to the Dane Guthrum who was now King of Anglia, and to his jarls. They in turn presented gifts themselves, and Sidroc's to Godwin was of especial richness. Amongst this treasure was a full pound of amber, in pieces the size of hen's eggs. Godwin had given a third to his mother Modwynn, a third to his wife Edgyth, and a third to me; a most generous gift. I had taken my share to the goldsmith at Kilton, who with his fine-toothed saws and sharp drills had formed scores of flat round disks, linked one to the next with a golden chain.

"A necklace," gasped Ælfwyn. She was wearing a gown of light green, and the moment she clasped the linked amber about her neck it sang out against the gleaming colour of the silk.

"It should have been yours anyway," I smiled and said. "It was from the store that Sidroc gave to Godwin."

"What will you wear?" she asked, and peered within my little jewel chest. In a tight-tied leathern pouch was a sum of coinage, but little else. I had worn almost no jewellery since my loss, and had in fact packed only the silver brooch Ælfwyn had given me, one of twisted gold from Modwynn, and a few bronze mantle pins. At the last moment I had put a lone necklace into the chest, a single large pearl hanging on a silver chain. Godwulf, the old Lord of Kilton, and Modwynn had placed it about my neck the night they had heard of my coming babe.

Ælfwyn saw it now and drew it forth. "You must wear this, Ceridwen: it is so costly and rich and will look so fine against the yellow silk."

She looked at me, my hands long bereft of rings, wrists bare, my gown unadorned save for its own shimmer. She slipped the pearl around my neck.

Now I had to blink back tears. "When I was growing well again, after Gyric died, I recited my will to Dunnere the priest. In it I left this pearl to you."

"Hush, hush," she whispered. "A pearl is the egg of new beginnings; just as your in-laws told you back then. And so you shall have another beginning, Ceridwen, here at Four Stones; the start of a new life for you."

We walked with Ceric between us through the side door of the hall. It was fully dark now, and the moment we entered the passageway heard a hall full of noisy cheer. The hall held a vast numbers of tables, most of them already filled with men and women. Even in the dim of the torch light I could see it was transformed. It was nearly twice as long as it had been when Ælfwyn and I had first come to Four Stones; Sidroc had rebuilt it to again meet the foundation stones that gave the hall its name. The once sooty timber walls within were lime-washed, and the alcoves that pocketed each long side hung with colourful curtains. The fire pit, blazing now, was centred in the old space, but the stone floor of white and red was swept and bright. We stood near the treasure room, which sheltered both Sidroc and Ælfwyn at night and the greater part of their costly goods. The high table was the same, I saw so at once; for there was at one end a deep burn mark that I recalled from years ago. On the far side I saw Æthelthryth and her husband Asberg, together with the three-fingered Jari and a number of other Danes; all Sidroc's favourites to have won a place at his own table. Also at this end was a small older pinched-face man dressed in the way of a priest, who nodded to me.

At one side was a table crowded with children old enough to take their meat in the hall, and Ceric ran to where Hrald and Ashild sat with Burginde and Eanflad.

Sidroc was not there, but as we approached the table he came through the press of tables and benches from the end of the hall. Some of his men called out to him as he did, and he stopped and spoke a word or two as he made his way to us. His brow was knit; with the hall-moot tomorrow he must be much occupied.

I knew well from my brief life amongst them that the Danes cared as much for fine clothes as we, and Sidroc had dressed with care. Over a pale linen tunic of fine weave he wore a blackened leathern tunic stamped with scrolled

44

patterns. His dark brown hair just rested above his shoulders and was evenly cut and combed smooth. On his right wrist shone the silver bracelet which he ever wore, and on the left this night he sported a massive band of twisted gold. He stopped before us, and his flint blue eyes went to the brilliant necklace adorning Ælfwyn.

"From Ceridwen," she smiled. "She had it made from the amber you gave to Godwin."

He looked at the necklace, looked then at me.

"My treasure has returned," he said. "The Gods favour me."

I cast my eyes down a moment.

Then he turned to Ælfwyn, and just touched the amber disks as they lay upon her breast. "This gift is worn well," he told her with a smile.

She smiled back at him, and then glanced over her shoulder at the ever-noiser crowd. I too scanned the faces of the men and women that packed the hall.

"All eat here, but many of them sleep in the second hall," she explained, and gestured with her hand toward the newer hall which lay outside in the yard.

I watched Sidroc as he looked out over the throngs eager to begin. Ale was going around the tables, and bronze ewers carrying the wine I had brought ready to be tipped over the cups of those who sat at the high table. I tried to gauge the numbers of those who filled this large hall, and looked back to Sidroc.

The Claiming

"How many men have you?" I asked.

"Right now, one hundred and thirty," he answered.

I shook my head. "That is twice the thegns that Godwin has," I said, in my awe.

He gave a laugh so that the scar which rose above the line of his dark beard went crooked. "Yes. He is a smarter man than me."

We drank first of the Frankish wine, Ælfwyn rising and as Lady of Four Stones filling each lifted cup at the high table. All praised it by word or act, and I watched with some little pride as the men looked down into their cups, and brought them slowly to their lips as the fragrance swirled to meet their eager mouths. Ælfwyn, giver of good things to these folk, smiled upon them, and I saw she murmured to each whose cup she filled that this was my gift, for cups were raised in salute to me.

It was indeed of rich savour, and Ælfwen pressed two cups on me. I drank it readily, letting its sweet warmth fill my belly and lighten my head. I sat at her side and she urged the best bits of the fine meal onto my brass salver. Sidroc sat at the right of Ælfwyn, and next him Asberg, with Æthelthryth, his wife. Asberg was now Sidroc's chief man, his most trusted warrior, and the two men spoke much to each other. Ælfwyn almost never turned to Sidroc, so careful was she of my comfort; and the heartiness of all about me made it difficult not to take pleasure. Ceric was laughing with Hrald at something Burginde was saying, and I found myself whispering in Ælfwyn's ear, "I cannot believe that I am here, at a Four Stones such as you have made it, and that my son sits laughing with yours."

46

The Claiming

The table boasted all the finest fruits of late Spring, for with much milk at hand there were cheeses, herbed with sage leaves or dotted with fennel seeds; and boiled eggs seethed in fat butter. Great joints of roast oxen were brought out, crisped and crackling, and many domed loaves of wheaten bread milled of flour so fine that it rivalled that of Kilton's. There was a browis of pounded pease and onions, and another of barley meal and parsley and fowl, both ladled steaming into pottery bowls, and we had big copper spoons to lift it to our mouths. When we could eat no more and the tables cleared save the cups that lay circled in easy hands, a man came forward with a harp, and sat at one end of the high table and sang the sagas of Sidroc's people.

When Yrling lived and ruled at Four Stones he had kept no skald, as the Danes named their scops, for having sailed to Lindisse and wrested this land from its lord he had no man about him save warriors and those who forged their weapons. But now with peace, the men farmed, and Sidroc had had brought from his blue-shored homeland a singer of songs. He sang in the tongue of the Danes, but the names of the Gods in their tongue is close to those my father and kinsman used, and their names and stories I had known since girlhood. I caught in his mellow words these names, for he began his song tonight by praising Odin, All-Father, magician who found the secret of the runes, and strong-armed Tyr, seeker of justice, ever valiant, and harvest-bringing Frey, and his sister Freyja, goddess of lust and battle. I closed my eyes, and heard him sing of Thor, who my kinsman named Thunor, and his magical battle-hammer which crushed anything it was flung at and unfailingly returned to the red-headed God's hand.

These were the Gods my heathen father and kinsman had honoured, and their names and stories I knew well from my kinsman's hall, and now I sat in a far greater hall and heard them sung of. I felt a child again, with a child's gladness, and opened my eyes as the skald struck hard his painted harp and saw Sidroc's eyes upon me, and a smile upon his lips.

"The hall-moot is beginning," said Ælfwyn next morning as we broke our fast together in the bower room. She had come to the bower house with a serving woman and a tray, and now we two sat and looked forward to our first real day together.

"Dobbe's broth," I said, and sipped at the warm liquid. I had yesterday greeted the old kitchen-woman, knew that despite her growing palsy she still lived. We had also fresh loaves and sheep's cheese and sweet yellow butter, and I woke to this goodness after having slept well and deeply. Ceric peeked in through the open door from the garden, Hrald at his side. Now Hrald ran to his mother and whispered in her ear, twisting his hands together as he did. Ælfwyn smiled and spoke.

"The boys wish to ride their ponies to the fish pond," and looked for approval to me. "Mul will ride with them."

Mul had been a stable boy of twelve or thirteen Summers when Ælfwyn and I came to Four Stones, and risked his life by stealing one of Yrling's many horses for Gyric to ride on our escape. My face must have lit at the

48

sound of his name, for Ælfwyn went on, "You will see him soon."

Ceric now joined Hrald, and I could not deny their hopeful faces as they stood before us. Hrald would be tall, like his father, and tho' two years younger than Ceric was fully as big as he. They stood side by side, rocking gently from heel to toe, awaiting my answer.

"Only do not get wet," I smiled.

They were off like flown arrows, and Ælfwyn said, "Better to have them out from underfoot today, with the hall so crowded."

"Tell me of the hall-moot," I invited. "Is it like those your father held at Cirenceaster?"

She laughed. "These are noisier, but each year they grow closer to those we had in Wessex. The biggest change is that now they are held indoors, in the hall, and that Wilgot the priest writes everything down."

This was all interesting to me, and I bid her go on.

"At home Sidroc's folk hold their hall-moot, or gathering-time, out of doors, in Summer, and fine weather. Something about the Gods being able to listen in. None of them read, save for those who know the runes, nor do they have written law-codes as we do here in Angle-land. Old men - Sidroc calls them 'rememberers' - sit with the chief and advise him; they are supposed to recall all the earlier grievances of the people and what judgements may have been decided.

"So that is the way Sidroc first held them. Then when Wilgot came to live at Four Stones, Sidroc saw it would be good to have a scribe to write the judgements down, and so now the priest writes down what Sidroc decides. This all used to happen out by the valley of horses; Sidroc threw some runes and decided that was a favourable place for the judging. But when it rained Wilgot complained his ink and parchment got spoilt. No one can grumble more than Wilgot; he is just like an old hen. So tho' there was much grudging and fearfulness amongst his men about having it within doors, Sidroc made it so the hall-moot is held in the hall. And anyway," she ended with another little laugh, "they are all supposed to be Christian now, so whether the old Gods listen in should not matter to them."

"Are women allowed?"

"O, yes; many come to watch and listen, and then there are those directly named in the grievances."

She stood up. "Come, I wanted anyway to show you our old chamber, which is now my weaving room. Since we must pass through the hall to get there, you will see all you like."

Within the hall a table had been set up fast by the fire pit, and all that gathered there circled around it. The men seemed numberless to me, ranged about on benches, resting their jaws in their hands as they leant forward to eye the speaker or sitting with arms folded across their chests as if their minds were settled on the subject. A handful of women were amongst them. At the table sat Sidroc, with Asberg at his right, and at one end, surrounded by leaves of loose parchment and two pots of ink, perched Wilgot the priest. Off to one side sat three old men, next each other on a bench, and behind them sat an old woman, quite alone, who was leaning forward and whispering to them. On the other side of the fire pit stood a man, who was talking to those at the table in a rapid way, his brow showing his agitation. Not far from him stood another man with a pursed mouth, waiting to be heard.

Asberg was repeating what the man had said, and we were close enough to hear that the words were in our own tongue, and not those of the Danes.

"On the fifth day the well ceased to bubble," he was saying now, "and Grinulf claims that Halle had dug a ditch to carry off the water source so Grinulf's well would no longer fill."

Wilgot was scribbling away as fast as his quill would scratch, and we moved away as Halle, who could contain himself no longer, began to refute this claim in a bleating voice.

We gained the passageway near the main hall door that led up to the short flight of stairs to the upper level. This was so unchanged that I paused as we mounted the first step, and was not surprised to hear the familiar squeak from the third tread. Our old chamber still held three beds, and three large looms stood up against the walls. But the broken shutters on the windows had been mended, the walls lime-washed to add brightness, and the three females within were now Burginde, Eanflad, and little Ealhswith.

Burginde stood spinning wool, her fat fingers drawing forth thread of such fineness, and so rapidly, that my eyes widened to once again behold it. Ealhswith was at her feet, playing with a tuft of carded roving, ready to be spun. To my surprise Eanflad worked away at one of the looms, her hands deftly thrusting the weaving sword up against the weft to tighten it to the warp.

Burginde grinned and greeted us as we came in, and Ealhswith toddled over to her mother. Ælfwyn glanced about. "And where is Ashild?" she wanted to know.

"Off riding with the boys, as you bade her do," Burginde answered with a sniff. "Leaving her spindle behind, with yarn so full of lumps a whole lamb might be hiding in it."

"I never told her she could go; she never asked me. I thought she was here, spinning with you, as she ought to be," returned Ælfwyn with a rueful smile at me.

"Ach!" answered Burginde, "she be as wild as an eagle, that one. 'Twil be no supper for her tonight," she declared, but the way in which she said this made me doubt the threat would be carried out.

I crossed to the table at which we had so often sat and picked up a spindle from a workbasket. "I myself shall spin Ashild's share today," I promised, "and hope that my spinning conceals nothing larger than the burr that must be in Burginde's shoe."

That night in the hall of Four Stones we at the high table had again the good Frankish wine to drink, for the pot held enough for two night's worth. It had been a day of quiet pleasures for me, foremost that of being once again in Ælfwyn's company. Hrald and Ceric and Ashild had come back wet and muddy and happy from their outing at the fish pond, and now, their food eaten, were scampering about the hall together. The skald did not come forth tonight, but sat at a table with some other Danes, tho' I would have welcomed his flowing words and loud plucking on his painted harp. Instead Wilgot cleared his throat and stood. He was a small man, with a round belly under his black surplice, and a fringe of dark hair streaked with grey above his narrow face. Glancing into his cup, he began to speak to us.

"The goodness of all blessings recall us to our Saviour, the great chieftain of salvation, who willingly let flow his blood like wine for those his followers who heard his message. One night Christ, greatest of chieftains, went up to Galileeland, to a hall at the place Cana owned by a rich merchant. This merchant's daughter was to be wed that very day, and so the feast would be a fine one. And Christ, the great chieftain, travelled with his dear Lady Mother to this feast, as well as his picked men, his closest companions. The bride and groom had clasped hands, made their vows to each other, and the feasting began. Serving men poured out fruit wine into the cups held by all the guests. There was much happiness amongst them, all were laughing and full of cheer. Then the wine ran out; every drop of wine was gone. This was made known to Mary, Lady Mother of Christ, and she was troubled by it; she was a gracious lady and did not want any shame to fall on this merchant or his household for running out of wine. She went to her son, greatest of chiefs, and asked him earnestly to do something, for she knew he could.

"Then holy Christ ordered that six large stone vats be filled with clear water, and he watched them be so. He spoke words of power over them, moved his hands above them, and then told the servants to dip out the wine that was within.

They did, and saw at once it truly was wine, and Christ said to them, 'Take it to the most important man here, the greatest of guests in this fine hall, and give it him to drink.' And this was done, and the guest, who was a powerful war chief, said 'What is this? In our land it is the custom to serve the best wine first, and after it is drunk and the tongue loosened and the taste numbed, to serve then the poorer wine. But you have saved the best wine for last.'"

We were all attentive to this speech, for tho' Wilgot had no harp and his voice quavered in pitch, he spoke loudly and without hesitation. Sidroc had leant forward, his elbows on the table, his golden cup clasped in both hands, listening with lowered eyes. Ælfwyn smiled at me, and smiled too her praise upon her priest for his cleverness in so framing this familiar story. Looking at the faces of the Danes I saw they had heard this tale before, and envied any man the power to make clear water into wine, and found this a fitting feat for a God.

"You often say good comes to those who wait, and the best will be saved for last," Sidroc now questioned him. "Yet in my life all good I enjoy came from my own actions. It is hard to wait. To wait for something which may never come is hard indeed."

"Rewards on Earth perish, those of the spirit are everlasting," responded the priest, but it was clear from Sidroc's face he was not thinking of the afterlife.

In the morning, after the cares of the hall had taken Ælfwyn away, I crossed through the yard and went out to walk along the palisade walls. I could see the tops of the trees that grew down in the hollow to one side, and made my way there, walking through new growth of wild grasses. Before me, far from the noise of the hall, was the Place of Offering, where Yrling had sacrificed gifts of cock fowl and captured weapons before the carved wooden image of Odin.

I was drawn to it, and walked on. Rising from the centre of the shallow offering pit was the tall pole with the painted face of one-eyed Odin, All-Father, he of mysteries. Grass was growing in the pit, covering bits of bright metal that glinted there, and the ground about it was untrammelled. Few visited here now.

My eye travelled to one end of the pit. There a stake, shaped at its end almost like a hay-rake, had been driven into the soft ground, and upon the tines of the rake the carcass of a small pig lay caught, held to the heavens as Offering.

I stared at it. Sidroc's first words to me had been: I will offer a piglet in thanks-giving for your safe journeying; and now I stood before his deed.

The sow was sacred to Freyja, and she the goddess of lust and battle he had often compared me to, and this the thanks he made to her. He had taken baptism with Guthrum three years ago as part of the Peace. But this was his true faith; his Gods, those I still silently honoured.

A crow flapped over my head and startled me as it landed upon the carcass. A breeze ruffled its feathers, and it stared at me with unblinking black eyes. Then it cawed loudly and pulled at the innards of the piglet. I moved a few steps on.

A small grassy mound lay at the northern end of the Offering Place. I looked at it, and knew it to be a place of burial.

"Toki lies there," said a man's voice behind me, and I turned to face Sidroc.

He looked beyond me to the burial mound.

"I rode all night to reach Four Stones," he began, and he spoke as if this deed of ten years past had happened but last week. "He claimed it all for himself, was mad with this thought of riches. We fought before the hall as the Sun was rising. We wore no ring shirts, would give no ground to the other. Both knew one of us would fall. I disarmed him with my sword, a blow to the upper arm. Then I lunged with my knife, caught him in the chest. He fell to his knees before me, uttered one word. 'Cousin', he said, and died."

He drew breath and looked from the mound to me.

"I picked him up in my arms and carried him here. In the hall I found his gold hammered helmet, brought his shield and favourite spear. All his weapons I piled upon him, then covered his body with brushwood. I lit the bale-fire, threw more wood upon it. He had given himself to Odin, and to Odin I sent him. The smoke rose straight into the dawn air; Odin took him.

"I killed my knife, broke its blade in the pit of Offering. I could no longer wear a weapon that had shed my kinsman's blood."

I recalled too clearly the hated Toki, and his yellow hair and sneering mouth. I said the next with all the fervour I felt.

The Claiming

"I give thanks to all the Gods you killed him, and so spared Ælfwyn."

He thought of this, then nodded. "Toki was a good warrior, but here," and he tapped his forehead, "he was a boy."

He looked down and shook his head. "I should have killed him long before; that night he grabbed you on the stair. I would have, too; I was in pain from my wound and angry that he had laid hands on you when he knew I had claimed you for my own. But then you were before me, eyes flashing, telling me to spare him. Like the shield-maiden you are, deciding who is to live or die in battle."

"I did not want him to die because of me," I told him, thinking on that fearful night.

"Toki died because of Toki, not because of anyone else," he answered.

I saw his wisdom in saying this. He did not disavow that he had killed his cousin, nor did he take pride in it. Toki, treacherous and greedy, had met at a young age the violent end meant for him, and Sidroc had simply been the one who most justly served the hand of his Fate.

I nodded, and as he looked at me a slow smile spread across his face. I turned a little, so that my eye again fell on the Offering. The crow had been joined by another, their glistening black wings held out from their bodies as they picked at the piglet.

"To Freyja?" I asked softly.

57

"To Freyja, shield-maiden," he answered, in a voice almost as low.

I knew I must find voice, speak about something, or go.

"How is it you are here?" I asked. "Ælfwyn said the hall-moot would last another day."

He glanced over my head to the palisade wall encircling his hall. "It will. The Rememberers are discussing something. I came out here to get away from it." His eyes roamed over the lengthening grass, and onto the Offering pit, unused and unvisited. "Here few come but me."

"I should leave you alone then," I said, and gathered my mantle about me.

"No," he said, with sudden energy. He looked as if he would speak again, but checked himself.

I did not wish to prompt him to speak. "I am going now," I said, keeping my voice steady.

"Then I will walk with you," he returned, and fell in beside me. We walked on in silence, past the near-empty pit, away from the huge beech tree, and through the path that ran by the weedy growth.

The crofts of the village neared, and the tents of those here for the hall-moot. Folk were moving about by the open palisade gates, and a woman in a gown of red came forward to meet us.

"Ælfwyn," I said, and returned her smile.

"One day soon we will ride out together, and you can truly take some air," she promised. She looked now to Sidroc. "That is, if the hall-moot be done."

"It will be," he said.

The three of us went on toward the gates.

"How goes it with the hall-moot?" I asked. "What are the things you are deciding on?"

He lifted his eyes to the sky before answering. "Land-theft. Water-theft. Strayed cattle that did damage to crops. A horse with an altered brand."

"And the Rememberers help you with this?"

"Yes, they are Law-Speakers; I brought them from home to help. But it is not simple here. The folk of Lindisse that were here before us recall their own laws, and wish for these. Guthrum has made some laws for Anglia, which we try to follow. And what worked at home does not always work here."

"Who is the old woman who sits behind them?" I wanted to know.

"Ah - one of their wives. She is smarter than all three together."

Ælfwyn and I smiled at each other, but said nothing.

"At least this year there are no disputed babes," said Ælfwyn.

"Disputed babes?" I echoed, not knowing how any woman could not know which was her own.

The Claiming

"This was one babe, claimed by two women," smiled Ælfwyn. "Like what was brought before King Solomon."

My lips parted in astonishment, but I looked now to Sidroc, who was scowling and shot a dark look over to the wooden chapel we were passing.

"That priest," he muttered, and I could see his anger about this still smouldered.

I feared to ask, but Ælfwyn answered with a broad smile. "When this case was finally explained to him, Wilgot was in a flurry. He was eager to show Sidroc the wisdom of the great kings and fathers of the Holy Book. So he got up and with care explained what Solomon demanded to settle the case." She was laughing now, barely able to keep on talking.

"It would not be so funny if your priest had been killed," Sidroc told her, but then gave a short laugh himself. "He said something a mad man would utter - that the child should be cut in half with a sword. As soon as the women heard it, one of them flung her knife at him. She missed, but it let the air out of him still. He threw himself behind a bench and sputtered that Solomon only said that to see if the real mother would beg for this not to happen."

The thought of Wilgot cowering behind an overturned bench in return for teaching the wisdom of the great king made me put my own hand to my mouth to stifle a smile.

"But," ended Sidroc, "in a way he helped decide the case, for only the real mother would risk hurting a priest, so she took the babe away."

Chapter the Fourth: The Duelling Ground

I awoke next morning before the Sun had fully risen, and lay abed in the dim light. All was quiet in the hall yard. No bird sang from the little garden, no ocean roared up its crashing greeting onto red rocks. Kilton felt far away. I was no less alone here in Ælfwyn's narrow bed as in the dragon bed in my bower house at home, but the emptiness seemed not so great.

I stretched and thought of Ceric sharing the alcove with Hrald in the hall, glad to think on the friendship he had found so quickly here at Four Stones. Then I rose and walked out into the coming day. Heavy dew stained the gravel pathways dark, and I pulled my mantle closer about me as I walked through the garden, glistening in the early light.

The yard was just stirring, a few serving folk moving about at their early chores. The great palisade door was cracked open, and I went to it. No village folk were yet afield, but a few smudged fires showed those huts in which broth was boiling and the morning's bread being eaten. I did not think to walk far, nor to any certain place, but as I moved along outside the palisade wall I jolted to a stop.

There, a little ways down the incline which led away from the hall and towards the Place of Offering, stood a group of men. The ground was damp here, with mist rising from it, but I saw almost at a glance what they were about.

Four slender wands had been stuck into the ground about ten paces from each other, marking out a square. Two small groups of men stood on opposing sides of this, outside the boundaries of the square, with another group, including Sidroc and Asberg, at one end. I had never seen this before, but knew it well from the sagas. It was a duelling-place, where men would face each other in combat, and the wands, hazel sticks which hallowed their fighting space.

The place they had chosen was a no man's land: outside the paling of the yard, beyond the fields of the village, not yet part of the Place of Offering. Wilgot was not amongst them; I knew he would rail against and forbid this heathen thing; and all about it had the furtive air of those practising a near-forsaken act. The earliness of the hour, the few men gathered to witness, the place itself, neither of the realms of men nor the Gods, all spoke of it.

So some men sought a higher justice than Sidroc had meted out, and would fight until one yielded or died to claim it. I did not wish to see this, and dug my fingers deeply into the soft wool of my mantle and began to turn. As I did the group of men nearest me glanced over. I shrunk back, aware that in such cases a woman's glance might blunt a man's weapon; and indeed, none but men stood there.

The men were unspeaking, and none raised an arm to drive me away. I began to move off. Then I saw the two small figures that stood behind Sidroc at one end. It was Ceric, with Hrald. They were looking not at me, but at Sidroc, staring up with wide eyes at him, and at what they were about to witness.

Ceric had often seen warriors training, and had delighted to watch the thegns of Kilton in their spear and sword play. But he had also stepped upon the gore-soaked floors of Kilton's hall following the attack that had nearly killed

62

Godwin, and had seen and heard first-hand the suffering caused by the terrible wounds driven home by the Danes on that dark day.

I did not think I wanted him to witness this combat, and yet was loathe to call him away to my side. I stood there, muffled in my mantle, and Sidroc glanced at me. There was steadiness in that glance, and no dismissal; he wanted me to stay from calling Ceric, and to stay myself.

Sidroc now stepped forward and spoke in a low voice. I looked at the men who prepared to fight. One was the man Grinulf, who had complained about his well drying up, and the other, Halle, who he accused. In the hall they had been dressed in wool leggings and tunics. Now they appeared before each other in all the armaments they owned, linked ring-tunics to the thigh, round shields at their feet, and swords and knives at their waists. Both men held iron helmets in their hands, and these they now slipped on over their heads as Sidroc dropped his arm as signal.

They took up their shields in their left hands and moved into the centre of the small duelling ground, and as wordlessly as they had awaited the battle, began to fight. The men gathered to watch were also soundless; no words of encouragement nor disparaging oaths fell from their lips. The only sound came from the dull ringing of the swords as they struck the edges of the iron rimmed shields, and the grunts of the two as they swung and thrust and parried.

Grinulf was the younger of the two, but Halle greater in size, and the bigger man drove Grinulf back towards the line marked by the hazel-wands. To step without meant forfeit, and Grinulf, seeing the nearing wand, redoubled his effort. He side-stepped so that Halle's next thrust missed him entirely, and the man nearly crossed outside the boundary himself. Halle rounded on him, charging, but the nimbler Grinulf flipped his sword hand and found flesh in Halle's forearm. The sword dropped from the bigger man's hand, and a stifled howl escaped his lips.

I closed my eyes, fearing that the aggrieved Grinulf would make Halle's blood flow in lieu of his well. But I heard the panting words of the one, and cracked my eyes to see him demand the other yield, for Halle stood with reddening arm and bowed his head before Grinulf.

Now Sidroc spoke, so that all looked at him, and he questioned both men, and they answered. Then Halle walked unsteadily off the duelling field to where his group of men waited, and they led him away, and Grinulf too, flushed with the victory of justice, pulled off his helmet and swaggered off amidst his followers.

The whole time the boys had watched this with their round eyes, and Hrald had stood so near his father that he was touching his leg. Sidroc walked to the four wands, and pulled them out of the ground, and then laid them in the centre of the duelling place, two crossed over two.

Men were drifting off now, and the Sun fully risen. Sidroc came over to where I stood. Asberg was still at his side, and he nodded to me, and the two boys who followed behind looked up at me uncertainly.

"Foolish to bleed for stealing a man's watercourse, when in Lindisse it rains so much," said Sidroc. He looked back over the duelling-ground, and then at the boys. They nodded up at him.

His eyes went again to the boys, and then met mine. "Perhaps Ælfwyn would not like to hear of this," he said now, softly and to me.

Sidroc had not approved of this duel, and had made it clear to the boys he found it foolish, but still he would defend his men's right to follow their ancient ways and so fight.

"She will not hear," I told him.

He smiled at this and fell in beside me. The boys walked along with us, and broke into easy chatter, already planning their day's outing. Each wore a knife at his waist, hanging from a belt of leather. Hrald's was small, as a boy of seven Summers ought to wear. My eye went to Ceric's belly, and the large seax there. The leathern cord that Godwin had so tightly bound around the hilt of the weapon was now clumsily knotted around it.

"Ceric," I asked, and my tone made him look up at once. "Did you untie the Peace Band on your seax?"

He hesitated, his eyes rolling, and pursed his lip. "I wanted to show the blade to Hrald," he excused.

Sidroc lifted his hand slightly and so silenced me.

"Then that is Yes?" he asked. His tone was mild, but Ceric's eyes betrayed his unease. He nodded his head, fearing what might come.

"Now you can show it to me," Sidroc continued, and Ceric looked up to see if I assented. I nodded, silently, and his fingers fumbled at the knot he had tied. He placed his small hand upon the horn hilt, and drew out the shining blade. Sidroc placed his hand over it and took it from him.

65

"Pattern-welded," he said, looking down on the rippling design in the twisted bands of hammered steel. In the gathering Sunlight the blade truly seemed to shimmer and to dance. The pommel topping the hilt was dressed with pure gold, set with incised silver wire.

"This is a fine weapon, one of the best," he said, and slid it back into the carved and stamped leathern scabbard. He took the leathern cord from Ceric's other hand and twisted it strongly about the guard, securing it to the scabbard.

"It was Merewala's," I found myself saying.

Sidroc's head jerked around at this, and he rose from where he was crouched by Ceric's side.

"How came you by it?" he wanted to know, and wonder was in his face, and in the soft tone he used. I did not know who had killed Merewala in the battle for Four Stones, whether it was Yrling or one of his war-band or even Sidroc himself.

"Your old kitchen woman, Dobbe, had it hidden, and put it in my food-sack when I left here."

I did not fear that Dobbe be punished for this act of defiance of ten years past, and wanted to speak the truth of this weapon's tale in front of my son to the man who now ruled the hall of the fallen lord.

"Gyric wore it ever after, and used it to slash a bandit we met upon the road in Mercia. And it was this blade that later saved the life of Godwin, for Gyric cut the throat of the Dane who was about to take his brother's life."

These were the feats of a man blinded out of Danish spite, wrought with a blade once worn by he who died defending his rightful hall.

"Then it was used well by Kilton's brother," answered Sidroc after a little pause. He considered, and added, "Such acts take courage."

"Gyric had more courage than any man I have ever met," I said.

He searched my face and nodded. He looked to where both Ceric and Hrald stood unmoving, watching us.

"Fine weapons must be always well-used, such as this one has been," he told them.

He crouched down next the boys and pinned them in turn with his eyes. "You must never draw your blades against the other. Never." The warning in his low voice made the eyes of both boys grow wide.

Sidroc lifted his hands to his face and parted his dark beard on the left side. "You do not want to look like me," he told the boys, as they gazed at the long scar on his cheek.

Ceric shook his head and Hrald gravely nodded his pointed little chin. Sidroc winked at them, and then stood up.

We walked on, and he said, "Can Kilton hold a shield?" - for this was the way in which he named Godwin, by his hall.

"No," I told him, for despite all the leech-skill of Edgyth he could lift nothing heavy in his left hand following the spear thrust that pierced his shoulder.

"Is the arm dead?"

I shook my head. "Not quite. He can still hold his horse's reins, and use it at table."

I wondered what made him think on this; mayhap my mention of that same battle in which Gyric had saved Godwin's life. I glanced at him, but he was looking straight ahead. I thought of Godwin's words to me on the day I sailed - I do not trust him - and wondered if the same be true for Sidroc.

I was leaving the croft of Witha the Dyer, for Ælfwyn wanted more yellow wool for a new mantle she planned to weave, and I had begged her to put me to some work that I might feel useful. The Dyer wiped her stained hands on her apron front as she placed in a basket a range of bright wool from which Ælfwyn could choose. The hanks were still slightly damp from the drying racks whence she had hung them from her steaming vats. "The Lady thought well to send you now," she told me, "'tis all yellows this week; mustards and tansy-heads and Baptist-wort; last Summer's fine crop. Next will be blues, when the woad ripens, or greens, if the weather dampens."

I thanked her and headed back down the road to Four Stones. I heard a squealing cry of delight, and there in front of me appeared Ceric and Hrald, running from behind some cottar's outbuildings, where they ought not be. The cooper in the yard had given them iron hoops from his barrel-work, and the boys drove these rolling before them down the hard clay road.

The Claiming

Nothing had gladdened me more these past weeks than seeing Ceric's happiness; he had known too little since his father and sister had died. Even his shyness with Ashild had passed, and sometimes as the two little heads bent together in play, one covered in copper curls and one in honey coloured tresses, Ælfwyn and I would glance at each other and hold the same unspoken wish for their future in our eyes.

I was thinking on this when I heard the jingling of bridle bits behind me, and stepped off the road to let the riders pass. One did, and I saw it was Asberg, Æthelthryth's husband, who raised his hand as he rode on. The second rider was Sidroc, and he swung down from his bay and fell into line next me. The boys ahead had clustered around Asberg, begging to be hauled up on his big black horse, and he obliged, pulling Hrald before him and Ceric behind. With their iron hoops in their hands they made ungainly progress for the patient Asberg, and I smiled after them.

Sidroc too was grinning.

"You named Hrald for your own father," I recalled aloud.

His eyes went to his son, and he nodded Yes.

I realised I knew nothing at all more about his parents.

"Tell me of him," I invited.

His horse came up and nudged him on his shoulder, and we started walking. "There is not much to tell," he began, and looked across the line of cottar's huts on either side of us. "He had a farm on the banks of a narrow river. The land was not good and it flooded often. To put more food on the table he would take his small boat down river into the sea to fish. One day he did not return."

"I am sorry."

"It was late in the season. Storms come up quickly on such days."

"How old were you?"

"Hrald's age, I think; seven or eight Summers. I do not mark the years as well as you."

I thought of him growing up fatherless as I had done, and my own son would do.

"And of your mother?"

"She was not my father's wife."

I only nodded and wondered if he would say more of her.

"She was a kitchen-woman. After I was born she went to another farm and left me behind. I do not know her name." He shot a glance at me. "Just as you do not know your mother's name."

So in this too we were alike, with nameless mothers who could not raise us.

"What happened to you?" I asked next.

"After my father did not come back, his wife wished to wed again. She had three children with him and no longer wanted me. Yrling rode to the farm and took me away with him. He was no more than fourteen or fifteen Summers

70

himself. He was my father's youngest brother, and lived with his sister and her family. She was Toki's mother."

I closed my eyes. His tale was nearly my own. Taken from our childhood home and our birthright to be raised elsewhere, I to the priory, he to his kin.

"So Toki's parents and Yrling fostered you?"

"Yes, but it was not many years before Yrling joined up with a ship of raiders. He had heard what a rich land this was and was restless to try his hand." A smile played about his mouth as he spoke on these days. "They would sail in good weather, as soon as Summer broke, make a few strikes, gather slaves and silver and come home again."

"And when you grew old enough you joined him."

"Yes, me and Toki both. Just as there was no room for me at my father's farm, there was not enough room in my homeland for me to have what I wanted."

I knew he had not much more than twenty Summers when he first sailed for Angle-land. "And you knew what that was, even then?"

"I always knew. I knew I could fight. I wanted treasure." He stopped a moment. "Then I saw you, and I wanted you." His eyes rested upon my face. "The treasure I have won, beyond my reckoning."

"Few men can say as much," I murmured, but would not look at him. "You must be content indeed."

"It will not last." There was no sharpness in his answer; it was as simply said as any fact. "Men like me do not live

71

long. All that I have I gained by fighting, and to keep it I have to go on fighting. A few times in battle I have already met my match, but the Gods looked kindly on me and I bested them. One day I will meet my better, and I will die."

It was odd to hear him say this, a rich and powerful jarl, on the road leading to his own hall; and I felt troubled at his words, and troubled more at the easy way in which he spoke. But I myself had seen how quickly peace can be shattered.

"Godwulf, the old Lord of Kilton, was six and sixty when he died," I said in protest. I tried to think of any other war chief who had attained close to his years, but in truth I could not.

"His God favoured him," replied Sidroc.

I knew this was true and so said nothing.

"It is strange, fighting a man who you know is as good as you are," he mused. "When you are young and cocky you think you are better than everyone. A few close calls and you learn you are not. You watch a man who you know is a better warrior be hacked down. You learn it is not just the strength in your arm or your speed that keeps you alive. You begin to see the shield-maidens above you on the field. They choose who will live or die; you may do your best to win but they will decide."

I looked at him from the tail of my eye as we kept walking. He had ever been an enemy to my people, but never to me. He was a warrior of renown, and freely admitted it was not only his skill that had kept him whole. I could not be surprised at it. He had always thought much, but in these latter years he seemed to have questioned all, as well.

The next was hard for me to ask. The Sun shone above us, and peace and plenty was all about. "You think then more war will come?"

"I have been in this land for twelve Summers. The first nine were all hard fighting. The last three have been almost as hard, keeping peace." He thought on what he said, and went on. "Ælfred's grip is tight, as is Guthrum's. And here in Lindisse all goes well. But there will always be those with little to lose, eager to challenge, to win what they may." He looked towards the palisade gates we had nearly gained. "Here I am likely to be killed by one of my own men over a judgement I have made; or trying to settle some drunken squabble." And he laughed.

Chapter the Fifth: Treasure and Ashes

THE weather blew rain for a few days, and kept us all about the hall and yard. Once it hailed, too, sending bits of streaky ice pummelling against the walls of the bower house and the hall. But the Sun returned, and with it warmth, and Ælfwyn resolved that we should ride out to the valley of horses and look upon all the animals pastured there. Her chestnut mare had foaled again that year, and was amongst them.

When the boys heard of the outing they must needs join us, and Ashild, who could ride as well as her brother, would likewise not be denied. The three of them were already upon their ponies when Ælfwyn and I arrived at the doors of the great stable. There stood a lean young man with a rough-hewn gawky face, which creased into a ready smile as he saw us.

"Mul," I greeted, and smiled back as he bobbed his head to me. He had grown so tall I could not keep from saying, "You are quite a man now." In fact he had but a year or two less than me, so was as much a man as I was woman.

He grinned again. "And with a wife and two sons," he answered. He nodded to where the children stood their ponies. "Your boy's a fine lad on a horse, Lady," he said, which made Ceric grin himself. He looked beyond us. "The lord be fetching your mounts," he told us.

In fact, I did not know that Sidroc would join us, but there was his horse ready saddled. Now Sidroc crossed the

74

yard from the smaller stable, leading two saddled mares, one so pale a grey as to be nearly milk-white, and the same bay mare he had met me with at Saltfleet. She was a beautiful animal, with a full black tail and a long mane shimmering over her dark red coat. It was so like the morning years ago when he had presented Ælfwyn with her chestnut mare as Yrling's gift, and me a bay mare as his own. I wondered if Ælfwyn too was thinking this. I could scarce look at him and nodded my head wordlessly as he boosted me up into the saddle.

We set out. No dust billowed from our horses' hooves, for the road lay damp and hard beneath us, and the air was washed and freshly moist upon our faces. The children rode ahead, Ashild leading the way on her roan pony. Beyond the common fields in which grew wheat and barley and rye we turned onto the beaten grassy track which led to the valley in which the horses kept their Summer pasture.

The great timber long house which had been the first dwelling of the Danes was still there, and a few huts and fenced crofts told me that some of Sidroc's men had settled here to farm. To one side lay a field marked off with stout wooden fencing.

"Your flax," I said to Ælfwyn, for its slender stems crowned with blue flowers proclaimed it. She and her women wove fine linen from this field, and I smiled to recall our joy at finding a few young sprigs growing there on our first ride to the valley so long ago.

But my eye was carried away from this by the horses just beyond. There were score upon score of them, greys, blacks, chestnuts, and bays. Even better, it seemed half of them were mares with young ones at their flanks.

We reined up, and I looked at the wealth of this horse-flesh. There was no nag amongst them; they were all fine beasts, fat with good feed, glossy-flanked, with thick manes and tails streaming to their hocks.

"What treasure you have," I said, with all the awe I felt.

"Yes," agreed Sidroc, and eyed them himself. Now he patted the arched neck of his bay. "But I can only ride one at a time." He looked over to Ælfwyn. "Likewise with jewels. Even the woman who covets them has only two wrists and one neck to hang them from."

Ælfwyn laughed, and I smiled with her.

"That is why it is good to have many, so one does not tire easily of them," came her ready answer.

Sidroc leant forward on his saddle bow and regarded the horse herd. "If you possess what is right for you, you do not need much," he remarked.

I thought of his silver bracelet which he wore each day; and thought too of his single-mindedness in other things.

He went on. "If a man has one good horse, a sword he trusts, and food for tomorrow, he has most of what he needs to be content."

"You did not think this ten years ago, when that was all you had," Ælfwyn reminded with a gentle laugh.

The children had now ridden to the edge of the herd, and called back in their excitement that they saw Ælfwyn's chestnut mare and foal. She touched her heels to her horse's flank and joined them.

The Claiming

Sidroc moved his bay forward, and we walked our horses slowly past the herd. Above us the Sun was dropping from its highest point. Summer was nearing its fullness and showed it in the height of the tender grass stalks that swayed as our horses parted them. The forms of Ælfwyn and the children shimmered in the distance against the mass of horses behind them.

He did not speak, nor did I. At last he reined his horse to a standstill.

"What will you do now, shield-maiden?"

I was silent so long that he was forced to speak again.

"I will ask another question: What do you want to do?"

I shook my head and gave a short laugh. "That is another question indeed." I lifted my face and looked out over the expanse of pasture lands to the dark green of the sheltering hills. A sigh escaped my lips. "I want to sit in a pleasure-garden and look at the sea."

He was quiet some little time, and then said, "You are very young to do that, and nothing else."

"I do not feel young any more, Sidroc," I told him, and turned my face to him.

He looked at me a moment and then down the clay road that led to Four Stones. "You could stay here."

With effort I kept my voice light. "Even if I did not have a duty to do, that would not be wise."

He made no such pretence. "Duty? You have already given them sons. What more can they ask of you?"

I did not answer, and at last he spoke. "Will you be forced to wed again?"

I paused, thinking on how I could answer this. But he did not give me the chance.

"Or maybe not. Likely Kilton wants to keep you where he can look at you." Now I turned from him, and he added, "That is what I would want."

I felt weariness, and no anger, at his words.

"I am the daughter of a forgotten heathen war chief and a nameless Welsh slave woman. I owe everything to the folk of Kilton, from the first day I arrived. Godwulf and Modwynn received me with honour, named me their daughter, and made me a rich woman. Now Godwin and Edgyth rule all with justice and open hands. I have found a home there beyond my imaginings. Widowed, I am treated with esteem and kindness. To them I owe everything."

I was not prepared for the force of his answer. "To them you owe nothing. You carried back one of their men, stolen from my own keep, and returned him alive through great dangers. Kilton himself could not do this. They are a dying tribe; you brought them hope. You have given them ten Summers of your life." He looked up at the sky, drew breath. "You have given them both sons. You owe them nothing."

"What would you have me do? I am still young; you said it yourself. I must go on."

Our eyes locked and I read his answer.

"I cannot stay here. For all our sakes."

From across the grassland the children came trotting to us, laughing and calling, and I urged my mare forward to meet them.

"Godwin must have forged many alliances," said Ælfwyn.

We were sitting in her garden outside the bower house on High Summer's day. We had gone to see the fire the village folk had built to welcome Summer be lit, and now it was late afternoon and the yard still empty. We had not been speaking of Godwin or even Kilton, and her words made me stop a little before I answered.

"Yes, all throughout Wessex," I told her. It was hard to think of Godwin on this day of all of them in the long wheel of the year, for it was on High Summer's day four years ago that he had come to my bed for the first of four nights.

"Is there...some lord is he is indebted to?" she now wanted to know. Her lap was full of flowers that cottar girls had given her, and they lay against her green gown as if they had been heaped upon a grassy bank. She stroked the small soft petals of a white rose as she looked at me.

Now I understood. Ælfwyn had rarely been interested in affairs of state, and she was not now.

I found myself biting my lip, but I nodded my head just the same. I had been widowed now for nigh onto two years; I was rich, and sister-in-law to Godwin, most powerful of all ealdormen in Wessex. Modwynn and Godwulf had had no daughters who lived beyond childhood, and thus lacked the ability to strengthen bonds with neighbouring lords through the giving of those daughters in marriage.

I smiled at her and tried to keep my voice light. "There is...a kinsman of Modwynn, at her home in Sceaftesburh. It is some miles inland, and said to be rich farming country, with a good and hardy folk. It was her father's hall; he was bailiff; but Modwynn had no brothers. It was left to her and for some years she had an overseer care for it. It was always her plan that one day Gyric should have it."

Ælfwyn's pale eyebrows lifted. "Then..." she began, and faltered. She took up the thread of her thought again. "If Gyric had not been maimed, and he and I had wed, it was the place I should have lived." She said this with some wonder, thinking on it all.

"Yes," I said. "If he had been whole, Sceaftesburh would have been for Gyric and his wife."

I was quiet again until she asked her next question. "What happened to it?"

"Modwynn passed it to a cousin of hers. Now he is widowed."

Her brows almost touched as she looked at me. "And they wish you to wed him?"

It was not an easy question to answer. "I know Modwynn would like it," I said at last, "and she has been, as you well know, very good to me."

"And Godwin? Is this his bidding too?"

I thought of what he had said to me at the port of Swanawic as I had boarded the ship: Do not think of the other matter. In truth, he would neither bid me wed the man nor ask me to stay at Kilton. He had not so much tried to take my hand in the years since I had borne his son Edwin. Yet now that his brother was dead I thought his possessiveness towards me growing stronger, and not weaker.

"I am a resource; he must use me like any other to help his shire."

"Yes," she nodded. "No bond is as great as that made by marriage, and no doubt this would bring Sceaftesburh and its wealth near as close to Kilton as it could once have been."

Ælfwyn knew well of what she spoke, for she had been given in marriage as part of a peace accord; and tho' it failed and her husband Yrling be killed by Godwin, she lived on to give her mother and sisters the peace and plenty they had lost in their home of Cirenceaster.

"Tell me of him," she prompted now, and her tone was almost playful as she thought on this. "What is his name, and is he fair to look upon, and how he has spoken to you."

I had to smile at her. "His name is Heahstan." I thought of how to describe him. "He is in, I think, his fourth decade. He has light brown hair. He is not over tall, yet he is not short."

"Has he children?"

"Two. Sons, of about sixteen and twelve Summers."

Her brows rose in a brief frown. "So Ceric will not inherit."

"No. But that which is rightfully mine from Gyric will be his."

"You say Sceaftesburh is inland," she posed next. "Then you will miss the sea."

"I will," I must admit.

"Is he fair to look upon?" she asked again.

"I have only seen him twice, the first time years ago, the last at Gyric's funeral feast," I confessed. "I did not notice; I did not think to notice."

"He does not sound fine. You would have recalled him if he were." She looked down at the blossoms in her lap. A few were starting to brown in the warm air. "And he is kind?"

She did not wait for my answer. "He must be, or Modwynn would never bid you wed him."

I nodded in assent.

"Will you do it?"

"I do not know. I cannot stay for ever at Kilton, and do naught." Tears had watered my eyes, and I blinked them away.

She put her hand over mine. I felt ashamed; I had married once for love, a gift never given to Ælfwyn.

"It would not be difficult to wed such a man if it were not for the marriage-debt," she considered. "Being a willing bed mate can be hard indeed, even if the man be kind."

I had never felt the duty of the marriage-debt; my nights and mornings spent in love were just that, and no mere fulfilment of a man's claim on my body. I knew too, that many men of high estate must wed women for whom they held no affection, and this burden of all landed folk must be borne with good sense and good grace.

She leant over and kissed my cheek. "Do not think on it now; we have still over a month of pleasure awaiting us," she reminded.

Sidroc had ridden to Saltfleet to check on the progress on the pier and storehouses being built there. He took with him a few men and a waggon, and also Ceric, Ashild, and Hrald, to be dropped off at Oundle on the way to the coast. A visit with Sigewif was considered a great treat by Ashild and Hrald, and since Ceric had met the abbess on our way to Four Stones he too looked forward to the stay.

"She makes them say their letters, and practice forming them in wax tablets, and they work out sums with counters; all the things Wilgot makes them do here," Ælfwyn explained with a smile, "only at Oundle it is all fun and no drudgery for them to do so."

With both Sidroc and the older children gone it was quiet indeed about the hall. We were sitting now in the treasure room, a place Ælfwyn did not spend much time in other than to sleep, for her weaving and spinning she did upstairs in the weaving chamber, and she was much about the kitchen yard and storehouses in her daily tasks.

The Claiming

When I had first seen the treasure room on my return to Four Stones, I remarked on the transformation she had wrought in it; yet there was such about it that still gave me a chill. I recalled too clearly the night we readied Ælfwyn for her first as Yrling's wife, and left her clutching at the bedclothes awaiting his entry to the barren room. Indeed, the wolfskin spread her mother had made as wedding gift still lay upon the bed. I thought too of the awful afternoon when we had first learnt that Gyric be a captive beneath in the cellars, and how she had dropped upon her knees on these floorboards and placed her hand on them and uttered to me her love for him.

The room now had many comforts that it had lacked when Yrling lived. Ælfwyn had had the walls lime-washed, like the rest of the hall, to give it lightness, and deerskins now covered the floor boards, lending their warmth underfoot. A large copper wash tub sat in one corner, where she might bathe, and near it upon the wall hung a silver mirror of a size that the whole face might be seen. But the greatest change was that most readily seen, for there were I think ten times the number of chests and casks of treasure within that room; all that Yrling had won, and all that, so much more, won by Sidroc. This treasure took the form of chests of weaponry fallen from the stilled hands of Saxon thegns upon the field of battle; and of armaments such as helmets and ring shirts stripped from their bodies. There was silver and gold, both in coinage and in jewellery taken as booty in numberless raids upon halls and storehouses of now-dead lords and reeves and bailiffs. Here too were things gained in trade from distant lands; precious beakers of glass, and baskets of fur pelts from northern animals.

Today we sat at the little table, amidst all these treasures. It was late on a rainy afternoon, too soon yet for the hall to fill for the evening meal, and all was still. Only the rain pattering outside through the single barred casement made any sound.

Ælfwyn had been showing me a pair of golden bracelets Sidroc had given her at Ealhswith's birth. She did not often wear them for they were too large for her slender wrists and Four Stones had as yet no worker in gold or silver skilled to cut them down for her. They were things of wonder; twists of gold that met in the faces of gaping beasts. One had two rubies set for eyes, the other sapphire or lapis. Even the tiny casket that housed them was fine, for it was carved of whitest walrus tusk.

I praised them, both for their beauty and the kindness in the giving of them to her.

"He has always been very good to me," she said, as she pulled the bracelets off. "He has given me complete freedom in running the hall and over the village. In all these years he has rarely spoken a harsh word to me. But his fondness for me does not run much deeper than it did when I was Yrling's wife."

I opened my mouth to protest, thinking on the years they had spent together.

"You are as beautiful as ever," I began. "You have run his hall ably and well all this time. You are the mother of his children."

"All this may be true, but when he turned to me in the night I knew it was from his man's need, nothing more." She looked away now, and her voice dropped so low that I leant forward to hear her. "In the morning he would fasten the silver bracelet upon his wrist, and it was as if he were putting you on."

I tilted my face from her; I had to. Tears welled in my eyes but I could not speak.

"When we wed I thought he would give me that bracelet, since he valued it so highly. Then I saw it was the only part of you he had left. He had made you accept it as payment for dressing his wound, and thereafter you had worn it each day on your wrist. Then you ran away from him. It was what you left behind to beg your pardon. And every day for the last ten years he has worn it."

"Ælfwyn, I...I am so sorry; this is terrible, terrible for you." I could scarce control my voice and feared I might sob. "A part of you must hate me."

"I could never hate you, Ceridwen. None of this is your fault; you were always blameless. Nor is Sidroc to blame. I do not think he chose this for himself. He has suffered, wanting you."

She shook her head before she spoke again. "The only man I ever loved was Gyric. It was so long ago, I was a girl. I loved him, and wanted nothing but to be his wife. But I could not love him maimed. You could, and did - you were more worthy of him than me." She looked at me and smiled, tho' there were tears in her blue eyes. "You have had two men to love you, all this time. Your Goddess has found you most deserving."

I almost could not bear to hear this. I had loved Gyric well and truly. It was he who had first awakened the stirrings of womanly passion in me, and despite his ever deepening sorrow at being blinded I had known at times true joy with him. Then I had betrayed my vow to him and yielded to Godwin's desire, and let him enter our bed, and bore him the son he so yearned for. I had suffered greatly by my act, in the pain I had caused Gyric; but Kilton had the heir it needed, and I had grown to see that I had played a part for good in bearing and then giving up this child to Godwin and his wife Edgyth.

Ælfwyn knew none of this, none save that Gyric and I had given up our second son to be Godwin's, which is what all of Kilton believed; none knew the child to be that of the lord himself. Only three now lived who knew it, and the third was Sidroc.

I knew no words to speak, nor would my clenched throat open if I did. But she in her goodness took my hand in hers, and wiping away her own tears with the other, smiled upon me.

Chapter the Sixth: The Thread of Life

ÆTHELTHRYTH and I were in the kitchen passageway, sorting and numbering brass drinking cups. Those who sat at the high table drank from cups of silver, some of which were studded with gems; and these were carefully kept in the treasure room until they be needed each night. The rest of the cups were of beaten brass, and today Ælfwyn's sister and I had set scores of them along the narrow tables in the passageway.

"These need a hammering," said Æthelthryth, pulling out several which were badly dented.

"And here's another has been dropped," I said, fingering the crack in the rim. There were many to be mended, and an equal number to be newly made, for in a large hall things such as brass cups were often lost or carried away.

We had propped open the door to the kitchen yard for better light and now Ælfwyn walked through it. Her smile reversed itself as her eye fell upon the number of battered cups.

"What do they do, step on them?" she wondered aloud, picking up one that looked almost as if it had been treated thus.

Burginde was just behind her. "Just fling them at each other's hard heads," she answered.

We had not stopped our laughter when she went on, "The lord be back from Saltfleet."

We all went out to greet him. Sidroc had been gone four days, and I expected to see the children, or at least Ceric, with him, for he was to have stopped back at Oundle. But he was alone, save for the men he had ridden with, and the dour oxcart drover.

"And the children?" Ælfwyn asked.

"They chose to stay on a few days at Oundle, all of them," he answered, with a glance at me.

Ælfwyn nodded in approval, and tho' I was gladdened at Ceric's happiness, I felt almost a pang. He did not miss me, and he was all I had left on this wide Earth. I shook this thought from my head, but not before Ælfwyn had read it; I saw it in her tender smile. Sidroc was already unlacing the oiled tarpaulin over the waggon back. There over the rear axle sat two stout wooden casks, stopped with broad disks of wood. I knew what lay within from the rim of dull lead sheeting that lay folded over the edge of the casks.

"Salt," said Sidroc, as he and another man pulled the casks forward.

Æthelthryth and Burginde looked in as Sidroc lifted one of the stoppered tops. "Our meat will last the Winter now," said Burginde with satisfaction as she gazed upon the first cask. It was brimful of greyish salt in coarse chunks, the kind used to lay by meat for the lean days of Winter and early Spring. The second cask, not so large as the other, held fine flakes for the table, and these were of a cleanness and whiteness that a King would not disdain.

We were remarking on this when Ælfwyn spotted the other contents of the cart. "The new mill stone," she cried, and her gladness was in her words. "At last!"

I peeked in. There, well forward over the front axle and lying upon planed timber boards was a thick circle of flecked stone, broader across than my arms' reach.

Sidroc laughed. "It is from Frankland, where the best such are quarried, and we have waited two Summers for it."

"Better bread, and more of it," said Burginde, clapping her hands together.

"The Lady of Oundle bids you come yourselves next week," Sidroc finished. "She has even got Hrald cutting goose feathers to hold ink."

This was a wonder we must see, so we resolved to go. Ælfwyn wished to see her mother, and soon Ceric and I must leave for Kilton, for St Mary's Day be but a fortnight away.

Sidroc had Asberg and a few men ride with us, for the new milling-house was being built and he must stay that all be right with it. It was an easy trip in fine weather, and as it was so fair we rode rather than be jostled in a waggon. The three children were scrubbed and waiting for us in Sigewif's yard, and the Abbess stood behind them with a broad smile upon her face. I almost started when I saw Ceric, so much had he grown this Summer, tho' I only saw it now that we had been parted a few days. I wrapped my arms about him and kissed the head now a bit nearer to my own.

Sigewif gave us a rich meal in her snug hall, and after the nightly clamour of Four Stones I welcomed the quiet and calm of it. Tho' two score men and women sat at tables within, there was naught heard but the shuffle of the serving folk as they moved amongst the tables bearing bread or ale.

"You have well taught Ceric his letters," the abbess told me after the children had been sent off to sleep.

"It is the Lady Modwynn has worked most with him, in wax," I told her, "and will be glad to hear her skill praised by such as you."

"It is his facility with the quill that most impressed me," she went on to my surprise. Ceric had been an able student with a stylus and wax tablet, but had never yet asked to handle quill or ink.

"Come and see," Sigewif invited, and we rose and followed her through the stout door that divided the hall, and went into a room that served as the treasure room, just as it would in the hall of a great family. Upon a narrow deal table sat several scraps of parchment. Three stools were drawn up to the smooth edge of the table, and a flat tin tray held a handful of ink-stained goose quills.

She held a burning pottery cresset over the scraps and its light flickered upon them. Each child had begun to write the alphabet, and two of the parchment pieces showed the large unformed hand of a child's work; one had run out of room after ten letters or so. The third showed small well defined letters, spaced in mostly even rows. My lips parted as I looked upon it.

"He has a gift, which I hope you will continue to nurture," Sigewif went on, with real pleasure in her voice.

Ælfwyn had picked up one with a smeared thumb print upon it. "Hrald's," she laughed, and tho' I laughed with her reminded he had but seven Summers to Ceric's nine.

"Ashild has strength in her hand, which I like," said the Abbess, pointing to the third. "Next time I will find her a larger piece of parchment, so she can finish the letters," she smiled. "But Ceric," she went on, "I hope will be made to copy out something every day, for by doing so he will learn to read as well as to write." She folded her hands as she looked at me. "Your priest at Kilton must be proud to tutor such a boy."

I had to lower my eyes. Dunnere had never shown much interest in Ceric, but I wondered in truth if it was not because I had never shown any in the priest. I stood dutifully in Kilton's stone chapel each Sabbath, and made certain Ceric said his prayers, but Dunnere, I felt, knew me still to be heathen, and so could not like or trust me.

The Abbess now left us, but Ælfwyn's thoughts ran on, for she turned to me with the eagerness of a thought she had grasped upon.

"Ceridwen," she said, "why do you not leave Ceric with me? He will live with us at Four Stones, and Wilgot will make him do his letters, and he can often come here to Oundle so that Sigewif may instruct him."

I had lifted my hand, but she did not give me time to speak.

"And look at how he and Hrald and Ashild care for one another, and how happy he has been - you know he has. And best of all, by leaving him here now I know you will return to me next Summer to fetch him." She paused for a moment and then ended. "It will give you a needed rest from Kilton - or Sceaftesburh - wherever you may be..."

"I...cannot," I began to say. "He is all I have left," I forced out, before my throat grew too tight for speech. I felt the selfishness of my words, and the wrong in denying Ceric of what I well guessed he would truly desire. His father was dead, and I was bound to marry a man at Sceaftesburh or some other burh and take Ceric away from Kilton anyway.

Ælfwyn's arms were already around me. "Please to forgive me, Ceridwen," she whispered. "Think no more on it."

I swallowed the lump in my throat, and tried to smile at her. "I must think on it, all at Kilton are; and you are right to speak of it."

In truth, there was no reason, none at all, for me to balk at going to Sceaftesburh. It must be fine, if Modwynn loved it, and if she had meant it for Gyric. Heahstan would be kind; no one at Kilton would wish a brute on me. He would be good to Ceric; and then they must hope too that I would bear more children and thus add to the lineage. I must take up the thread of my life again, I told myself, tho' it felt as if it had been snapped too short to grasp.

She read my silence, as she was ever skilled at doing, and asked, "You must be sorry you cannot take the veil. Many widows do, and so find peace. How Sigewif would welcome you here at Oundle. My mother too." She touched my hand. "How I should love to have you here! It would be almost as if you could be at Four Stones with me."

I knew that many found peace and content in holy-houses, and knew just as surely that I could not be one of them, even tho' I now longed for quiet and a place of refuge.

She answered for me. "Thinking as you do, you could not in good faith do that."

I shook my head to agree with her. There was no refuge such as nunneries for those who still worshipped the Old Gods.

"Then let us at least be sure we will see the other soon," she went on. "Leave Ceric with me, and come to me yourself next Summer, to take him back." Her eyes were shining, and her words tumbled forth. "You would not wed until Spring, and even if you are got with child it will be early in your course."

She lifted her hand to where the two boys now walked across the dusty yard. Ceric had his arm slung over Hrald's shoulder, and the two small heads were close together, as if they shared a secret.

"If Ceric wishes it he will stay," I answered. "You and I must be parted again, but if our boys are together I will feel closer to you." I made myself smile as we looked at our sons. "And I will come back next Summer."

I said it with a conviction I could not feel, for to make a declaration is to tempt uncertain Fate.

Chapter the Seventh: A Ship Unlike All Others

THE day of leave-taking came; St Mary's Day fell on the morrow. Sidroc and a few men would ride with me to Oundle, and after an early start the next day, on to Saltfleet. Ælfwyn and I took a final walk together, and arm in arm thought aloud about my return the next year. Ceric, never seen without Hrald, now grew quiet and left his friend's side for my own. He had seized upon this chance to stay another nine months, and his eagerness made me both proud and a little saddened.

Now the waggon was ready, and the same hoary Dane sat upon the waggon board, the reins in his still hands as my things were loaded in the back. It was past mid-day; Oundle was not far. The men who served as escort mounted their horses, and Burginde and Ælfwyn's sisters bade me Fare-well. Ashild gave me a handful of flowers, and kissed me, and I bent to kiss Hrald as well. Ceric would show no weakness for his mother before all who stood waiting, but I let myself shed a few tears as I kissed him and bade him be good. His eyes grew wide and he nodded his head quickly and I knew he did not trust himself to speak.

Sidroc came out of the hall in front of two men who carried between them a long and low wooden chest. It was newly made, the wood untouched by beetle or worm, the metal work upon it still bright. He pulled open the tarpaulin flaps and they slid the chest inside next my bags. I was arm and arm with Ælfwyn and he gestured us closer. He lifted the lid. A pure white sheepskin lay folded within, and I saw from its outline it held a sheathed sword. Sidroc parted the sheepskin and we looked upon the hilt of horn, wrapped in silver in wondrous designs. The sheath too was richly worked, of dark leather stamped all over with twisting beasts.

"It is the best of my store," he told us. There was a small casket of carved wood, and he opened that next. Inside was a broad armlet of hammered reddish gold, glinting against a woollen cloth of red. He lifted a second box to reveal a silver drinking cup set with garnets and lapis stones around the footed base.

Only one word could describe the richness of these things, and I said it. "Magnificent." Ælfwyn too murmured at the beauty of them.

He turned to me and said, "You are leaving me your boy. I send these things to Kilton, not in trust, but freely, so that he knows the boy will be well-cared for." He looked over to where Ceric stood with Hrald and Ashild. "I would send him my own boy, but he is too young to foster. If he wants him in a few years I will send him."

I felt Ælfwyn start at these last words, but she did not betray this further, and I gave her arm a squeeze.

Then in a haze of tearful smiles I parted from Ceric and Ælfwyn. I took my seat next the old driver, and Sidroc swung up upon his horse.

I looked back a long time. When at last I could no longer see the faces of those I left behind I tried to square my shoulders to the road before us. Open meadows greeted us, and I was glad to let the breeze bathe my hot cheeks and cool my brow.

The Claiming

It was a quiet ride to Oundle, and we were received there by its Abbess with courtesy once again. In gratitude I slept in that peaceful hall. We were up before dawn, for I knew Sidroc wished to be there waiting for the ship when it arrived, and give no cause for concern to the wary thegns sent to fetch me. I did not look forward to appearing before them without Ceric, and hoped they would not question me harshly. He was my son, his father dead, and I had the right under Ælfred's law to foster him as I pleased; I did not need Godwin's consent. Yet I felt uneasy about seeing them, and uneasy too about leaving the boy I loved so well, tho' I believed it best for him.

"What if the ship is not there?" I asked Sidroc. It was fully day and we had been on the road for several hours. I had been quiet for so long I think my words roused him.

"It will be there," he answered. "Or if they have had trouble with the tides or some mishap, they will come ashore as soon as they can." I know he thought of the grim faces of the thegns Godwin had sent as my body-guard. "What is important is that we must be there, as we said."

But in fact no ship was there. We neared the little settlement, glimpses of green sea peeking through greener trees. We saw the new pier, now finished and jutting out into the water. The tide was low and an expanse of rippled sand lay glistening in the noon light. A few men were gathered about the small timber buildings near the pier end, and turned and walked towards us as the waggon rolled to a stop. Sidroc got off his horse and spoke to them, and his men joined him, and I stepped down from the waggon board, wanting to feel my legs again. In truth I was not sorry to think I had yet another hour or two upon the land before I

97

must board ship and suffer the pangs of the sea-sickness again.

Sidroc came back. "The tide is still low; and there are shoals. The ship will be taking care not to run aground. The tide will lift in less than two hours." He glanced around. There was not much more than the storage sheds there, and nothing to do. "Would you like to ride a short way? Not far is a small hill, a bluff above the water, with a long view." He shrugged. "We might see Kilton's ship."

There was nothing to tempt me there at the pier, and I did not care to sit in the waggon waiting. I nodded. He came back with his own horse and one of his men's, and helped me up upon it. We rode from Four Stones with five men, and he had three of them stay with the waggon and two of them fall in behind us.

We turned out of the little clearing and followed a road of pounded clay that ran along the shoreline. It was mostly shrubby growth with some trees, but the bluff he mentioned was in plain view. We left the road as we neared it, and made our way closer to the base of it, following a path there made by others who had also wished to view the sea from this vantage. When it narrowed we stopped our horses. Sidroc left them with his two men, and pulled off his heavy ring tunic too. He and I went on by foot.

Although the day was hazy the Sun felt hot above, and warmer still as we climbed. The walking was easy, though, for the ground was not stony, and it felt good to be amongst the trees and shrubs before I must take ship again. We could not always see the sea, but at length came to a clearing, and then another, with a wide expanse of green water before us.

The Claiming

Sidroc had been quiet throughout, and now as we stood together I was most aware of how alone we were. There were many things I should say; I wished to speak to him about Ceric, to thank him for his rich gifts to Godwin, and most difficult of all, tell him with all the truth I felt that I wished him well. But I did not say any of it.

It was not that there was more ease in silence than in words, for his nearness worked upon me just as it had when I had been a maid years before. I felt his strength as a man and both the fear and protection of it, and felt within my own breast the queer mix of safety and alarm that being with Sidroc had ever stirred. Most of all I felt his regard for me, and with a keenness that was almost a pain, the abiding regard I had borne for him. He could not know how much his life and safety had meant to me through the long years; my actions had not conveyed it, and I had no right to tell him now. But the knowledge that Sidroc lived was like a signal-fire on a shore I could not hope to gain. It burned, a beacon through day and night and storm and joy, through war and harvest feast, constant and unchanged. This was what he had meant to me these ten years.

We walked and stood together untouching, a hand-span away, and a part of me sought to speak and tell him this. But no good, only sorrow to us both, could come from these words now. If I had but laid my hand upon his arm he would have turned to me and clasped me to him. I knew this, and clenched my hand to still its movement towards him. I would not wrong him, nor harm she who was his faithful wife. I moved not, said nothing, just felt the keenness of his presence at my side.

We wandered a little on the clearing, and turned to the North and followed a pebbled path. The path was overgrown but gave out on another view. From it we could see into a cove beneath the bluff. Standing in the water there was a large ship, and Sidroc stared down at it.

"So it is come," I said, knowing that we must turn at once. I glanced down at the wet rocks below. "The tide is far from full."

Sidroc said nothing, and stood motionless studying the ship below. "That is not your ship," he said, almost under his breath. "That is no ship I have ever seen."

He turned away from it, put his fore fingers to his mouth and let out a piercing whistle. "We are going, now," he told me, and the urgency in his voice made my heart skip. He drew his sword, and started down the path before me. He went so quickly that I must gather up my skirt so I would not trip and fall.

We were halfway down when they came upon us. From out the shrubby growth on either side of the pebbled path jumped blue-clad figures. They were warriors, and unlike any others to come before my eyes. The swords they held before them were short and curved, and the men themselves had amber-coloured skin. They were dressed all alike, and all in blue, and wore curious full leggings of much fabric gathered together instead of wool tight against the skin. Even their tunics were odd, full and gathered at their waists, and they wore blue sashes that trailed along their sides. Most of them were clean-shaven, and so too were their heads, and upon their heads was wrapped more of the blue cloth.

They did not yell or hoot as did other warriors, and made no sound at all, only extended their curved swords at us. There were six of them, and stood in circle around us and took a single step closer.

When they first leapt out at us I had nearly run into Sidroc's back. I held tight to the edges of my mantle and tried to stay my trembling. My stomach churned and my head emptied. I did not cry out; there was no time to, and I heard Sidroc's quick release of breath. He stood still, with his sword before him. The men too were motionless, and then one of them, with a sash a lighter blue than the rest, spoke.

His voice was high and fluting and more like song than any speech I have ever heard. None of the men were tall, but this one was shorter than the rest. He had a long dark moustache that framed his full lips. He moved his sword in the air as he spoke, and tho' his dark eyes were sharp, his voice did not sound angry.

He looked at us carefully, and with, I thought, a practised eye. I was dressed for sea-travel, but my thick mantle of dark green wool was trimmed in brown otter fur down the front and pinned at my throat with a finely wrought bronze pin. My russet gown bore but one jewel, but that was of silver, my gemmed brooch. From under my head wrap of thin linen trailed my chestnut hair.

Sidroc, so tall that he stood more than a full head-span above the taller of these strange men, wore a brown leathern tunic worked with scrolling designs, over a dark blue linen tunic. From his belt glittered the silver-wrapped hilt of his seax in its painted scabbard. Upon his wrist was the silver disk bracelet, and that hand held a sword the worth of which would buy ten of ordinary make.

The Claiming

The man smiled now, showing in front a tooth wrapped in gold. He spoke in his high, song-like voice, to Sidroc, and gestured once with his curved sword that Sidroc should drop his.

Sidroc moved not, but I saw the tail of his eye flick from man to man as he took the measure of those who circled us. The man spoke again, and the one closest to me extended his arm so that his sword tip lay inches from my face. Sidroc lowered his sword.

At once the men closed in around us. None of them touched me, but they unbuckled the weapon-belt from around Sidroc's waist, placed his sword in it, and passed it to the moustached man. He spoke the whole time, both to order them about, and it seemed, to us; for he looked at us and nodded as he spoke. One of the men drew from out a pouch at his sash a long leathern cord, and two others each took one of Sidroc's hands and pulled them behind his back. As the moustached man looked on they lashed his wrists together, pulling tightly with the cord. When they had finished all six men stood before us. Their leader spoke to them, and pointed to two of them. Still holding Sidroc's sword-belt he turned and disappeared through the shrubs with the two, leaving three to guard us.

I stood unmoving where I had stopped when they had sprung upon us. They had pulled Sidroc away from me, and I could not see his face. I yearned to speak to him but my throat was clenched, and I did not know what to say, or if speaking would anger our captors.

The three of them stood before us, swords drawn, and regarded us closely. One began speaking to the others, and tho' the second answered him shortly the third laughed at what he said. The first man glanced about in the direction the moustached man had gone, and turned his eye steadily upon us, and then upon me. His eye roved across my face and hair where it lay loosened along the sleeves of my gown, and he said something with a grin. The other men laughed at this, and the first went on, gesturing at me with his sword.

Now the first sheathed his sword, and began to untie the blue sash at his waist. The others joined him and held their swords before Sidroc. There was a small tree nearby, not more than a sapling, but they backed Sidroc towards it as if they would tie him to its slender trunk. They had not bound my hands, and my fear was so great I spoke at last.

"Should I run?" I asked him.

"No," he said, without taking his eyes from the three. "Do not give them cause to get you alone."

They had tied him now and I was almost panting with my fear. The first man turned to me and leered as he passed his sword to one of the others. One of them spoke angrily to the first, but he answered with a harsh word of his own. Two of them now gestured to me, their grins growing across their faces. I moved back, and the first man stepped in front of Sidroc and towards me. But they had misjudged the reach of Sidroc's long legs.

"You are wrong," said Sidroc between gritted teeth, and lunged forward as he shot his leg out. It caught the second of them around the ankle and tripped him up so that he fell, staggering against the first.

"Scream," yelled Sidroc, and I did.

The men were scrambling to their feet and whirled around. I kept screaming as loudly as I could as the first man wheeled on Sidroc and swung his fist up against his right temple. The second closed in on him as well, but then the shrubs behind me were thrust aside and the moustached leader appeared with the two men he had left with. He kept his voice low but his anger was made clear in his flashing eyes as he looked upon all of us.

Sidroc had been knocked to his knees by the force of the blow to his head, and the little man himself hastened forward to help him to his feet.

"Your men have been at sea too long to trust them with a woman," Sidroc told him, and tho' the man could not understand, he nodded almost as if he did. Sidroc's voice was strong but the tone of his words even, and the man replied to him in a way that made clear his regret.

Sidroc looked now to the two he had tripped. "A willing woman gives more pleasure," he said, but the men would not look at him. One of them had split his lip in his fall and a line of blood dribbled down his chin.

The moustached leader turned and berated his own men, shaking his fist at them and furrowing his brow. Although I was the one who was endangered, he said nothing to me, and scarcely glanced at me the whole time.

Now the leader made us form a single row, with him at our rear, and we took another, less worn track, and started down it. We reached the bottom of the bluff and pushed through a ring of elder shrubs to see a small boat in shallow water. Within was a single man, and beyond in deeper water waited the ship we had seen from above.

They hurried us across the pebbles and into the cold water. It was just past my knees when we reached the boat. The men hoisted me over the side and ordered me with gestures to go to the bow. There were three large barrels in the boat already; they must have come ashore seeking fresh water. It would be crowded with all of us within, and Sidroc, walking carefully with his bound hands, sat down at my side on the narrow bench. Then four men took up oars and we were off. The water was flat with no breeze, and we moved quickly out of the cove.

"I have never before been taken," he said to me, as he settled upon the bench. "You will have to tell me what to do."

His tone was mild, as if he jested, and I turned to him in wonder. The bruise about his eye was already beginning to colour, showing that soon the eye itself would close.

"But I have a feeling you did not make a good captive," he went on.

"I was not a good captive," I allowed.

"Did you fight back?"

"Yes." My thought travelled away across the water to where other waters lapped the rocks at Kilton's shore. "But he had a spear, and I a poker. After he knocked it from my hand he struck me. Then he cut the sash from my waist and tied me to an upright timber."

"Who killed him?"

"One of the men pledged to Gyric. A warrior-monk. He came up behind him and ran his sword through the Dane's body."

"Good," he said. "When I reach the Halls of the Slain I will kill him again." He was silent a little time. "You said a monk killed him? One of their holy men?"

"Yes, Cadmar is his name. He was a prized warrior in another hall before he turned himself over to prayer. You saw him at Kilton; he sits at the high table. A dark curling beard and twinkling eyes."

He laughed. "I recollect him. Strong wrists. He bested me one night at arm-wrestling."

I tried to smile too. "Yes, that is Cadmar."

"He is a good man, that monk." He looked across the sheet of water to the ship that grew ever larger before us. "I would he were in this boat with us now."

He said this as lightly as one who wishes a friend were along for a pleasure sail. Then he dropped his voice and asked, "Are you fearful, shield-maiden?"

I looked down. "Yes, I am fearful."

"I too am fearful, for myself, and most of all for you. But I will not let my fear ride the same horse as my cunning. It must follow behind."

The ship was unlike any I had so far seen. Its prow and stern were curved, like onto the ships of the Saxons and the Danes, but its breadth was much greater, and sat higher out the water. It bore not one but two sails, the larger off a tall mast of dark wood that rose near the centre, and the second that shot off the stern. The sails were slack and partly furled and coloured a deep red. As we neared it a number of men, also clad in gathered trousers, came to peer over the edge at us. The man with the moustache called up to them, and as we reached the side a hempen ladder with slender wooden slats was thrown down to us. One of the men grabbed the end of the ladder, and I nearly fell from my seat as the little boat we were in scraped and bumped along the straked planks of the ship. Five of the men clambered up the ladder in quick order and were lost to view over the side of the ship, so that now only the man with the moustache, Sidroc and I, and the boatsman remained. The man with the moustache now spoke to Sidroc, and gestured that he would untie him so he could climb. He smiled at him and held the curved sword up to his own throat, and Sidroc nodded. Sidroc turned to me, and made a gesture that he would help me go up the ladder, but the moustached man grinned the wider and shook his head. He sliced through the cords with the point of his sword, and waved his hand with the gesture, Go.

Sidroc grasped the ladder and began the climb. The little boat we were in was pitching up and down, and the large one was moving slowly away from us. It looked a long way to go, with nothing but deep water on either side of us, and little to hold onto. He made the climb surely and was met at the side by the men aboard. They were already retying his hands behind his back.

The moustached man smiled again, showing his gold tooth, and waved his hand at the ladder. I turned from him and pulled my gown up a handspan and retied my sash so that my hem was a little above the tops of my boots. I was fearful of tripping and hoped this would help. I shook my hands in the air to feel them again, and grasped the hempen lines as I planted my foot on the slender tread. I moved up three steps, and of a sudden felt the arms of the moustached man on either side of my waist, startling me so I jolted. He said something in a low tone and I heard Sidroc call to me. "Do not look down."

I nodded my head and kept my eyes upon the strakes in front of me, smelling in the warming Sun their softening tar, counting worm-holes to calm myself. With each step my toes bumped against the side as the ladder swung gently against the boat.

Then I was up and two men reached out to pull me aboard. The moustached man came just behind me. Before us was a score of the blue-clad warriors, all bearing at their waists the shining curved swords, and all of their heads wrapped in blue. Boatmen amongst them now began to haul up the little boat, and swiftly hoisted it over the side and set it upon the deck.

I moved to Sidroc's side. The men were lost in their speech with each other, the moustached one gesturing. I looked the length of the ship. There was no fraying to the edges of the red-dyed sails, and the hempen lines lay coiled about pins of brass so brightly polished that they shone like gold. I had never seen a ship laid with such order, or with goods so neatly stowed. There were chests and casks all sorted as to size and shape, sealed with great flattened lumps of lead and stamped with thread-like letters. There was a rowing pit along each side of the smoothly sanded deck, with perhaps thirty oars to a side. Men at rest at the oars looked up at us from them. They were ill-clad, many of them bare-chested, with ragged hair and beards, and I saw that these were no free men who sat there, but slaves, for they were shackled with chains that ran from ankle to ankle through their ranks.

Now my eye fell on two together that made me jump, for their skins were as dark as a Moon-less night, but with a waxen darkness that shone of itself. They had but short crimped hair upon their round heads, smooth faces upon which no beard grew, and eyes as black as their skins. Their limbs were long and slender. Sidroc too spied them, and said in a low voice, "They are from far to the South, the men who hunt the great cats, the pelt of one which I gave to Kilton." He looked long upon them himself, so I thought they were new as well to his eyes. None of all these shackled men spoke out, but some began making faces. One of them bared his teeth to us, and I looked away.

Now I heard Sidroc call out something loudly in his own speech, and saw he looked down the rows of men on either side. Some looked up at him but none responded. The moustached man clapped his hands in anger, and Sidroc said no more.

The man called out, and his call was echoed by another, and the slaves in the rowing pit pushed down upon their oars. The ship hesitated and then moved forward, and the oars stroked down, up, and around. I looked back at the bluff we had so lately stood upon. It seemed so beyond our reach that it may have been a thousand leagues away. Now we were moving from it, and I turned my eyes back to the ship that bore us away.

Near the tall mast was a little wooden structure like a small house, and before this house was a row of fabric screens of the same brilliant hue that the men wore. The screens blocked my view of part of the house, and in the noonday Sun the fabric flickered with a sheen and richness that only silk gives. I looked at these silken screens, billowing softly in the breeze, and wondered what they hid.

"What will they do to us?" I asked Sidroc, as softly as I could.

"Their captain means to treat us well; he has not taken our jewellery but only my weapons." I saw he looked at the slaves at the oars. "I think they will ask for ransom."

I gazed again upon the armed men, dressed all alike, at the trimness of the ship and the number of chests and casks of goods lashed upon the deck. Their war-lord must be rich indeed. "Who are these folk?" I wanted to know.

He shook his head. "From the South, and then East, I think. Abbasids or Khazars; I have not travelled enough to know. They are a long way from home."

Before we could say more the moustached captain turned of a sudden to face us. He spoke to Sidroc, and pointed with gathered fingers to his own mouth, and then clapped his hand over his heart and staggered. Then he shrugged. He did this twice.

"I think the man they once had who spoke our tongue is dead," Sidroc told me. He nodded his head at the man to show he understood, and the man pointed out across the waters and spoke a single word twice.

Now we heard another voice, a sharp, rasping woman's voice, and all turned to it. The blue silken screens that hid our view were a hand's length above the deck, and we glimpsed dark-shod feet moving behind it. The voice called again, and the moustached man answered it, and then two women, clad wholly in gauzy fabrics of dark blue, appeared from behind one of the screens and lifted it up. Even their faces were wrapped, so that little but the eyes could be seen, but those eyes were lustrous and large and dark. The forms of the women were graceful and behind them stood more, dressed just the same. My eyes went to their feet, for their boots were curious. They were of leather stained dark blue, and so soft that they had been sewn with a separate shape for the great toe, like onto the thumb on a glove. No gems could be seen upon the women, indeed naught but their slender dark wrists and darting eyes were revealed.

The man with the moustache bid Sidroc and I come with him, but no others of the men did so. We walked to where the women held the screen raised, and they dropped it behind us. There in front of the little house sat a woman on a thick cushion covered in blue silk, and this cushion sat upon a plush weaving of red and blue and gold, wonderfully worked. Tho' she was as swaddled as all the other women it was easy to see it was she who had called out, for the skin about her eyes was mazed with lines. The movement of the cloth that veiled her face told that she was chewing something. In form she was nearly as broad as she was tall, and sat upon her cushion with her eyes snapping like an angry rook's.

The moustached man bowed to her, and I saw he did not raise his eyes to look her in the face. Seeing her to be a great lady I dipped my head to her. The man stood between us so I could not know if Sidroc showed this old woman any homage, and I dared not speak in front of her to bid him keep his eye from boldness.

Her voice was harsh, and she questioned the man and he answered her in a mild tone, showing often his golden tooth. I raised my head to her and saw her bright eyes fast upon me; and I glanced too at the other women, who with widened eyes looked back at me. The old woman looked too at Sidroc, but with a movement of her plump hand dismissed him. At once the moustached man bowed again, turned to Sidroc and pointed that they go. I too made to move off with them, but the women who had pulled open the blue screen now snapped it down in front of me. I could just see the feet of the men outside, and the brown boots that Sidroc wore.

I turned alone to face the old woman on her cushion, and dipped my head again. She unwound the blue cloth about her head, and I saw the lower part of her face bore a design of dark curving lines pricked into the skin around the chin and mouth. I could not smile at her, my heart was beating too fast, nor could I know if this would give offence. Her snapping eyes met mine and she raised her hand and spoke. Two women came to me and lifted my mantle from my shoulders. Another stepped behind me and I felt her hands under my hair, untying my head wrap. She then moved to my sash and with deft fingers removed it. The two who had taken my mantle now returned and took up the damp hem of my gown. I could feel the loosened hair at the nape of my neck begin to stand of its own. They drew off my gown from over my head and dropped it, and the cool breeze lifted the fine hairs on my bare arms as I stood before the women in my linen shift. This too they grasped and drew off, and I stood naked before the dark eyes of these women, wearing naught but my low stockings and leathern boots. I would not close my eyes but stood staring straight ahead, the Sun striking my face and breasts and thighs and warming me not.

Now the blue-clad women broke silence with their soft laughter and mirthful speech. One of them drew the length of my hair out to the side and let it drop slowly from her fingers as the others, with chiming voices, exclaimed over it. The old woman moved her short finger in the air, and another woman gave me a gentle push at the shoulder that I turn before her. I did so, and came to my starting point to see the old woman gesture me to her.

I came before her, and she reached out her hand and grasped my breast, and then poked at my belly. Her blunt fingers were hard and cool, and I knew I flinched as they groped my flesh. She ran her hand along my thigh, and then spoke at last. Whatever she was chewing had stained her teeth dark, and her tongue also was nearly blue. She said a few words to me and nodded and smiled with tight lips at me.

She spoke to the women, and they stopped their tittering and looked at her, and she pointed to me. She nodded again, and looked well satisfied, and with a flick of her fat hand had them bring my clothes. She spoke to one of the women and the woman went to work, pulling the bronze pin from off my mantle, taking the silver brooch from off my gown. She passed the two jewels to the old woman, who closed her hand about them.

At a gesture from her I put on my shift and gown. I reached for my head wrap but the old woman spoke and it was taken from me. I draped my pin-less mantle about my shoulders as the old woman gave another order. I watched the same woman who had pulled off my jewellery go to the door in the wooden house, open it by its brass handle and go within. I caught a glimpse of more stuff of blue, and many cushions, and of oil lamps like onto cressets hanging overhead. The woman came back and stood before us with a string of coloured glass beads in her hand, which she passed to the old woman. In her other hand she held a long scarf of the same glistening blue she wore. She drew the scarf over my shoulders and with rapid strokes of her brown fingers plaited my hair and bound it up close to my neck, and then wrapped it in the scarf so that no strand could be seen. The old woman fingered the bead necklace and placed it herself around my neck, and said something with a soft laugh.

With another flick of her hand she bid me go, and I turned from her and the eager, mirthful eyes of all of them. The silken screen was pulled apart for me to pass through, and snapped back down again.

I walked out onto the deck and heard the voice of the old woman ring out behind me. The moustached captain called back in answer, hastened to the screen and was let in. A group of his men stood to one side, shifting from foot to foot and talking amongst themselves. Sidroc, his hands still tied behind his back, was sitting alone on a bench. His eyes latched onto me. No one stayed my action so I went to him and stood near. He kept his voice low, and I did not look at him as he spoke.

"What did they do to you? I saw your gown fall to the deck."

"The old woman wanted to see my hair. And my body."

He blew out his breath. "She wants you for her chief, to be one of his women."

114

"I do not think he is aboard," was how I answered this. "I saw into the little house and it looked to be empty."

"What else?"

"The old woman took my jewellery, and put this strand of beads around my neck. And they wrapped up my hair to hide it." I looked at Sidroc from out the tail of my eye.

He shook his head once. "She has marked you for sure." He was silent a time. "You are safe from the rest of them, from all of them, until we reach their war-lord."

I hung my head, but could not find words to answer.

He moved his leg slightly. "I have a small knife, on my left leg, above the ankle."

I looked and could just make out the slightly raised line beneath the wool leggings, strapped over by leathern wrappings. I could not take my eyes from it, thinking of what this could mean. I moved a step nearer him.

"What should I do?" I breathed to him.

He gave out with a low easy laugh. "Nothing," he answered, and stretched out his legs in front of him. He crossed them at the ankle as he looked over at the group of blue clad men. "There are three-and-twenty of them. I would need five good men at my back to make a move now. I tell you this just so that you know it."

I sat down upon the bench but not too close. The men were looking at us, but I folded my hands in my lap and looked down. The ship rocked steadily forward and a few boards creaked. The Sun was lowering in the sky, and the breeze beginning to pick up. Soon there might be enough wind to hoist sail, and we would only go the faster. I glanced across at Sidroc. His eyes were partly closed, and he leant back upon the bench with his legs out in front of him.

Then the silken screen opened, and out stepped the moustached man. He smiled at me and pointed, and held the curtain for me to go through.

"They will part us now," said Sidroc in his low voice.

I stood up but could not make myself walk. I did not know what might befall me with the strange women, or if I would see Sidroc again, either on this ship, or ever in life. Perhaps I would be shut behind the screen with the other women for the rest of the journey, and could not imagine where that might end. The captain hooked his finger at me, and I found myself moving towards the curtain that he held.

"I will see you soon, shield-maiden," called Sidroc softly after me.

Chapter the Eighth: Amongst the Women

THE blue silken screen dropped behind me. The old woman was still upon her cushion, and the other women came and went from the little house, carrying out cushions of their own, workbaskets and small chests. They threw themselves down upon the cushions and unwrapped their faces. All of them were comely, and many of them were very young, some perhaps of thirteen or fourteen Summers, but with their small pointed faces I found it hard to judge. Their brows were dark and their faces unmarked by the curving lines the old woman bore. I stood there, all unknowing what to do. The old woman was talking to one of them and paid me no mind. Then one near to me rose and made a slight gesture with her hand. She vanished into the dimness of the house and returned with a cushion, which she dropped near her own. I sank down upon it and said, "I thank you."

She smiled at me, showing white teeth, perfectly formed. I smiled back, and then she lifted the lid of her work box and drew out a piece of cloth dazzling to the eye, for it was all of silk, with thread work of every colour laid upon a ground of blue silk. She went to work on it, with a needle of such fineness that I marvelled to see it in her fingers, and all the women bent over this or that piece of fine work. I looked around at them and saw the old woman with her eyes closed, and wondered if she drowsed as she sat.

The sky was now deepening to the same blue as the silken screens that surrounded us, and from beyond them I heard the voices of men calling out. I heard men grunting, and then a glad shout as the sails were unfurled to the

117

freshening wind. The huge sail was hoisted over our head by unseen hands, and cast us in deep shade of a sudden; then the ship rolled and strained forward.

I wanted some work to take my mind off the movement of the ship, and what it carried me to. I looked down at my mantle, which without its fine pin I now must hold around my shoulders. I pulled it off and began picking at the hem at the neck edge of it; if I could cut there I could make ties.

She who had brought me the cushion now looked over and saw what I was about, and opened her workbasket. She took from it a small pair of shears so marvellously worked that they made me blink, for they seemed to be cast from pure gold, and were shaped in the likeness of a bird, with the points forming the bill. I exclaimed over them, and she smiled and nodded, and passed them to me. When I held them to the thick wool I knew at once by their great sharpness that gold they could not be, but of some fine steel dipped in the precious stuff. She waved her hand over her workbasket to make me free of it, and after I had cut the hem away I choose one of her thin needles and some silken thread and set to work.

After a time the old woman awakened with a start and began to order the other women about. Some of them rose and brought out from the little house slate cooking slabs which they set upon the wooden deck, a large brazier, which took two to carry, and pots and baskets. Water was dipped from the barrel outside the house, and a fire begun in the brazier from the lit cresset hanging within. The women laughed and talked amongst themselves as they did this. Soon a large pot was bubbling away, and a savour unlike any I had ever smelt rose from it. Pottery bowls were fetched from the house, and a few of the women carried the bowls to the rest of us. A flat-bowled spoon also was given to me, of copper with a long twisted handle. All the women fell to and I was quite hungry myself. Within our bowls was some sort of grain, round and large like onto barley, but much softer to the tooth and golden in colour. Cooked with it were peas and onions, and shreds of some other kind of root I did not know, and all of it was delicious.

Now cups were passed out. These were small and of well-worked bronze. Within them was not ale, but a sort of fruit-water, sweet and tangy on the tongue.

After I had eaten I began to wish I had not. The sea had picked up its swell and the ship moved up and down upon it so that my full stomach lurched with each wave. The women were collecting the bowls and cups now, and I stood up. I felt I must stand rather than sit on the low cushion on the pitching deck. I did not want to be sick in front of them; I did not want to be sick at all, for the shame of it and the weakness it showed. Standing I felt better for a time, but I could see nothing but the silken screen that enclosed us, and when I raised my head to look up my dizziness grew worse. I went and stood by the little house, and leant against it.

I did not know their speech, and was their captive, and likely headed to the camp of their chief as a slave. Sidroc was bound and so outnumbered that there was nothing he could do, and we were now within a swift moving ship carrying us far from his men. I felt it my fault; he would have never been on that bluff at Saltfleet if he had not ridden to escort me there; and tho' I knew the acts of these people were their own, I could not help but bitterly condemn myself. In my mind's eye I saw Sidroc's men riding back to Four Stones with my abandoned packs, leading the great bay stallion; and squeezed my eyes shut as I saw Ceric and Ælfwyn react to our vanishing.

The old woman had taken from me the only jewels I was wearing, including the silver and emerald pin which Ælfwyn had given me so long ago. I had nothing save the clothes I wore, no comb, no linens, no vial of scent nor polished mirror nor any other thing that was my own to remind me of my home and people. Thinking on all this my face grew hot as I stood there, and my throat clenched as I swallowed back tears.

I fought to calm myself and fought also to stem the sea-sickness rising within me. At every pitch the back of my head struck lightly against the wood wall of the house, and I kept my thought upon this, and upon any other thing I could think of to lend me some ease. My face and hands were damp with sweat tho' the breeze was cool. A bird passed overhead; I could see its shadow flicker across the deck in the lowering Sun, and thinking of his freedom I bit my lip to keep from crying out.

I sank down upon the deck with my back braced against the wall, but straightened up again as my mouth began to water. Now I knew I would be sick, and only looked for some place to be so. I put my hand out and turned towards the door, and the woman who had been kind to me was standing there with another woman. She looked at my face and reached for a basin, and as she passed it to me called ahead to a woman near the silken screen. I saw the screen open before me as I retched into the basin, and I ran, almost falling as I went, over that unsteady deck and out of the women's quarters.

I went to the bow near where we had been taken aboard. No one was there, save the men in the oaring well below, and a single blue-clad man to watch them. I stood clinging to the top rail and hung my head over. I was sick with violence and lost my meal quickly, and then bitter bile filled my mouth and I spat and spat. I rested my head upon the rail and let the wind fan my hot forehead. When I felt everything was out I turned and looked to see if there was a water barrel nearby where I might rinse my mouth. I walked not too steadily to the group of barrels and casks lashed together and saw one bore a copper dipper chained to its rim. I took a mouthful and rinsed my mouth, and spat into the basin, and walked back to the side and dumped the contents over the side.

Now that I was out I did not want to go back, and knew I must. The slave men closest were beginning to chatter at me, and I moved as far from their view as I could, but anywhere I stood some of them could see me. I looked down the length of the ship to where Sidroc and the other men must be, at the stern end. Only a narrow walkway passed around the edge of the silken screens, and they must be beyond that.

The Sun was sinking behind us, and I saw we went steadily East. The water was darkening faster than the sky, and I looked long at it. At last I turned and made my way to the screen, hoping that I would not be sick again. I pushed at it and let myself in, and saw a woman crouched near the cushion I had been sitting on. She had my mantle in her hands, and was ripping the otter fur trim from it. I cried out at her, I could not help myself, and she raised her head and I saw it was she who had pulled off my jewellery and plaited my hair. Her eyes looked full of resentment, and her mouth sneered at me as well. I hurried to her as her small brown

121

hands ripped pelt after pelt from the thick wool. I looked up at the old woman, but her eyes were hard and she spoke no word. The other women looked away, and I stood there until she had stripped off every pelt. She twisted her lip to me as she gathered them in her arms and vanished into the house with them.

I finally slept that first night, upon cushions on the open deck with the rest of the women. The ship seemed not to pitch so much or my weariness grew so great that it did not matter. In the morning I was sick again, and again had to run to the bow where I retched up nothing but bile from my empty belly. I wept then, clinging to that rail, and cared not who saw me. The pale blue sky looked down pitilessly above me, and beneath the keel the water foamed as we split the dark waves.

When I went back to the women's quarters the kind woman spotted me and vanished into the little house. She returned with something small in her hands and came and sat next to me. It was a cream-coloured root, knobby like that unto man-root, but when she sliced it open with her sharp work knife and held it to my nose I knew it was not. She took a thin slice and bid me open my mouth, and trusting her, I did so. She placed it upon my tongue and my eyes at once began to water, for the root almost burned within my mouth. She clamped her hands over her own waist to show this would help my sickness, and made chewing motions with her mouth. I bit down and tried to chew. Its flavour was so sharp it made my mouth fill with water, but it did not make me sick.

She brought me also a little of the fruit-water, and bid me drink, and by taking small sips and chewing of the hot root I began to feel less liable to retch. Her kindness to me in my distress moved me greatly, and I had no way to thank her, and no token to give her. I made bold to clasp her hand, and this she understood, for she nodded at me and smiled.

Four days and four nights the ship sailed swiftly East, without pause or stopping to land. Much of the time the winds were fresh, and the dark red sails over our heads billowed so that the mast creaked. But whenever the winds lessened, the sound of the men straining at the oars served as a steady background as the hours passed. From the gap under the silken screens I could see the feet of the blue clad warrior who urged them on, and heard at times the crack of a lash.

The women worked at their coloured thread-work, and played games with tiny counting pieces, and napped upon their cushions. When I felt strong enough I stood and walked about the silken enclosure, tracing again and again its small confines. Behind the windowless house was the covered pail that served as latrine. The women put out buckets of slops from our meals beyond the screens, and none of them ever ventured outside. The old woman did not stay my going, so whenever I felt too unsteady I went to the bow. At times we passed by land so close I thought if I cried out some one might hear me, but no building met my eyes on those flat shores. Much of the time there was naught that met my view save endless seas, and I more than once looked down at the deep waters and wondered if drowning be a painful death. Then I would curse my weakness, and turn and look down towards the stern I could not see, and whisper my hope that Sidroc be well and strong.

On the fore-noon of the fifth day I stood again at the railing of the ship. There was a strong wind, and the men were rowing but lightly.

"I stood with Odda at Ethandun."

The voice was husky and low, but I could not mistake the words. A man near me had stood in the shield-wall of an ealdorman of Ælfred's upon the field at Ethandun, and fought the great battle three years ago last Spring that had been won against the Danes. I raised my head, but dared not turn it, hoping he would speak. "I stood with Odda at Ethandun," he said again.

My throat unclenched enough for speech. "I am of the hall of Kilton," I answered.

A moment passed. "You are sister to Godwin?"

"Sister in marriage to Godwin," I said. I shot a glance to my left. Three rows back, his hands on his oar, sat a man with a tangle of yellow hair. I looked back over the water. "How came you here?"

"The lust for gold brought me," he said. "Tho' I have found nothing but sweat and the lash."

"What will they do to us?" I asked him, and swallowed hard.

124

"You are destined for the Caliph's men, or mayhap even his own sons if you are found pleasing enough. They will put you ashore when we return to their coast, and take you overland to Fès. She will expect a pretty trinket in return for you, or she would sell you herself in the market at Fès."

I had lowered my head to the railing.

"The big Dane they will find good use for. They need endless slaves to row their ships and work their mines."

"He is a powerful war-lord, Sidroc of South Lindisse. He was one of Guthrum's jarls at Ethandun."

"You are with him, were captured together?" he asked.

I made bold to turn a little so I could see his face. "He is a friend to me," I answered, but he scowled at this. I thought of what else to say. "He has much treasure. Will they not wish to ransom us?"

"In their land a woman has no wergild," came the aweful answer. "You will be worth only what you can bring in the markets as a flesh-slave." I squeezed the tears from my eyes and he went on in a low musing voice. "I hear the Caliph keeps a whole hall of women for the use of his picked men. None but women dwell in this hall, with a few gelded men to guard them. To even look upon them is death. The women are of the choicest, and live there in comfort, and also behind the high walls of a garden he has made for them. Babes born to them are flung over the wall onto the rocks below."

I tried not to sob out my misery, but for a moment covered my face with my hands. I had no way to know if this was truth, and spurred my thoughts away from it. I drew breath and looked over the side at the water swirling as it parted against the ship's side. "Will it put your life in danger to speak for us?"

It took a while for his answer. "I know but little of their speech, but half-alive as I am I do not have much to lose."

I turned to him again. "I truly thank you," I said, and hurried from him towards the stern of the ship. I skirted the edge of the silken screens and stood upon the walkway at its narrow point. I could not see around, and was afraid to go much further, lest there be a guard who I startle. I stood there and called out.

"Sidroc," I called, as it was the only name I knew to call.

I called again and a blue-clad man appeared from around the other side of the walkway, holding his hand on the hilt of his curved sword. I did not know what to say and gestured helplessly behind him. Then a second man appeared, and it was the man with the moustache, and I beckoned to him. I recalled his own gesture and grouped my fingers and pointed them towards my mouth. He looked at me with wide eyes and then gave a little shrug. I pointed towards the bow where the slave was. Then I pointed to myself, and beyond the moustached man, and he nodded and said something like Ah. He turned and came back in a few moments with Sidroc before him.

His black eye was now purple, but the swelling was gone, and his face showed at once his gladness at seeing me. He was dressed as he was when we had parted, and looked clean, and with no sign of hurt upon him. His hands were again tied behind his back and it was not until he came up next me that I saw he wore still his silver disk bracelet upon his wrist. The moustached man was chattering away at his side, and the guard who had come first was walking behind him.

"There is a man from Wessex here, at the oar, who can speak their tongue," I told Sidroc. I did not want to tell him what the man had said.

"You are good to have learnt so much," he praised, and looked at me closely. "How do you fare?"

I knew my face must be pinched and pale. "I am sea-sick, that is all," I told him. "But I am well treated. Are your wrists always tied?"

"No. They tied them again just now, so I could come out."

The men at the oars were looking up at us as we passed them, and now we stood before the yellow-haired man. I turned to the moustached captain and pointed down at the slave, and the captain called out to him and moved his hands.

The yellow-haired man looked up at Sidroc and squinted against the Sun. "I stood with Odda at Ethandun," he said again. His eyes ran the length of Sidroc's frame. "It was only the second time I saw you Danes turn and run from us."

Sidroc was not quick to anger, but I could not guess what he was about to do or say. He turned his face to the sky a moment, and tapped his boot once on the deck. He stared down at the Saxon at the oar. "I have seen your back more than once," he answered, with no rancour. "Now we are equal."

Sidroc gazed at the man shackled at his oar-post, while he stood with his hands bound upon the deck.

127

"We will be equal when you sit beside me on this stinking bench," returned the Saxon.

Before Sidroc could answer the captain spoke, gesturing both to Sidroc and to the oarsman. His impatience was made clear by the shortness of his words. The Saxon nodded at him and looked up at Sidroc.

"What do you want me to say?" he asked.

"Whose ship is this?" answered Sidroc.

"That I can tell you myself. It is one of the Caliph of the Idrisids."

"He is their war-lord?" Sidroc wanted to know.

"He is their King."

"What place does he rule?"

"The Idrisids claim the land across the water from Cordova."

"Cordova," Sidroc repeated, and his face told me he knew of it. "Yet we sail East."

The Saxon shrugged at his oar. "I do not know where we are heading now, only that we will return to Fès."

The moustached captain spoke again, and Sidroc turned to him.

"Tell him my men are looking for me, and will bring great treasure to buy our lives."

It was not a simple task for the Saxon to speak the tongue of the Idrisids, and tho' both men spoke slowly it took some little time before the Saxon was sure the other understood.

"He says the Caliph sits on a whole mountain of gold and does not need yours."

Sidroc turned back to where the captain stood, with his thumbs hooked into his blue and gold sash. "What does their Caliph want us for?"

The Saxon spoke to the man, gesturing both to Sidroc and to me. The captain grinned and held his hand far above his own head, and pointed to Sidroc as he spoke.

"You they want for the Caliph's court guard," the Saxon said. "It is made up of all tall men. I have heard of it; men from all over are in its ranks. At Fès you will be forced to fight so that they can gauge your skill. If you survive they will take you into the guard." He spat down near his own bare foot. "It is a very good life, I have heard. Much food and women, too. I hope you die at Fès."

"How far is Fès? How many days?"

The Saxon showed his teeth to Sidroc. "He will not tell me when we will return there."

Sidroc looked again at the moustached man. "This lady is a noble-woman in the land of King Ælfred."

The Saxon gave a short laugh. "She will see Kilton no more. I will tell you what I told her. She is headed to the women's hall of the Caliph's own men. The beads about her neck tell me that." He looked at me then, and lowered his eyes a moment. "I sorrow for you, Lady," he said.

Sidroc turned to the captain and tried again. "Tell him I wish to give my treasure to him, and not to his King."

The Saxon began speaking, and Sidroc watched the face of the Idrisid closely.

"Tell him I have silver, and gold. Also furs from the North, they are of the best."

The Saxon went on, slowly and with much repeating. The eyes under the moustached man's furrowed brow lit up, and he exclaimed, but his look was one of anger.

"Tell him I have also much beeswax, the purest sort," Sidroc went on, and I could see he wracked his brain thinking on those things that might tempt the Idrisids, "also walrus ivory, hard and white, and -"

"I do not know how to say all these things," complained the Saxon. But now the Idrisid spoke up, and the Saxon only listened. At last he said, "He is a man of honour and should be angered, for he does not steal from his Caliph. He thinks only of pleasing his Caliph. You will be a trophy in the guard, and his gift of you will win him much favour."

The captain was nodding his head at all this, as if he understood, and re-hooked his thumbs in his sash. The Saxon gave another short laugh. "If she were not aboard," and here he jerked his head to what lay beyond the silken screens, "he would deal with you quick enough!"

"The old woman? Who is she?" Sidroc asked. "Will she deal with me?"

"The Caliph's kin, or an old favourite; I do not know for sure. No. She will care nothing for you, and has already chosen the lady. It is finished."

Sidroc turned back to the captain, and moved a little closer to him. I could see from his face that he would say anything, and he did.

"Tell him I will also bring many women with bright hair, to take the place of this one. Maidens."

The Saxon went to work, gesturing at me and Sidroc both, but the captain rocked back upon his heels. He shook his head and shot his thumb behind him at the little house.

"No, no. The lady belongs to her, and you to him."

The Idrisid now spread out his hands before him, shook his head again, and gestured that we move away. I did not wish to believe it was over and felt rooted to the spot; and Sidroc too moved not. The man spoke again, more harshly now, and we both began to move. Then Sidroc turned back and looked at the Saxon.

"How long have you been at the oar?" he wanted to know.

The Saxon lifted his eyes as he answered. "Over two years."

"I wish you two more years," Sidroc said. "And that you live to avenge yourself on your captors."

Chapter the Ninth: The Cord is Snapped

IN my dream I was a girl again, and the Prior was lifting me upon the back of his scrawny horse. I could hear my kinsman's men lamenting his death, and as the Prior rode off with me I kept turning in the saddle, for a last look at my kinsman's hall. The wails of the men grew louder, and I awoke on the deck of the Idrisid ship.

Dawn was streaking the dark sky. The air was clammy with mist and my mantle damp with morning dew. The shouts were real, and as I pushed myself up on my cushion I heard the yells of men, and the sound of feet pounding up and down the deck. The women rose up around me and cried out in alarm, and the harsh voice of the old woman sounded from the open door of the little house.

Men everywhere were yelling now, and I heard the crack of the lash over the oar slaves. The women were snatching at their scattered cushions and hurrying into the house. One of them grabbed me but I pushed her away. I ran to the silken screen and blundered against it. I could not find the opening in the dim light and tore blindly at one panel, ripping it from the hempen hanging line. Out on the deck Idrisid men were running and shouting, and three of them now lashed at the slaves. The dawn winds were light and the sail above my head scarce moved. The deck of the ship seemed level and I did not think we were sinking, but I could not know for sure. Through the ripped screen I could see two Idrisid men sliding a bar across the door of the women's house, and locking it with an iron lock. I shuddered for the women, herded into that tiny place, and now bolted within.

I went to the bow. One of the Idrisid men yelled at me but quickly turned back to snapping the lash over the slaves straining at the oars below. I reached the rail and looked backward down the length of the ship, and then I saw it.

There, nearing the stern, was a sharp-prowed ship, whose deck teemed with men. The sky was lightening fast, and I knew from the beaked head that rose from the strange ship's prow and the war-whoops of its men that these were Danes.

Their ship came up along the Idrisid ship, and bumped it side to side with such force that I was thrown to the deck. I stood again and saw the Danes hurl huge iron hooks across the narrow gap of water. Some of these fell short, but most caught over the railing of the Idrisid ship, and the Danes hauling on their lines pulled the two ships close.

They were a ragged lot. Their round shields were saw-toothed from having been hacked at, and the painted designs upon their leathern shield faces were flaked and faded. From the belts that cinched their bellies were suspended long knives in leathern scabbards. The men held spears in their hands, and I saw swords as well, but only a few wore helmets and none ring-shirts of iron.

There were so many of them that I could not guess how their ship held them, for it was far smaller than that of the Idrisids. They let go a volley of spears, and the Idrisid men returned it with light throwing spears of their own. Now the Danes began to haul wooden ladders from their midst and to swing them against the rail of the Idrisid ship. The deck of the Idrisids' was higher than that of the Danes, and many of the first Danes were cut down by the curved swords in the hands of the waiting warriors before they landed. But still they came, while others amongst them pulled at the lines between the ships and narrowed the gap to an arm's length. Soon the ladders were covered with Danes, and more and more of them swarmed aboard.

Idrisids hacked at the lines holding the iron hooks, trying to free their ship. The Danish ship slid closer down the side of ours, and spears whistled by. One of them sunk into the back of an oar slave, and an Idrisid shoved him away from the oar and took it up himself. But soon he abandoned this, as few slaves were now rowing, and the drag of two ships grew too great.

The damp air was filled with war-cries and yells, and the screams of men as they met the steel of spear or sword. I crouched down behind the railing, and crawled to the small boat that lay upon the deck in which we had been rowed at our capture. It gave some shelter, but a spear falling a hand's span away told me how little. I resolved to crawl back to the rail where I could see, and grasped the still-shuddering spear in my hands and pulled its point from the deck. I stood and for a moment faced the tumult before me. The rising Sun shone gold upon the water, and I squinted to try to pick Sidroc out from the forms that crowded the stern and mid ship.

Now Idrisids were coming my way, being driven back by the onslaught of the Danes. The slaves in the oar wells, seeing this, let go their oars and hooted and whistled and slammed their chains against the foot blocks. The Idrisids came, their backs to me, and some of them fell as they did so, Danish steel having found home in their blue-clad bodies. One of their swords rolled a half circle towards me and skittered to a stop at my feet. I bent down and took it up, and with the sharp sword in my right hand and the heavy spear in my left, moved closer to the base of the mast. I could see the faces of some of the Danes now, who rushed with bared teeth and howling oaths. As the next Idrisid came close I flung out the sword in my hand and swept it like a scythe against the back of his body. I was trembling badly, and there was not much force in my hand, and at the moment of the blow I closed my eyes; but as I swung I thought of the two who had wanted to ravish me.

I heard a howl and saw the man crumple to the deck, then watched as he rolled away the growing line of blood streaking the blue cloth at his waist. Idrisids and Danes were surging past me, grunting, yelling, with spear and sword glinting in their closed fists. Another blue-clad warrior backed near me, and when he came within my reach I again swung out the shining curved sword, and cut him across the back of the legs. He fell, almost at my knees, and for a horrible moment looked up in surprise at me before a Dane plunged a sword in his breast.

The Dane was Sidroc. He pulled his sword from out the man's chest, and knocked the Idrisid sword from my right hand with his left. His left arm swung around my body, and the spear I held fell, and then his arm closed about my neck as he dragged me to the side of the ship. He was yelling, but not at me. He was bellowing across at the men still upon the Danish ship. He rammed his sword between the opening of the rail and the deck planks, and then hoisted me with both arms into the air. I clung to him, crying out his name, but he was yelling all the time at the Danes, and then cast me with violence over the side of the Idrisid ship and into the water.

It took a long time to fall. I heard my own scream, and kept on hearing it as the side of my body hit the dark water. My mantle flew up around my head, and as I sank my opened mouth filled with cold sea water. I went down, and down, and my brain and ears and nose felt like they would burst. Then I was up, choking and screaming, and my arms felt as lead under the weight of my heavy wool mantle and gown. The mantle billowed around me but my legs could scarce move, trapped in my wet clothes. I sank, and the water closed again around me, and I knew I had been grabbed by Ran, the greedy Lady of the Sea who hungers for the drowned.

Her hands were clenched about me, and my nose and mouth were filled again. All was darkness and cold and the heavy bursting feeling in my head. Then I was up once more, and there in the water with me were two Danes, and they were laughing.

One of them was clean shaven, and one had red hair and a long beard, and both of them were grasping at my body as I struggled in the frigid waters. I grabbed at them as I went down again, and felt their reaching hands touch my arms, my waist and breast; and as I thrashed they kept on with their laughter. Then one of them swung me around and held me almost as Sidroc had, with his arm about my neck, and I sputtered and choked as I tried to turn and take hold of him. In the water nearby I glimpsed the floating bodies of a few blue-clad Idrisids, and some too of the Danes.

Now we were moving to their ship, and the clean shaven one took hold of a rope where it dragged in the water, and they both turned me about and I wrapped my arms about the neck of the red haired one as we were hauled up the side of the Danish ship. We bumped up against the side as we went, tho' the man tried with his legs to keep me from hitting too hard.

We were met at the rail by two others, who pulled me over the side. When I let go the red haired man I saw I had some of his beard in my fingers. The clean shaven one followed us up, and the two of them laughed together.

The sea battle was nearly over. I stood dripping upon the deck of the Danish ship and saw the few Idrisid warriors left cast down their weapons and throw up their hands. The Danes were ranging up and down their ship, seeking out any others who might resist. The air rang with their calls and shouts, but now they were the sharp joyous cries of victory and not blood-lust. Some of them had begun to swing or jump back from the Idrisid ship, and I moved down the deck to the bow and sank upon a bench near a pile of roped casks.

Two of the Danes, who looked to be chiefs amongst them, began calling out orders as they moved between the ships. All of the men were busy and none of them paid me any mind. I could not see Sidroc and felt sick with not knowing how he fared. At times I stood up upon the bench to try and see better, but some of the Danes now began to look at me so I again sat.

I had pulled off my heavy mantle and wrung it out, and spread it over a cask to dry. There was no place I could go to take off my gown and shift and wring them, and they both clung to my skin, but I did the best I could a handful at a time. The blue head scarf was still tightly wrapped upon my head and I shook it out, and unbraided my sopping hair and combed it with my shaking fingers.

Then I saw Sidroc in the stern of the Danish ship, and I jumped up. He looked straight and hale and I could hear his voice. He was talking to three Danes, including the two who had leapt in after me. He moved towards me and raised his hand in greeting.

"They tell me you do not swim very well," he said with a laugh.

"I do not swim at all," I answered, and tried to keep the anger from my voice.

"One day I will teach you." He looked down at me, and now his tone was grave. "First you must remember that the shield-maidens do not themselves fight, but only urge men to do their best in battle."

"I cut two of them," I said back.

"Yes, I saw. You are very bold. I will always take pride in what I saw you do just now. But you are no trained warrior. The third man would have turned on you and you might be dead now."

He looked now to the men and spoke to them, and then back to me. "They have no women's clothes aboard; you will have to stay wet for a while."

"I will be all right," I said, and wrung out the hem of my gown again. In truth it was all I could do to keep from shivering. I had caused the maiming and perhaps death of two of the Idrisids, and then swallowed great gulps of sea water. My body hurt from being slammed into the hard water, and my skin was bruised and tender from so much man-handling. My nose stung and my throat was raw from screaming. I felt shaky and weak from it all.

"I did not mean to fright you by throwing you overboard. I had to keep you safe."

His voice was low, and the sea water still streaming from my hair hid the tears that welled in my eyes.

"I will teach you to swim," he said again, "so that one day you will love the water as I do."

I could do nothing but nod.

Now I saw that his legging was ripped open at the left ankle, and the leathern wrapping from that leg gone. He answered my unspoken question. "When the Danes struck I ran to the Saxon at the oar. He pulled the knife from around my leg and cut my hands free. I shouted out to the Danes and found a weapon." He looked across at the ship of the Idrisids. "I do not much like those curved swords; they are sharp as razors but have no reach. It took a while to find a dead Dane and get a real sword."

"What happened to their captain, the one with the moustache?"

"He was killed as soon as the Danes boarded." He thought a moment. "He was a fair dice player."

"Is that what you did together?"

"You do not need to talk while throwing dice," he returned. "But whenever my hands were untied one of his men had his sword at my throat."

Now one of the chiefs called out to Sidroc and he went over and spoke to the man, and two others with him. They spoke a long while, sometimes it seemed in jest and other times almost in heat.

When he came back he sat down next to me.

"Do you know these men?" I asked.

"None by face. Some by name."

"But they know who you are," I said in certainty.

"No," he said quietly.

"How can they not? You are one of Guthrum's jarls, one of the richest."

"Because I will not tell them."

My mouth opened in surprise.

"If they knew who I am, they would want much treasure for me," he said. "Right now I bargain only for our freedom and a small share of the booty."

I nodded my head in understanding. "What wisdom you have," I breathed.

He laughed again. "That is not wisdom, only craft." He looked over to where the men stood talking. "It is not to my advantage for them to know who I am. I helped them take the ship and they expect to give me a share in the plunder."

My eyes followed his. "What did you tell them of me?" was my next question.

"Only the truth. That you are my wife."

His eyes were still fixed on the Danes as he said this, and then he added lightly, "I will see if I can find you a blanket."

The Claiming

Sidroc and the rest of the Danes spent much of the morning going back and forth between the two ships. The first time he returned with his own sword-belt buckled around his waist, and both his fine sword and seax within it. The importance of this to him could be read in his face at a glance. A man such as he lived and died by his steel; and his was of the best, known to him, and trusted through hard usage. He came back three times with arms full of different things, blankets and hides and sheepskins and such, and a plain Danish knife, and dropped them at my feet. I saw some men's clothing as well. He spread the things around for me to see.

"I did not bring you any of their clothes. I do not want you dressed as a slave-girl."

I nodded my head in assent.

"But I brought you this." Under the blankets and bolts of cloth was one of the women's workbaskets. I opened it and found it full of silk thread, a full quill of their fine steel needles, a sharpening file, and most wonderful of all, another pair of the sharp bird-shaped shears. I lifted the top out of the basket and beneath was a small well-wrought mirror of polished silver, a fine-toothed comb carved of bone or even ivory, and a pair of tweezers with points as sharp as pins. There were also two tiny pottery pots, so small they would rest in the palm of the hand. I pulled at the waxed stoppers and peered within. The first held a black substance like powdered charcoal, or ground oak gall. I held it up for Sidroc to see. "I think it is ink, without the apple gum added," I told him.

He shook his head. "No. This is for the eyes, to make them more beautiful. Both men and women decorate their eyes with this at Haithabu."

I looked up at him and he went on, "One of the trading posts at home. I went there a few times when I was young."

He reached for the other pot and opened it. Within was a ruddy ointment, with a sheen like beeswax. "And this is for the lip," he said, and dipped his finger into it. "But only women use this one."

Now that he had it on his finger, he did not know what to do with it. He reached over and touched my lower lip with it.

I thought my cheek might flame and I lowered my head.

I looked at all the things, and thought upon she who had lost her workbasket, and asked him, "What will they do to the women?"

He shrugged. "You were their captive. You should not care."

He saw this would not satisfy me, and went on, "They will be no worse off than they were. Since the old woman is important, perhaps the Dane will try to ransom them back, should he wish to try his hand in the South."

We both turned our heads and looked over to the ship of the Idrisids. "I could not find your jewellery," he went on. "The women are hiding things upon themselves and the Dane does not want them touched."

"I do not care about the mantle pin, but the brooch was the silver one that Ælfwyn gave me."

"O," he said. "Well, we will be someplace soon where I can get you silver, and maybe gold, too."

I looked away from him. He took a breath and spoke again. "Look at this."

He had unrolled before me a small weaving of moss green, with blue and gold and red in it. But it was not the kind of coloured weaving that I made at my loom at Kilton, for the woof did not lay flat against the warp. This was like onto the one that the old woman had sat upon. The woof stood up against the grain of the warp, and each yarn thread lay so close upon the next that it was like the fur of a cat or dog. It was wonderfully soft, like a cat, and had a lustre like silk.

"It is too heavy to wear, but it will be soft for you to sleep on," he said.

"It is most beautiful," I returned, and meant it.

Now came a great deal of noise and shouting from the Idrisid ship and we stood up and looked over. All the rowing slaves were standing upon its deck, and the Danes were walking amongst them, looking at their teeth and testing the brawn in their arms. Some of the slaves were young and hale, but some were so weak they could scarce keep their feet.

"What are they doing?" I asked Sidroc.

"Dividing up the slaves between the two ships."

Now a few were picked out and made to understand that they were to swing from the deck of the Idrisid ship to the Danish one. Most did this on the first swing, but a few pushed off so feebly that they swung back over the deck of the Idrisid ship, and with much laughing by the Danes, were pushed hard to breech the gap. One man even let go the rope and fell in the water, and thrashed gasping until they lowered him a rope and hauled him in.

After a number of the slaves had swung over so too did one of the head Danes. Sidroc walked over to the man, and began talking to him, and as he did, pointed to one of the rowing slaves. I saw it was the yellow-haired Saxon.

Sidroc kept talking, but the Dane he spoke to was scowling. Finally he spoke, and Sidroc pointed again to the Saxon, and gestured to him, Come. The Saxon made no move.

Sidroc spoke to him, and his words were firm and steady. "Saxon, I give you something you have not had in many a Moon: I give you a choice. You can be their slave, or mine."

The Saxon looked at Sidroc, perhaps recalling their words together, and looked at the oar well on the Danish ship. He then went to stand by Sidroc.

Sidroc turned his back on the Dane, and the Saxon followed him to where I waited. When they got within a few feet of me Sidroc turned to him and said, "You have cost me nothing but a few words. Your life then means nothing to me, and I will kill you in an instant if you anger me. You understand this, Saxon?"

The Saxon nodded. Now Sidroc looked at me. "Do not speak to him," he ordered me.

I did not even answer, and Sidroc pointed to the deck as he looked at the Saxon. "Sit there and do not move or speak until I return," he told him, and the man dropped to the deck.

As Sidroc moved off to the other Danes I knelt down and began to sort through the things he had brought. I glanced at the Saxon from the tail of my eye. Even through his tangled beard I could see his lips were pursed. He had said the lust for gold had taken him to the land of the Idrisids, and I wondered if he would try to now escape to reach Wessex again. As I moved about, folding and stacking things, I saw old lash marks upon his Sun-weathered back. It was not easy for me to guess his age; he might have thirty Summers or thirty-five.

Sidroc came back and tossed a pair of dark boots at the Saxon's bare feet. They were of the Idrisids, for they were stained dark blue. He squatted down next to me and sifted through the pile of men's things I had started, and pulled out a tunic and a pair of leggings, and also tossed them without a word to the Saxon. He moved his hand to show the Saxon to put these things on, and the man stood behind us and stripped off his ragged leggings and did so.

I did not think Sidroc wanted me to speak and could not think what to say even if he did. It felt awkward to have the man so near to us. I looked down the length of the Danish ship, but did not let my eyes rest on any one man. I wondered what would happen next, whether the two ships would part or travel together. Sidroc had said that soon we would be somewhere where he could get gold and silver, and I wondered where that might be.

Now there was more noise coming from the Idrisid ship, and we stood to see better.

Upon its deck were the two men with skin as dark as blacked iron, and the two chief Danes were before them, arguing. I could guess by their gestures that each chief wanted them for their own, and neither would give them up to the other. Then they resolved to settle the matter by each taking one, but when they gestured one to swing over to the Danish ship, he would not do so without the other. Their distress at being parted was great, and I was moved with pity for them. With their shining skin and huge eyes they had peculiar beauty, and their loyalty each to each was deep.

"Likely they are brothers, or kin of some kind," I said aloud. "They may sicken and die without the other."

At last the Danes drew straws for the two, and the longer straw was pulled by the chief who had claimed the Idrisid ship. So the two blacked men returned to the familiar oar well, while the other Dane showed his disgust at his poor luck. Sidroc looked upon all this and said, "Their Gods are with them, and they will not be at the oar long. There are folk at home who will pay just to look at them."

Now both ships made ready to unfurl their sails.

"We are staying on this one?" I asked. It was more crowded and far less clean than that of the Idrisids, but I was not eager to return to the ship on which we were captives. I hugged myself in gratitude that we lived, and were well, and freed from the ends I had feared for us.

146

"Yes," said Sidroc, as he busied himself again with his battle-gain. "The other is turning West. We will sail East a while longer."

He did not look at me as he said this. I knew we had already sailed eight days to the East, far out into the Northern Sea, and this did not seem right; but I said nothing.

Both crews were now hard at work, and Danes called out Fare-well from ship to ship as they drew apart. The woven sails filled and we surged forward. Sidroc rose and we moved to the rail and looked out at the Idrisid ship. The red sails luffed as it tacked and then billowed as they caught the wind. Seated in the oar well we could glimpse some of the Idrisid warriors, now chained as once their rowing slaves had been.

Sidroc looked after them and gave a hard laugh. "I have already served in my own King's body-guard," he said. "I do not need to do that again."

He glanced at me, and his smile left his face. "Take off that necklace," he said. I had forgotten it was still there, and I drew the string of glass beads over my head. He put his hands within it and with a quick snap broke the silken cord, scattering the beads over the surface of the blue waters.

Chapter the Tenth: The Baltic

NOW that we were under way the men began to go about the tasks of the ship. The wind had picked up and a mixture of Danes and slaves from the Idrisid ship sat at the oars, but did not need to row hard. We had no wounded aboard; all the Danes who had suffered hurt had stayed upon the Idrisid ship which was heading West. Those with us sorted through their plunder, and talked and boasted of the battle just won. Their gains did not look great, and I thought that most of the riches of the Idrisid ship had sailed off with the chief Dane who had claimed it.

An ale cask was opened, and the men hooted when it was tapped. We stood to walk in line before it, and were handed wooden cups. When we rose Sidroc gestured to the Saxon that he come too, and the man did, and stood with us. I had wrapped the long blue scarf about my damp hair like my own head wrap, but I was most aware I was the sole woman aboard. I kept my eyes down, but those of the men at the oars still met mine. I thought they looked at all three of us, and could not guess what they might be thinking.

Near the ale cask stood a man with a basket, and we each too got a brown loaf, and a bit of smoked meat. We returned to the bench we had been sitting on, and the Saxon sat upon the deck. Only now did I begin to feel how hungry I was, and thirsty too. I took my wooden cup of ale thankfully. It was beginning to sour, but it was strong and chased the salt burn from my mouth.

We ate in near silence, and once in a while I looked at the Saxon crouched off to our side. Sidroc spoke harshly to him when he spoke at all, but he had clothed the man and made certain he was fed as well as he himself was. The Saxon knew of Godwin, and may even have met him, and I yearned to speak to him of Wessex amidst all these strange men.

Now I turned to Sidroc and spoke to him in a low voice. "Why do you not let him talk?" I wanted to know.

"It is dangerous," he answered.

This did not make sense. No one of the other Danes could likely understand our speech, and even if they did, the man had made it clear he wished to go with Sidroc, and not them.

"Can we not even ask his name?"

"He is my slave. Slaves have no name."

I tried again. "He is no common slave. He is of Wessex, and surely free-born; mayhap even a thegn. Should we not try to trust him, and -"

He turned on me, his voice hard. "I trust no man," he said. "That is why I still live."

"He will want to get back to Angle-land, as we do," I persisted.

"If he had the chance he would kill me and rape you," he shot back.

My shoulders slumped and I was silent.

He went on, but with no anger. "You think that because he is from your land and far from home that he will be friendly to you. You know nothing of him. He is likely outlawed in Wessex, a deserter to your King, or worse."

All these things could be true, or none of them; but just then I was too overcome by my own weariness to argue. I knew I wished to speak to the man to feel less alone; we had escaped a common enemy and now shared the uncertainties that awaited us with the Danes. I looked around the crowded ship. Men sat at every oar, and others sprawled across the narrow deck between. In the stern their chief stood at the steering-beam, squinting at the sail overhead. A cluster of men stood at his back.

Since he had come aboard Sidroc had spent much time talking with these men, and most especially the chief and his closest followers. By their sideways glances I saw how they studied him, and I thought some muttered beneath their breaths about us. I could not know who they thought he truly was; but it was clear that they noted well the worth of his arms, the fineness of his clothing, and the jewelled-hilted seax on his belt, which told them he had fought in Angle-land. None of them, even their chief, or the richer chief who had made off with the Idrisid ship, had weapons or clothes to match his. Although he talked and jested with them I thought Sidroc felt we had something to fear from these men, and thinking this made it hard to feel any real ease about being amongst them.

The Sun had not been strong and my clothes would stay damp until it was. The sky was beginning to pale to its evening hue, and I shivered as the wind crossed my face. At least I was not sea-sick, only tired in every bone of my body.

"You need sleep," Sidroc said, and I opened my eyes. He squatted down and unrolled the plush weaving so that one edge lay along the hull of the ship. "I will lie at your back."

I sank down upon it and pulled at the pile of random cloth at my feet. As it surged forward the ship rose and fell gently under me, and the creaking of its timbers and noise of the men grew fainter.

I do not know when Sidroc lay down that night, but I awoke, cramped and sore, to find him already on his feet, and peering through the dawn mist. "Is there land?" I asked.

"No, and the winds have lightened so much that our going has been slow."

I came and stood by him, and rolled my aching shoulders as I looked out. The sea and sky were nearly the same grey colour, and the drifting mists made it hard to tell where one ended and the other began.

"Where are they taking us?" I asked him, and hope I hid the fear I felt.

"They are not taking us anywhere," he said, and gave a low laugh that put me more at ease. "We are sailing with them until they reach the trading posts they seek."

I squinted into the gathering light, trying to find the Sun. "We have sailed so long, we must be far past Frankland," I said, and tried to recall all the charts I had seen, both at the Priory, and the few at Kilton, that showed these lands to the East.

"Yes," he agreed, "we have passed their coasts, and sailed both North and East."

"There is nothing but wildness beyond," I said.

He again laughed. "My home is there, and it far from wild. But we have passed those shores, and are now further East, in the sea known as Baltic. Its shores yield much amber. We have amber at home, but the finest washes up on these Southern shores."

"Then it is a rich place?" I asked, hoping this meant that many ships put in there, some of which would be heading West.

"It is, as you said, a wild place, but great riches in the form of furs and amber and slaves and salt are traded in these parts. There are trading posts to which folk from many lands come in the Summer. They are run by the Wends, the big tribe here. It is late in the season and some of the posts may be shutting down soon."

"Have you then been here?" I asked hopefully, for a familiar place is surer than a strange one.

"Never. Not near this coast. But some of my people have traded here in Summers a long time."

He did not have any sense of ease in his voice as he said this, and he went on. "The Svear range here."

"Who are they?"

"The tribe that rules the land directly East of my home, over the water."

"Are they then like you? Like the Danes?"

"Yes, and no." He looked across the empty waters. "They are warriors, of the best."

"Then they are raiders."

He only nodded, but from the little he said I knew these Svear were men to be feared.

We were both still, and a little shiver ran through me. The bloom of Summer was past, and I looked over the grey seas through which we ploughed. "No one sails these waters in Winter," I said, feeling it to be true.

He nodded his head in agreement. "There is ice in the water then, small mountains of it."

The sailing season was short, four or five months, perhaps, before the Baltic could not be crossed until the following Spring. "And the folk in the trading posts, where do they go?"

He waved his hand in no particular direction. "Those who have sailed there for the season sail home. Those who have come overland, from further South, start earlier to make it before the snow flies."

So those who did not hasten home would be stranded on these wild coasts, I thought; but this I did not say.

I had been aship enough days to learn that the winds at dawn were always light, but morning came fully, and the sail hung limp in the still air. The chief, after staring at the sky and the water, ordered the sail furled, and called out to his men to begin rowing. A mix of slaves from the Idrisid ship and the Danes themselves manned the oars, and they struck out strongly and the ship glided forward under their efforts.

We had each gotten a cup of water, a cup of ale, and another loaf. I sat with Sidroc on the bench as we ate, the Saxon not far from us, crouched upon the deck. I gave my ale to Sidroc; it was too sour for my taste but he downed it in almost a single mouthful. I sipped at my water to make it last and used a bit of it to dampen my face. There was no water aboard for washing; each precious drop was to be drunk, but I could no longer bear the salt feel of the sea water upon my skin. My hair, too, hung in ropey lengths along my back. It had dried, but with the salt in it. I took out the delicate comb from the workbasket Sidroc had brought me. The teeth were so closely spaced that I could but only place it to my scalp, or comb out the tips of my hair. The women of the Idrisids must have fine hair indeed to use such a comb, and mine was thick and fell in curling waves.

The Sun refused to show her face behind the thin blue haze, and the morning wore on. The men at the oars had worked steadily, and their bodies glistened with sweat. The chief, still at the steering-beam, called out again, and men answered, and those who had been rowing answered loudest. Sidroc of a sudden stood up.

"Well, Saxon," he said to the man who had been watching those at labour, "your God is good to you, and you are going to get your wish. Now we will row together, as you had hoped."

154

He spoke as if he were laughing to himself, and unbuckled his sword-belt and laid it down upon the bench at my side. "This I entrust to you," he smiled. My face must have shown some alarm, because he went on, "No one will touch it."

He unlaced his tunic of scrolled and carved leather, and drew it off, and pulled off his linen tunic. As he turned to me I saw again the long curved scar under his left arm, the wound that I had searched and dressed ten years ago. The hair upon his chest was dark and I barely glimpsed the outline of the blue dragon pricked into the skin beneath it.

The yellow-haired Saxon too had stood and stripped off his tunic, and now followed Sidroc as he made his way to the oar well. I saw Danes nod in approval as he tapped a man upon the back and swung his long legs down against the foot block, and then take the oar from the man on the upstroke so that no power was lost. Sidroc had gestured the Saxon to take the place of the man in front of him, and the Saxon did so. Others of the Danes relieved the first group of rowers, until every oar was freshly manned.

I could still see no land, on either side of the ship, and I began to wonder how with nothing to sight upon the chief at the steering-beam could hold a course. The Sun crept across the sky, throwing no shadows, and again the chief called out and more Danes swung behind the oars. Sidroc and the Saxon stood up and headed back to the bow where I waited. Their bodies ran with sweat, even their dark leggings showed it; and I had no linens, only lengths of wool cloth, which I handed them. The Saxon nodded at me, the first time he had dared acknowledge me since Sidroc had claimed him. They dried themselves and Sidroc sat down next to me and stretched out his legs.

"My hands are as soft as a girl's," he laughed. I had to smile as well, for they were far from it; large, hard, well-calloused from riding and spear-handling; but still he held them before me. The palms were slightly reddened where a blister must be rising. "I have been too long at soft work," he went on, and I knew the last time he sailed he must have stood in the stern and ordered others about.

A Dane now came with ale, and a cup of water each, and the men drank. Sidroc pulled his linen tunic and leathern shirt back on, and as he did I saw one of the Danes closely watching him. It was a man who had rarely taken his eyes off of us since we had come aboard, and I had from the first wondered if he had heard of Sidroc and would guess who he was. As our journey had gone on his eye had become bolder. There might a score of reasons for his interest in us; perchance he had once seen Sidroc, and barely recalled him, or had kin killed by him; or simply guessed him to be valuable for ransom, and wished to collect it; or he may have only lusted for the fine sword and knife Sidroc carried.

Now the man stood up and began to cross over to where we sat. He was stocky, above middle-age, with hair that was more grey than yellow, and a round nose that had once been pulped. His scornful mouth showed long teeth.

Sidroc's sword-belt still lay upon the bench, and as the man came closer, Sidroc reached for it and in a quick stroke flipped his seax into his right hand. Even in the dull light the blade flashed. The man jerked to a stop. Sidroc leant forward and studied his own fingertips, and then with the tip of the seax began to pare his fingernails. The parings flicked to the deck, and he did not look up at the man.

A long moment went by. The Saxon sat upon the deck, his arms wrapped around his legs, and I upon the bench, pretending also not to see the Dane. Then Sidroc cocked his head, and looked up at the man, and said something. The man hesitated, looked at Sidroc, and then shook his head. After a moment longer he turned and went back to his side of the deck.

"What did you say to him?" I murmured, after I saw the man look away to sea.

"Only that I would be glad to cut his hair for him, but that my hand might slip."

The wind rose enough so that the sail could be hoisted, and Sidroc did not need to take another turn at the oars. But the wind seemed to come from all directions at once, making the ship pitch, and my belly unsteady. I sat upon the deck with my back against the hull, and tried to brace myself from the worst of the movement, but the ship was as a bobbing cork and me a speck upon it. I could not eat my bread and smoked meat when it was offered, but went up just the same to claim it so that I might give it to Sidroc. Just holding it in my hand made my belly lurch and I scarce made it back to the bow.

To keep my mind from my misery I traced again and again with my fingers the patterns in the plush weaving beneath me. At last I lay down upon it and turned my face to the dark strakes of the hull and tried to sink into sleep.

I did sleep, but fitfully, with the grunting of the men and the sloughing of the wind in the sail and the straining of the ship against it filling my ears. Once when I awoke I saw the brightness of stars overhead, and knew the haze had lifted.

I awoke again to the gladsome shouts of the Danes. It was fully day, and I rolled and stood and looked past them at they stared over the starboard side.

"Land," I said aloud, tho' no one be near me. A green mass rose in the distance in the clear morning air, and we were pointed towards it. Men worked at the oars, and looking down at the stern I saw the chief with his hand upon the steering-beam. Sidroc stood near him.

I dropped to my knees and began to roll up my weaving, and hastily to pile up the hides and sheepskins and other things. I did not know how soon we might land, but the ship was sailing so speedily that I wanted to be ready at once.

The sail swung, and I stood again to look out. We were running along the coast now, and I strained to make it out. Some of it was marsh, but most of it was forest. I saw no settlements, but surely they must be close or the men would not have cried out as they did. Some little time passed, during which I did not lift my eyes from the shore, and then we saw it.

It was a small out-post, of less than a score of buildings, none of them large. Some of them were ranged along a sandy shore, and others lined a single road that split the settlement into two. We were close enough to see folk moving about, and a team of yoked oxen, with the longest horns I have ever seen, hitched to a large wain. A few small boats lay in the water, but no ship such as the Dane's; and I saw at one end of the settlement a pier which had half-way fallen into the shallow water.

At last Sidroc came down the deck to me, the Saxon at his heels. I think I trembled with happiness, and with weakness, too; and held up my hands to him.

"Now we can go ashore," I said, with all the gladness I felt.

"We will not go ashore here," he told me.

I could not believe it. "No? But why?"

He turned from me with a shake of his head. "Not here."

I moved around him so he must look at me. "I am filthy, and sore. I have been captured, almost ravished, marked to be a slave-girl, and for days been sea-sick. I nearly drowned. I want to get off this ship."

He looked up at the sky a moment before answering. "There is another trading post, in two days' time. We will go ashore there."

None of this made sense, and I repeated it in wonder. "Two days? And further East?"

He nodded his head, Yes.

"We have already gone so far East. You told the Idrisids your men would be looking for you. Should we not then head back and try to find them?"

It took him some little time to respond. "My men will not find me," he said, and then looked me full in the face. "I do not want them to, for then I will have to kill them."

It took a moment for me to understand all this. When I finally spoke, it sounded as if my voice came from afar. "Am I then your captive?" I asked him.

He did not answer, and I went on in a whisper. "You do not want to go back."

I could no longer keep my feet and sunk first to the bench, and then to my knees on the deck. I did not weep, only knelt there huddled as this whirled within my brain.

I was aware of the ship growing closer, and of the action of the men upon it as they readied themselves to land, but I did not stand to see it. The Danes shipped their oars, and I heard the plash of other boats drawing near, and knew the Danes scrambled over the side and into the small boats waiting to take them ashore. At times I heard Sidroc's voice speaking to the Danes, and knew he walked near me, but I did not turn.

It grew quiet upon the ship, but across the little space of water I heard the hoots and shouts of the Danes, and knew they walked the single road of the trading post. I could not summon the strength to rise and look at them. I heard a man quite close and from the tail of my eye saw Sidroc's boots. He squatted down next to me, but did not try to turn me to him.

The Claiming

"They will bring fresh water, and food, whatever can be had," he told me, and his words were low and gentle. I nodded my head; it was all I could do.

After a time he went to where our possessions lay piled, and I heard him sorting through the heap.

"Saxon," he said, and I heard the man stand up, "when we land we will have to carry all these things, and need to do so easily. We have hides and can make packs. Come and work with me."

I heard them lay out the hides upon the deck, and Sidroc measure off lengths, and heard too the sound of a sharp blade slicing through the tanned leather. I listened to them a long while. Sidroc gave orders, and the Saxon spoke not; but I heard them working side by side. I had made many a hide pack at Kilton, and made them well, and the one which had held my silk dresses and into which I had burnt the running stags was one of them. At last I rose and went to the workbasket and drew from it the sharp bird-shaped shears.

I knelt down next to them. Sidroc had given the Saxon a knife, and he was cutting strips to serve as lacing cords. His hand was clumsy and the strips thin in places and thick in others.

"Let me cut them with my shears," I told both men, and set to work at their sides.

161

Chapter the Eleventh: The Trading Post

THE Danes were gone most of the day, and on their return made trip after trip in the small boats. They hoisted up water casks, and a tun of ale, and baskets and skin bags of food. They were noisy as they left, and noisier as they came back, and some of them were drunk.

When the tide was full we set off, into a freshening breeze. Some of the Danes were sprawled upon the deck in sleep, and others boasted and swaggered about what I could not guess.

Sidroc brought me a pail, filled with fresh water, all for my own use; and after I bathed my face and hands I took off my boots and washed them well. They would take a day or two to dry again, but now they were free of salt water and would not rot. I rinsed out my stockings and wrung them out, and sat like a cottar's daughter in my bare feet.

We had fresh bread, still soft, and roasted fish, a large piece each, and ale so strong and bitter I felt it at the first sip. I drank it all.

The next day we sailed always within sight of the green shore and its forests and marsh-lands. The winds were forceful and cool and I wrapped myself in my wool mantle. Rain began to fall at dusk, and dampened all it touched; but we had made three hide packs, and rolled as much as we could into them. I watched Sidroc take another hide and sling it between railings in the bow of the ship, and then push my plush weaving under it.

162

"You have been wet enough this trip," he told me, and I moved under the slight shelter. I had scarce spoken to him, but nodded my gratitude.

It did not rain long, and I awoke to see Moon-light fall upon the deck. In the faint glow I saw Sidroc stretched out on a sheepskin near me, and the Saxon beyond him, and heard them breathe in their sleep; and I lay there and wondered what this new day would bring.

We did not reach the trading post until late in the day, and the Sun already slanting far to the West. It was much larger than the first, with timber buildings and long houses and many score of smaller structures. Some of the largest buildings were right along the shore, and behind them ran a road of pounded clay, and from off this road ran three more trailing off, with small camps and sheds with awnings and little crofts of penned animals.

Built out into the water were two piers, of good and sturdy make, and in water deep enough so that the ship could oar up next to one. As we approached men came out upon one of these piers, and stood ready to grasp at the lines thrown them; and the Danish chief called out and spoke to the men waiting there. The men who greeted us had yellow-white hair and round heads with red cheeks, and laughed and gestured with every word they spoke. Sidroc stood by my side and regarded them well. "They are the Pomerani," he said aloud, "they and another tribe, the Polanie, range all up and down this coast."

The Claiming

Sidroc had stuffed everything we owned into the three packs, and so I knew he did not mean to return to the ship. Mine was the smallest, and I would carry too my workbasket, which had a handle and was light. Both men shouldered large packs, and Sidroc had rolled up my weaving and had that strapped to his as well, and he had gotten from the Danes two spears. One of them was of Danish make, and thus like those of the Saxons, but one was of the Idrisids, small and light. He carried both of these in his left hand and so with his sword-belt and seax was heavily armed.

The tide was full and we walked off the ship down a short doubled plank to the pier. I nearly staggered as my feet met the unmoving timbers of the pier, so weak and wobbly did I feel. Danes were walking ahead or dawdling behind us, and as Sidroc turned to speak to their chief a final time I saw the red bearded man and the clean shaven one who had dove in after me. They laughed again, and waved Fare-well, and I nodded to them. I stopped at Sidroc's side as the chief spoke to him, and looked at him closely for the first time. He was younger than I had thought, with sandy hair worn long in braids, and a broad well-muscled frame. We had much to be grateful to him for; he had treated us as well as his own men, and now seemed content to let us go our way. He glanced at me, and I nodded, and he smiled at me and said something about me to Sidroc, who answered with a short laugh.

Then Sidroc started down the pier, and I at his side, and the Saxon just behind him. When we reached the end of it we stopped and Sidroc scanned the buildings before us. The day was far gone and some of them were locked for the night, and outside the smaller sheds canvas awnings were rolled down. But folk of all sorts moved along the pounded clay road, men in many different sorts of dress and a few women too. We walked a short way to the base of the second pier, at which no ship was tied.

Sidroc dropped his pack and gestured that we should do so as well.

"I am going there," he told the Saxon, and pointed to a shed which had withy cages stacked around it. "Stay here with our goods until I return. You cannot run without passing me, and if you do will find this Idrisid spear in your back."

The Saxon nodded, and Sidroc gestured I walk with him the short distance to the fowl-keeper's. Along the side of his shed he had a small fire going, and I was nearly made faint by the savour of roast fowl. As we neared it I smelt too the stink of droppings and the dust that hens always have about them. The hens were speckled, and clucked and pecked at the bars of their cages and glared at us with their beady red eyes. An old man came around the side of the shed as we passed under the awning. He stood before a chopping block hewn from a felled tree and greeted us with a wide and toothless smile. Sidroc looked all about him. In the back, alone in a withy cage, stood a big cock rooster with red tipped feathers and a flaming comb. As we looked at it it began to crow, and Sidroc pointed to it. The old man rubbed his hands and went to the cage and bore the pecking that the old cock gave him when he drew him out. He motioned with his hands to see if he should kill the bird, but Sidroc shook his head No.

Sidroc reached his hand into his belt and pulled out a quarter piece of silver, and laid it upon the bloodied chopping block. The man took it up, held it close to his eye, laid it down, and with a small axe sliced off a fragment. Sidroc took back the rest and the old man passed the cock feet first to him. The bird was huge and thrashing even as it hung in Sidroc's hand.

We walked back to the pier, and went a little distance from where the Saxon waited, standing guard over our packs. Sidroc did not speak and I did not know what to ask him. We had no cooking gear, none at all, and the cock, old as it was, would be tough without long boiling.

We neared a timber post which thrust up past knee-high. Sidroc laid the two spears down on the wood planks of the pier, and in a quick motion wrung the neck of the struggling cock. He laid the still-living bird upon the post-end. He pulled out his jewelled-hilted seax, and held it above the feathered breast. He took a breath, and in his familiar gesture, looked up at the sky.

"For Odin, All-Father, who watched us with his single eye; I give thanks. For Thor, who sent my brothers to help us; I give thanks. For Tyr, who made strong my arm; I give thanks. For Freyja, who made my shield-maiden bold and kept her safe; I give thanks. "

This was his first act ashore, to make Offering; to give thanks for our deliverance.

He turned to me to see the tears well in my eyes, and held his seax so both of us might wield it. I placed my hand upon it, and he closed his own over mine, and together we plunged it into the deep breast of the Offering. The blood ran in a thin rivulet across the light feathers. Sidroc pressed his thumb into the blood and lifted it to his mouth, and I too stamped my thumb into the warm liquid and sucked it into my mouth.

He looked at me the whole time I did this, and I was most aware that not since I was a child in my kinsman's hall in Mercia had any man seen me make Offering.

When I had done he took the body of the cock and cast it into the waters over which we had come. He smiled at me, and lifted his hand to my cheek and lightly brushed away the tear that rolled there.

We walked back to where the Saxon stood. I could see from his face that he had watched us, but he cast his eyes down as we neared. Sidroc looked at him, and now spoke with no harshness in his words.

"I stand in no one's debt long. You have done me two services, Saxon, first in speaking for me to the Idrisid captain, and then in cutting loose my hands. For these I claimed you for my own, and freed you from the oar well. Now that we are ashore I cannot keep you from running. I have other things of greater concern on my mind. So if you want to go, go. I give you your freedom. But if you will serve me a few days, help me get what I need, then I will arm you and give you a share in our winnings. So again I give you a choice."

The Saxon stood still a moment, considering this. He had nothing but the clothes on his back, and even these were given him by Sidroc. He stepped forward. "I will stay with you," he said.

Sidroc nodded, and I opened my mouth to speak. Sidroc turned to me and did so first. "He will never know our names, and we will never know his," he warned me.

I looked from man to man, and then said helplessly, "But I told him who you were, on the Idrisid ship."

Sidroc looked at the Saxon. The man looked at me, then at Sidroc, and then shrugged. "I think I have forgotten it," he said at last.

Sidroc grinned. "Good. A strong back and a bad memory."

He again scanned the row of sheds before us. "Food," he said, and held up his finger to stay us. "I will be within sight, and hailing." He laid the spears across one of our packs, and then gestured to me. "Sit," he said, and I did so, tho' it was far from comfortable with the wooden shafts beneath me.

He walked rapidly back to the fowl-seller. He came back with a wooden platter on which sat two whole roasted hens. Beneath his arm was a pottery flask. We all sat perched on our hide packs and Sidroc drew the stopper from the flask and put it to his mouth. He drank and then grinned as he passed it to me. "This is kvas, what the Pomerani call their ale," he said, and as I tasted it I found it was of the same strong and bitter brew we had drunk on the ship. I handed the flask to the Saxon and he too drank deep.

Then we fell upon the fowl. I had a leg and a thigh, and the two men devoured all the rest between them. On the ship the Danes had passed food so that each man had the same amount. It seemed just but meant that the largest would be also the hungriest.

168

Watching him now I saw that Sidroc must have been hungered for days. I had been often sea-sick, and had no relish for food, but tried to eat as much as I could aboard ship so I would not weaken too much. The Saxon too was famished, and had not had such fare I thought, in the two years of his captivity; but he broke off pieces of the meat only after Sidroc had first chosen for himself. The strong ale went to my head at once, and I took but a single second sip of it, and the two of them drained the flask with pleasure.

A raven had been watching us from the top of one of the taller store-houses, and now swooped down and landed not far away. It croaked, and Sidroc tossed her a bone and said, "I may need your help, so remember me," as the big bird flapped off with its prize.

After this we sat in the lowering Sun for a while, and I began to feel some warmth and blood come back to my limp limbs, and to feel sleepy, too.

Sidroc looked over to me. "All will be better now," he said, with a nod of his head towards the Danish ship. I glanced at it and was indeed grateful to know I need not return aboard its pitching bow.

"You will need gowns, and shifts, and stockings, women's things," he said to me. He splayed out his fingers as he listed these things, and weak as I felt, I had to smile. Sidroc had lived long with Ælfwyn, and her sisters and mother, and her little daughter. He well knew the things that women want and need. "Scent and oils and ribbands. And we will need horses," he went on.

I looked at our meagre belongings. Horses were dear in cost in any land. The only thing of great value we had was his

169

weapons, and he could not sell or trade those. "We do not own enough to buy horses," I said aloud.

"I do not mean to buy them," he answered.

Now I felt real alarm. Horse-theft was so grave a crime that many times men were killed outright for it, with no chance to redeem themselves with silver. If it could mean death at home, it might mean that here too.

"But first we need hot water," he ended. "We have little silver; the Idrisid captain took mine away from me upon his ship. I was winning it back piece by piece at dice, but he did not live long enough for me to get it all. We will have to trade the cloth and other things we have for what we need."

We stood up, I a little uncertainly, and shouldered our packs. We passed first the fowl-seller's and Sidroc gave back the platter and flask, and the old man grinned his gaping smile and bowed at us. Many of the sheds and store-houses were closed for the day, but we saw a woman with racks of dried fish, another with baskets of carrots and turnips, a shed of good size festooned with all manner of cloth and animal hides, a salt-seller with his lead-lined caskets of the precious stuff, and much more, telling us that many needs could be met in this place for those with goods to barter or silver to spend. I saw more wains drawn by the long-horned oxen, and I wondered at the great span of these, capped with copper tips from which tiny bells hung and chimed each time the huge creatures shook their heads. As we moved along the main road we saw Danes from the ship going in and out of this or that store-house or shed, and saw too men and women like those who had first greeted the ship, stocky folk with yellow-white hair and laughing red faces.

The Claiming

We stopped at the beginning of one of the narrow roads which led off at an angle from the main road. It was lined on both sides with tiny fenced-in crofts, and these crofts were crowded with workman's sheds and sleeping huts and pens of long-haired goats and small black pigs.

"We will look for hot water here," said Sidroc, and led us up the narrow road. Some folk were in their small front work-yards and glanced up at us as we turned our heads from side to side. No woman would be still at her washing this late in the day, but perhaps one could be found at her cooking who would be willing to give us hot water and basins to bathe in.

A few crofts up a young woman in a dull red gown came out of her small house and emptied the wash-tub she carried into the road. She looked at us and I stepped forward and gestured to her. "Can we wash here?" I asked her, and moved my hands over my face as if I were at my bathing. She tilted her chin at me and smiled, and I repeated this as another woman came from the house to join her. They were as alike as sisters with their light hair and pale blue eyes and plump forms.

Now a man came out and regarded us from beneath a furrowed brow. He looked uneasily at all the weapons Sidroc carried, and his own hand went to the knife at his belt and rested there. But the two women chattered away at him, gesturing to me, and then beckoned us in. We swung open the gate in the low woven fence and walked on wood planks to a bench in front of the low door. We dropped our packs there, and Sidroc sat down upon the bench. "Call if you need me," he said, and kept his eyes upon the man as he did so.

The Claiming

I took my workbasket in hand and went with the two women along the side of their hut. In back their kitchen fire was ready burning, with a cauldron upon it and a mass of onions and turnips upon a work table there. A bronze wash tub lay tipped up against one side of the hut, and one of them righted it and began to carry dippersful of steaming water to it. The other fetched cold water from a barrel at the corner of the hut. There was no washing shed, but from three sides was strung a hempen line which they draped with heavy oiled cloth. I stripped off my soiled clothing and crouched in the wash tub as they added more and more of the hot and cold waters. There were no washing cloths of fine linen, no crushed herbs to scent the tepid water, but as I sat in that dusty side croft I thought I had never had a better bath.

One of them took my shift and gown and stockings and scrubbed them well with washing-lye and water, and wrung them out and hung them by the fire. I had unwrapped my hair from the blue Idrisid cloth and now tried to rinse it as well as I could. I had no oil to ease the tangles but one of the women brought from the hut a long comb of antler or bone, with teeth widely spaced enough for me to run it through my wet hair. The water I bathed in was rain-water, and soft, and this helped.

After I was done they brought me a linen towel so rough that it made my skin tingle as I rubbed myself with it. I stood for a while wrapped in it by their cook fire, and when my gown had dried a bit I pulled my clothing back on. It was still damp, but each piece was warmed by the fire, and was clean again.

The women had both looked at the bright blue Idrisid cloth I had taken from my head, and now I held it to them with both hands as payment. I did not want it, and they

172

seemed well pleased with it, and returned with a short piece of undyed linen for my own hair.

I took from the workbasket the small silver mirror and looked at myself, something I had not dared do for many a day. My skin was pale under the glow of the scrubbing I had given it, and my lips were chapped. I had no bees-wax nor wool fat to soften them, and then recalled the tiny pottery pots. I pulled open one and looked at the ruddy ointment within. It had a sheen like bees-wax, and holding it to my nose I knew it was. I touched a little to my fingertip and then to my lip as Sidroc had done, and looked at myself in the small round mirror. It lent some colour to my face and I did not look so wan.

It was truly dusk now and I had been a long time at my bathing. I gestured my thanks to the women again and made my way to the front of the croft. Sidroc was standing as I came around the corner and I nearly ran into him. He looked at me a moment and began to smile, and I thought he looked at the colour on my lip, and felt my cheek flame as well.

Sidroc went around to wash, but he did so alone, for the man would not let the women help him; and then the Saxon too washed. When we took our leave the skies were dark, but torch-light and kitchen-fires burned up and down the narrow road. Beyond the last huts were crofts left this season empty, or perhaps those who had been there had already left for their homes. We moved a ways down and Sidroc walked onto the clay of one of them and bent down.

"The ground is dry. This is as good as any place for our first night's camp."

The Claiming

We dropped our packs and in the little light cast by the waning Moon spread out hides. We had no way to make a fire but need fear no wild beasts in the trading grounds, and the night would not be a cold one, despite my damp gown. Over a hide Sidroc unrolled my plush weaving, so I had the best sleeping of us all on that hard ground. I lay under my mantle and pulled a wool blanket over me and fell into sleep at once.

I awoke to paling skies, and looked about me. Sidroc was standing up not far away, and the dawn was streaking through the trees at our backs. I sat up and blinked my eyes open.

The Saxon was gone. I turned my head quickly to the packs, and saw all three, and saw the two spears safe by them. Sidroc wore his sword-belt, so it did not look as through the man had stolen anything. Mayhap he was simply in the trees, gone there to relieve himself, but when Sidroc turned to me I could read in his face that he had been awake for some time.

He shrugged, and there was nothing I knew to say. He had freed the man, and the Saxon had said he would serve Sidroc, and now he had run away.

I sat upon my weaving and looked about us. There was stirring from the sheds and huts before us, and a few folk moved upon the narrow road. I upbraided my hair and took the fine ivory comb from my workbasket, and combed it as best I could. Sidroc came to sit beside me as I wrapped the linen around my head.

I had a hundred questions in my mind for him, and my lips would form none of them. I wanted to know what he had planned for our day, how he had hoped the Saxon would serve him, where he intended to take us. I could ask nothing because I could not get past hearing him say that he would kill his own men to keep from being found. He had told the Danes I was his wife, and at first I thought he said that only to protect me; but with each day that passed the distance between the lives and laws we had known grew greater.

As we sat in silence a man appeared in the road. He walked in a strangely slumped way, with his shoulders hunched, and as he neared us we saw he wore the blue Idrisid tunic Sidroc had tossed him. The Saxon slowed his steps and crossed over and knelt down in front of us. He was holding his breath and his face was red. He pulled at the lengths of fabric at his waist, freeing it from his belt, and two wheaten loaves fell onto the hide. They were freshly baked and steaming hot, and must have burnt his bare skin where they lay against his belly.

I was so surprised I could not speak, but Sidroc did at once, and his voice, tho' low, was stern. "You were not seen?"

"I was not seen," said the Saxon with a grin. "But I could not gauge how hot they were when I took them, or I would have waited for them to cool."

This was the first real time the man had spoken since he was at the oar on the Idrisid ship, and it was good to hear.

"It is foolish to steal in such a small place," Sidroc warned. "I did not free you just to put me at risk."

"You said you had but little silver," the man answered in his defence. "And you are feeding me, too."

Sidroc shook his head, but from his voice I knew he was not truly angered. "Do not do it again unless you wish to lose a hand," he ended. "If you are caught, I will not redeem you."

I picked up one of the loaves and tore an end off and handed it to him, and then gave a second piece to the Saxon. The fragrance from it made my mouth water and as I tore a piece for myself I said, "I thank you for this," and the man smiled at me.

After we ate Sidroc gave us each a knife. Mine was small and well made, with a sharp thin blade of bluish-hued Idrisid metal and a bone hilt, and I strung its leathern sheath through my sash. The one he gave the Saxon was a long knife of the Danes. In doing so he did much to show the trust the man had gained in his eyes; but only slaves went about unarmed. If the man was to serve us he must be able to defend himself.

When the trading post was fully awake we set off with our packs to the heart of it. We saw an iron-smith at work at his forge, and saw ranged around his shed the bits of iron work that ships require, as well as hay-rakes and spear points and common knives. Sidroc looked all about the shed, and then said, "No shoes," which made me pause until he said, "Horse-shoes. I have seen no horses yet in the streets, only oxen."

After how he had warned the Saxon about stealing two loaves of bread I could only be glad there were no horses here to tempt Sidroc. We saw the Danish chief not far away and Sidroc walked over to him. At the pier the ship lay tied, and its men were loading it with casks and chests even as we watched. He came back to us and said, "The Pomerani have horses, tough little ones such as we have at home, with hooves so hard they take no shoes. But they are all in Summer pasture lands now, he thinks."

We walked on and reached the stall festooned with draping cloth. "They may have women's clothes here, that you can trade for the cloth we have," he told me, and pointed that I step before the low counter. A man and a woman were there, but not the light haired red-cheeked folk of much of the trading post. These had dark hair and light brown eyes, and were slightly built. They smiled and bowed as I came in, as all merchants do to those who wear good clothing.

I grasped my gown at the skirt to ask if they had another, and the man turned and brought forth a bolt of russet wool dyed not unlike the colour I wore. I shook my head and again gestured, and pointed to his wife's gown, and they both nodded. She looked around the shop and from a single pile unfolded three or four gowns. It was odd to look upon and touch them, for I knew the women who had worn them must be dead; but I had no time to make a gown for myself and must thence buy one made by fingers now stilled.

Two of them were so worn as to be near worthless, but one was a linen shift, unlike mine, for it had long sleeves. I thought it must be cold where that woman had lived, but held it up to me and saw it would fit. I nodded and put it aside. The other of the gowns was of good make, well-dyed a rich golden yellow, and tho' worn still had use in it. It was long for me but I could tie up my sash to gather it until I had time to hem. I nodded that I would take it as well. This would give me two shifts and two gowns, so that I might never have to wear a wet or soiled one, and I was well pleased. I held my hands up to signify that I was done, but the man now clapped his hand to his brow and went to a chest against the back

177

wall. He lifted the lid and after sorting through a few things pulled out something of ember red and held it up.

It was a gown, of wonderful workmanship, so bright and so adorned with coloured thread work of blue and gold at the throat and sleeves and hem that it made my eyes wide beholding it.

It would be very costly, I knew this, but I could not stay them as they carried it to me and made me touch it. The wool was finely spun, as finely as that spun for good stockings, and the thread-work done by one who possessed much art in her supple fingers. It showed no wear, none at all, and for a sudden moment I wondered if some young maiden had made it for a wedding day she did not live to see.

I smiled and shook my head, and pushed it away.

"Tell them you will take it," said Sidroc from behind me.

I turned to him. "We cannot buy it; it will be too dear." I looked back at the merchant and again shook my head, and gathered up the two pieces I wanted. But the man was looking at Sidroc, and now spoke to him. Sidroc answered in his own tongue, and the man nodded and answered, and even brought the gown forward so that Sidroc might touch it. He did so, and lifted his eyes from the flaming cloth to me as he fingered it.

The two spoke again, and Sidroc opened one of the packs and drew forth several pieces of cloth that he had taken from the Idrisid ship. One was a piece of a blue silken panel from the screen around the women's house, and I flinched when I saw it; but the merchant's eyes opened wide with desire. It was by far the richest piece of fabric we carried, and could perhaps have bought us food and drink for a month's time; but Sidroc parted with it.

We owned so little that this was a huge price to pay for me to have a fine gown, and I feared we might go hungry or thieving because of it. The merchant rolled up the gowns and shift and I put them in my shoulder pack, and as we left the stall I thought I heard the Saxon whistle under his breath at this costly purchase.

We came out and saw in the bright Sun the sharp-prowed ship of the Danes unfurl its sail and the men drop their oars into the water. Watching them pull away I gave secret thanks I was not amongst them, yet would willingly suffer sea-sickness once more if their ship was heading West.

We passed a shop all hung with the precious amber that Sidroc had said was found in such quantity in these parts, but we did not stay to look. I recalled the golden amber necklace I had given Ælfwyn, and wondered if he thought on it too.

There were many women about, and this surprised me, but I had never before seen a trading post, and did not know what to expect. A number of stalls were kept by women alone, or by man and wife or father and daughters, and these women could be seen behind their wares, or going briskly up and down the dusty clay roads on some errand, baskets over their arms. But a few women walked slowly about, with nothing in their hands. I saw one of them look at us, and thought she studied well Sidroc and the Saxon, for she fixed her eyes upon them boldly. I watched the Saxon look back at her. She had curling yellow hair above hollowed cheeks, and many strings of coloured beads around her neck, and the hem of her gown was dirty. I knew it must have been a long time since he had touched a woman, but after a single look he turned away.

Before one brew-shed were men, well dressed in good linen, sitting upon benches, drinking the strong kvas, and Sidroc looked upon them but did not stop. Further down was a stall that seemed crammed with bits of everything, for the woman within had scraps of cloth, pieces of ironwork, pottery and wood bowls and cups, and diverse items of all sorts of use and fancy. I saw a quill of steel needles, and toasting irons, and brooches of cast bronze. Sidroc and the Saxon began looking through the things, and the woman, seeing what they chose, began bringing out more and more of every sort.

"We need things for our kit," Sidroc told me, and I stopped my browsing and ran my eye over what they had gathered. They had two pots, one of middle size and one smaller, a brass basin, two toasting forks, two pottery flasks with stoppers, a wood cup, and a few wooden bowls, amongst other things. The stall-keeper stepped back and looked over all this, and added a small brass box, which I guessed was for tinder. Sidroc slid it open and there inside was iron and flint and even a few scraps of lye-soaked wood shavings. He nodded and put it down with the other things.

The woman turned to me and held up another quill of needles, and recalling the fine steel ones in the workbasket, I shook my head. She then lifted up a string of beads and two brooches, and I again told her No.

"Anything else?" asked Sidroc. I had spotted some pieces of linen, for we would need towels, and chose the largest of the scraps and added them to the pile.

"I think that is enough," I told him, and studying the things before us tried to think of any other needful item.

Sidroc took from our packs a length of striped wool, longer than any she had in the stall, long enough to be made up as a gown, and offered it to the woman. She pulled it carefully through her hands, holding it to the light to be certain no moth-hole or tear blemished it, and finding it whole, nodded her head once, and held out her hands again. Sidroc shook his head, and without a word she turned and began taking things from the pile, first the tinder box, and then the basin. Sidroc let out his breath and pulled a tanned hide from another pack, and held it before her. She smiled and reached for it, and he reached for a larger brass basin to replace the one she had begun to take away. She shook her head, but he stood firm looking at her, and she shrugged and let him have all the things, large basin too.

By now the Sun was high overhead, and we found the baker the Saxon had earlier visited, and this time gave him a fragment of silver for several loaves and two small sacks of grain. We went to the fowl-seller and he fished ten eggs out of boiling water for us, and so we took this feast down to the pier and sat and ate.

The Saxon got up after a while and went down to the shore line, which was a pebbly one, and walked along it. He returned with a smooth piece of drift wood in his hand, a stave of some sort, bleached almost white by the Sun and waves. He took out his new knife and began to work on it.

"What do you make?" Sidroc asked him.

"A comb for your lady," he answered.

Sidroc jerked his head around to look at the man after he said this, but the Saxon's brow was unfurrowed, as if this were something anyone would think of doing.

"There is a comb maker here, but the bone he uses is not deep enough for such hair as hers. I can carve one better than can be bought."

Sidroc said nothing, and the man went on, "She cannot use the comb of the Idrisid women; they have dark hair that is thin and fine."

Sidroc turned to me, but I could not read if it was anger in his face, or just amaze.

"It is true," I told him, and kept my voice light. I looked over to the Saxon. "You are kind to do that for me. And it will save silver, too," I added, hoping this would stay any anger Sidroc might have.

Sidroc looked at the man a long moment. "What is your name?" Sidroc now asked, and the edge in his voice made me hold my breath.

The Saxon did not show any startle if he felt it. He glanced up from his carving. "We are not to know the other's name. I am here to serve you a few days, until you are content, and then you will send me away. Until then I will make a comb for your lady's long hair."

To break the quiet that followed I stood up and smoothed my skirt. "Now that we have kit we can do our own cooking," I started. I looked along the water-front to the line of sheds and stalls. "We have the barley meal we have just bought, and there is the root-woman there, too. I can make browis in our large pot. The fowl-seller has many hens and eggs. We will need salt too."

The men said nothing, and I asked of Sidroc, "You say this place is soon to close?"

He nodded his head and said, "There is nothing on these shores in Winter but snow."

The breeze was more than tinged with Fall that day, and I felt almost a shiver as I saw in my mind's eye the shut-up buildings and empty piers covered with snow and frost. "Then if these folk are soon to head home, they cannot take all their beasts with them. Perchance they will slaughter some of their pigs and we can buy those."

I did not know how much of any one thing we should try to buy, or how to plan for any of this, for I did not know what Sidroc had in mind for us. Instead I just said, "All of this will take silver, or goods we do not have."

Sidroc pulled at the inside of his belt, and looked at what he held. "Four pieces of silver, one half piece."

This could be a lot or a little, depending on how long we need live on it. He too scanned the line of timber buildings before us. "The men who drink all day are merchants, awaiting their ship to pick them up. They will have goods with them, and silver, too." He looked back to where the Saxon bent over his carving. "Do you win at dice, Saxon?" he wanted to know.

The Saxon looked up at him and considered. "I play at dice," he answered. "But my best game is bones, at which I have never lost."

"Never?" I could not help echoing. Men always boasted of their gaming skills, but he said it with such surety that I could almost believe it.

"Never," he told me, and then gave a snort and a toss of his head. "That is how I wound up behind the oar."

"Then you will remember that it is dangerous to always win," said Sidroc in a low tone which hinted at the actions of the cheat.

Bones was a game of many pieces, and much counting. The Prior had played it with guests when I was a girl, and I had watched him move the tiny counters about and wished to play with them myself. Edgyth was skilled at it, and had taught me so well that I won as many games as she, for I was good at sums and could add them in my head.

"I also am good at bones," I found myself saying aloud, "but I still sometimes lose."

Sidroc turned to me and said quickly, "You will not be there tonight to play."

This stung me and I shot back, "You do not need to say that. I know only a lewd woman games with men not her brothers or husband. You are neither."

His eyes flared, and I knew I had stung him too. Now I was angry, and angry I had said this, and I turned away. The Saxon was listening and watching this all, and I heard the sound of his knife as he sawed into the wooden comb he carved for me.

The Claiming

By late afternoon we walked back to the narrow road where we had camped the night before. One of the young Pomerani women who had helped me bathe was sitting outside her hut, pottery jars ranged about her on the bench. She smiled when she saw me, and waved me over. We came within her pounded clay enclosure and she pulled a wood top off one of the pots. Something dark glistened within, and the fragrance rising to my nose told me it was honey. She gestured that I dip my finger in for a taste, and I did. I smiled with the goodness of it, thinking of its sweetness paired with the hot loaves we had bought. But I shook my head at her. Honey was dear, and for those who had already all they needed, and could buy also those things they wanted.

There was an old fire-ring at our camp site, and I rolled the stones closer for our small pot as the men brought dry wood from the trees behind us. The honey-woman let me fill the pot at her water barrel, and soon we had a browis of barley meal, cabbage, carrots, onion, and fowl bubbling away. It did not take much to tidy up our small camp after this, and there was still much light in the sky when Sidroc turned to me. I knew his voice was low because he did not wish the Saxon to hear, but his tone was also mild.

"I do not like to leave you alone, even for a moment, but I want to try my hand with those merchants. I am taking the Saxon with me, but I will not be gone long. I want you to stay with the honey-women until I return."

I could not stay alone on the narrow road, it was true. The whole time we had been at the trading post no one had troubled us, but I was always with two men, one of whom was heavily armed and very tall.

I nodded my head and we made our way down the road. The honey-woman had taken in her wares for the night, but her door was open and she came out when she saw us. I went to stand by her and waved to the men as they walked away. She looked puzzled until Sidroc made a drinking motion with his fist, and then she began to laugh and nodded her head.

I had brought her three of the eggs we had got from the fowl-seller's, and she accepted these gratefully. Her sister joined us, and the man poked his head out of the hut to look and then ducked back in again. It was wearing not to be able to speak to them, but after a while the two women and I found that much could be said with hands and faces. Their speech was pleasant to the ear, not so musical as that of the Idrisids, but with a light, clipped sound that with their frequent laughter made me think of nesting birds. One brought out her comb, and I again combed my hair with it, and then plaited it into the flat braid we called the snake, and this they greatly liked. I did it for them too, and tried also to guide their plump fingers so that they might learn to do it themselves.

Dusk waned into dark, and the deeper dark of an unrisen Moon, and the women and I had moved into the shelter of their hut and sat against the wall on a low bench there. I heard footsteps, and saw from the opened door the spill of torch light upon the road, and stepped out to see Sidroc holding a rush torch, the Saxon at his side. I gestured my thanks to the women and hurried out to them.

The Saxon wore a grin on his face, and Sidroc, who I could not see so well in the glare of the torch he held, had also a slight smile on his lips. Perhaps it was only the strong ale they had drunk that made them glad. They did not speak, and I looked from one to the other expectantly. I had waited hours in a strange hut with kindly women with whom I could not speak, and now they would force me to ask.

"Did you win?"

Sidroc nodded his head. "Yes," was all he said.

"I am so glad," I told him, and meant it. "Now I will not feel so badly about the red gown."

He opened his mouth to protest, but glanced at the Saxon and stopped.

We had reached our camp site and the Saxon turned to me. "I told you I never lose," he said. "And we even saw some lewd women."

I could not tell if he was teasing, or if it was the ale talking, but I looked at him quickly.

It was Sidroc who answered me. "Wherever men game, and win, there will be women to help them spend it," he said, and gave a low laugh. "But we sent them off to comfort the losers."

He had planted the still burning torch in the softer clay by the fire-pit, and we spread out our sleeping gear. The Saxon was careful to set his up a distance from ours, but before he lay down he crossed to where Sidroc sat near me on his hide ground cover. He crouched down and pulled a small leathern purse from his breast. He had not had it before so I knew he must have just won it with the contents. He held it before him and his eyes flicked from Sidroc's face to my own. He dropped the purse on the sheepskin not a hand span from Sidroc.

The Claiming

No one spoke. Sidroc searched the face of the Saxon, who broke the night stillness.

"You told me that you would share out to me a portion of our winnings when I go. Until then all this is yours."

I could scarce believe this, and I think my lips parted in my surprise. The man spoke softly, and yet there was something of great boldness in what he said.

It took Sidroc another moment to nod his assent, but he did, and his hand took up the purse and the Saxon retreated to his bed roll and lay down upon it.

The torch began to gutter as it burnt low, feeding off the last of the oil-soaked rushes. Sidroc sat next me and I found words.

"How much did you win?" I whispered.

"Seventeen silver pieces."

"Seventeen!" I praised. "And all from the four you started with?'

He nodded, and then said, "The Saxon won six-and-twenty."

"Why did he give it all to you?" I now asked, and lifted my eyes to where the man lay stretched out.

"Because of his craft," answered Sidroc. "He has more cunning than any ten men I have met." He shook his head to himself, and I did not ask more.

He reached his hand into his belt and pulled out a tiny object. "This is for you," he said, and pressed it into my hand.

From the feel of it I guessed it was glazed pottery, and from the small size I thought it must hold something precious. "The vial is not so fine as the glass one I brought you from Jorvik, but the scent is the same."

I found the tiny stopper and pulled it out. A scent like every rose that had ever bloomed wafted forth. Tears sprang into my eyes but in the little light I hoped he would not see them. I was back in the bleak hall at Four Stones, a maid of not yet sixteen Summers; and I saw myself standing with Ælfwyn as Sidroc presented us each with blown glass vials of rose oil he had got from Jorvik where Yrling had sent him.

"One of the merchants had me in a tie at dice, and I bluffed him so well he added this to his wager." He had the same note of pride in his voice now that he had then, so full was his pleasure to lay something this choice before me.

"These things are easier to find here than in Lindisse," he went on. "You can use it more freely for your hair, and...any other place you like."

I knew it was still very costly, and thought again of the red gown he had given the length of silk for. He was doing all this to please me, and as if he read my thought he added, "All good things should be yours."

We sat side by side, and I could not turn my face to look at him for fear he would see my tears.

He leant a little closer to me, his voice low. "Will you put some on? I want to smell it on you."

The Claiming

I nodded my head and held the tiny vial to the hollow of my throat. A drop of the precious rose oil nested there, and its fragrant warmth filled the air about us.

He took a breath. His body was so close to mine that we nearly touched, and I thought he trembled to hold the space between us. Then of a sudden he pushed himself up, and turned from me as he murmured, "You should sleep now."

Chapter the Twelfth: Grey Within and Without

I woke in a kind of panic realising that I did not know how many days we had been gone. I lie looking up at the clouded sky and counted over and again. We had been on the Idrisid ship for eight days, or mayhap nine; and then upon the Danish one for four, I thought; and now this was our third day at the trading post, where every day seemed to be the same. I sat up. Sidroc lay not far away, and I went to his side and squatted down. He lay upon his back with his sword-belt under the rolled up clothing that served as pillow. He started awake and I said with urgency, "How long have we been gone?"

He pressed up on his elbows and blinked. "Why?" is what he said.

"I...want to know. Somehow, if we lose track, it seems..." I did not know what I was going to say; that not knowing felt like not caring, or that I felt further away and more lost to those we had left behind. "I want to count the days, that is all," is the best I could say.

"Ah...sixteen days," he told me.

"What will they think?" I asked him.

He sat up fully now, and glanced over to where the Saxon lay still asleep. "At Four Stones, do you mean?"

"Yes, your wife and children and my son, and all your folk."

191

He stared out into the middle distance. "That we are dead, or lost beyond reclaiming."

I sank back on my heels, my eyes fixed upon him.

He took a breath, let it out slowly. "My men had to have heard me whistle. I did not see them on the shore when we were rowed out; maybe they did not spot the Idrisid ship or were already dead. If the Idrisids had killed them they would have likely brought their weapons on board as battle-gain, so I do not believe that. If they saw the ship they would have gotten one themselves and given chase. Perhaps they could have persuaded the ship you were to have taken to give chase, but this I doubt. Also the Idrisid ship was fast and had the advantage in their quick start.

"From all this I believe my men lived and are now back at Four Stones. They will figure we were captured; they heard my warning whistle and we left behind horses and all your goods. What else they think, I cannot say."

"But it does not end there," I said.

"It could have. I could have been killed trying to prove my worth at Fès, and you might be on your way to the women's hall of their King."

"But we were not."

"No. The Gods spared us. White-armed Freyja long ago marked you for me, and now she has at last given you to me."

My words tumbled out; I could not stay them. "You marked me for you, not Freyja."

"Yes, I marked you from the first; but she made you the shield-maiden you are, so the choice was not mine." He looked up at the paling skies. "And I have worked hard to keep us both alive, and safe."

There was no anger in his voice as he told me all this; it was low and even, and without any edge of defence. But I felt all the distress I had known when I awakened, and tried to calm myself by swallowing hard. I caught the scent of the oil on my throat, and felt last night's tears rise again.

"Where are you taking us?"

"Away."

Late in the morning it began to rain, and we had no shelter. We could have gone into the grove of trees behind the camp-ground, where we might have strung tanned hides from boughs and kept off the damp; but since the many buildings of the trading post offered shelter Sidroc led us back into the heart of it. The large store-houses had roof overhangs, and the hide and oiled fabric awnings of the stalls also gave cover. No merchant men were about the brew-shed, for we went there to fill our flasks with ale.

A while later we saw some of them, for we heard a shout from the shore line and a ship rounded the little cove and hove into sight. Merchants within one of the store-houses were calling. We peered out into the drizzle at the ship. Like most it had sharp doubled prows, but the breadth of it told me it was a ship for hauling goods and not for fighting. Sidroc studied it carefully, and did not seem alarmed, but he moved us along one of the side roads, where we stood beneath a dripping awning and watched the ship land.

A few men had begun to cross over to the pier to meet the ship, and the Saxon eyed them.

"Hard to lose such a source of silver so soon," he said, and I knew they must have been those they had gamed with last night.

Sidroc looked at him and said, "They would not welcome seeing your face again so quickly."

The Saxon shrugged, and Sidroc went on, "That is why men who game well travel much. They are rarely welcome more than one night in the same place."

Although it was but mid-day, some stalls about us were beginning to close up, which seemed odd, for the rain was not heavy, and I thought the men coming ashore from the ship might provide fresh trade. We looked about at this, and then saw that within these stalls chests and casks were being filled with all manner of goods, and that those within them worked in haste.

"They will leave with the ship," I said, and felt a little running fear shoot through me. I thought of the trading post soon empty, and us without the few comforts we had found there, with a hard Winter coming on. I bit my lip to keep from saying more. I wanted to again ask Sidroc what he planned for us, but could not before the ears of the Saxon.

We headed back to the road we had camped on, and found the honey-women still in their croft, with no sign of their soon leaving. I was so gladdened at seeing their plump smiling faces that I almost ran to greet them. I turned to Sidroc.

"They have a covered drying shed; I will wash our clothes today." I wore that day the yellow gown, but would welcome washing my shift and stockings, and the men had worn their tunics and leggings many days running. Since they had clothes to spare from what Sidroc had taken from the ship they need not be hindered by this, and I did not want to wander in the drizzle with them. I walked a little way off with Sidroc.

"Do you have a quarter piece of silver?" I asked him. "They have been kind to me, and I want it for them."

It was a lot to give them but since he had won so much I made bold to ask for it. The women had done us all many services, and I had given them nothing save the blue Idrisid head cloth and some eggs, and now, feeling the time of my bleeding Moon was near, I must ask them for more linen so I might make the drawers I needed.

He searched my face a moment and pulled the silver from his belt. He passed me eight pieces as well as the quarter piece I had asked for; fully half of all he had won. "This is for you," he told me.

I was moved by this and could not answer, and only nodded my head.

The men changed their clothes and set out into the road again. The honey-women helped me with my washing, and soon their drying shed was hung with Sidroc's tunic, the one of the Idrisids which the Saxon had worn, their leggings, and my shift and stockings. I had already stitched up the tear on the left ankle of Sidroc's legging where the Saxon had retrieved the knife hidden there, but I had done it while Sidroc wore them. Now I ripped out my crude work and sewed it so there was but a narrow seam.

As I smoothed Sidroc's tunic and hung it near the brazier I looked well at the dark blue linen. The thread was so fine I knew Burginde had spun for it, and the stitches in the seams so even and closely spaced that I saw Ælfwyn bent over it with her needle.

I shook my head, fearing to weep as I stood there. The continuing kindness of the honey-women too touched me, for they gave me not only a small box of washing-lye for my own, but after we had dried our hands brought forth a golden cake of bees-wax with which to smooth our hands.

I did not see the man and still did not know if he was the husband of one or even both of them, for perhaps, as in Sidroc's home land, a man from their parts could take as many wives as he could keep. Their hut was dark but with the door open there was light enough for sewing, and few folk came up the now sodden clay road looking for honey.

There was pleasure in sitting with the two women. There were many awkward moments in the camp with Sidroc and the Saxon; we had no shelter and I need go into the trees past the common latrines to wash or change my gown; and tho' I had gained much strength and felt fit again now that I was off the ships, our life was of a simplicity and hardness that I had not known in years.

The Sun was lowering in the clearing skies when Sidroc appeared. The Saxon was not with him, and I looked down the road to see if he trailed behind.

"He wandered off," he said in answer to my unasked question. "He will return; I have his silver."

"He will not try to take ship with those leaving?"

"He would have to game to win his fare, and I doubt the merchants he won from last night will play him." He did not seem concerned about it one way or the other.

He stood with me in front of the hut, our open packs upon the bench. Our clothes were dry and I had them at the ready. As I finished packing them he said, "I will get you a serving woman soon."

I looked up at him and forced myself to speak. "Where will that be?"

"I do not know," he said quietly. "I do not know yet where we are going."

"Is the ship heading West?"

"I did not ask."

I straightened up and faced him fully. "I washed your tunic, the one that Ælfwyn made for you. Your wife. Will you turn your back on her, your children, and your hall?"

His dark blue eyes held me. "You are my true wife."

I closed my eyes but could not close my ears.

"Do you hear?" he went on. "You are my true wife. I know your bonds to her are strong, but mine to you are endless."

I turned away, and saw the Saxon coming towards us. Sidroc shouldered his pack and said, "When the tide rises the ship will sail. Tonight we will have a roof over our heads."

The ship oared away just before dusk, and we walked the roads of the trading post. Some of the stall-holders had knocked down the simple structures and taken them aboard, but others left their stalls and sheds behind them to await their return in the Spring. I did not know how many had left, I saw the dried-fish woman was gone, and her stall also; and guessed perhaps five or more had sailed with the wealthy merchants on the ship. We walked into an empty shed which had held a leather-worker, and dropped our packs. Now even if it rained we should have shelter.

Sidroc took a short length of line and strung it at an angle across one corner of the shed. Then he shook out the longest piece of cloth we had and draped it over this, as a screen. The Saxon and I watched him do this and I knew he made a separate sleeping space for me. A glance at the Saxon's face told me he thought that Sidroc would join me behind it, and I looked quickly away from him before he saw me.

The leather-worker had left behind a good fire-pit outside with a small supply of kindling wood, and we began to make our meal. Inside there were also two benches, one short and one long, and a rude table that wobbled badly. Best of all, there was a wooden plank floor, so no damp could reach us.

The Claiming

After we ate and I had washed up our few plates and cups, I turned to my workbasket. There resting on the lid was a wooden comb. It was large with deep teeth evenly spaced, and had even a carving of a hound or wolf sketched lightly in the wood along its spine. As I held it I kept myself from exclaiming over it, but I went to the Saxon with it in my hands and said, "I am grateful for your work. This is a fine comb."

Sidroc was sitting not an arm's length away, and I saw the tail of the Saxon's eye twitch in his direction to try and read his mood. In the end he said nothing, but only nodded.

We had left the door of the shed open and some light still streaked the sky. The Saxon rose and went to the doorway and leant against it. I watched him pull his yellow beard from his face and with his knife begin to cut away at it. His beard was long and his hair straggled down behind his shoulder blades. He had done me a service and now I wanted to do him one.

I drew out the sharp bird-shaped shears from my basket and went to him. "It will be easier with these," I said. He knew I had the shears and I thought he did not ask me for them because he feared Sidroc's anger.

As he took them from my hand his fingers just touched mine, and he said in a whisper, "Such hair as yours deserves a far better comb than I can make."

I turned my back on him and went inside. I did not look at Sidroc but I felt his eyes upon me just the same. I still had the comb in my hand and put it within my basket.

"Will you go to the brew-shed tonight?" I asked, and tried to make light my voice. I came and sat across from him. I could see a few men passing our door, and guessed they might be headed there.

"No," he answered, and said no more.

The Saxon came in. He was careful not to hand me the shears, and set them down upon the table. He had clipped his beard close all over his face, and snipped off his hair to the back of his neck. His face was not unpleasant, and he had a fine straight nose. He was well-spoken, and well-knit in his body; there was nothing brutish about him. But I was troubled by his looks. Tho' he rarely lifted them, his pale eyes were restless under his brow, so that his aspect was always one of the hunted animal. The only time he had looked boldly at us was when he sat in the rowing pit on the Idrisid ship. Now he sat down on the worn floor boards and rested his back against the wall.

The shed was small, and somehow being under its roof made the awkwardness even greater between us than in the open camp. We sat a while in silence, and then I rose and went behind the screen.

I slept much later in the morning, for the shed was dark within and so the dawning Sun did not wake me. It was warmer inside too, and I had had the luxury of taking off my gown and sleeping only in my shift. I had a wool blanket to cover me, and also my green mantle, thicker than any blanket and long and full. I thought of the otter fur trim the Idrisid woman had ripped off, and how I had liked to pet its softness, and shuddered to think of that ship.

The Claiming

I heard the men moving behind the woollen screen as I unbraided my hair and combed it out. I looked carefully at the Saxon's handiwork. It was indeed a fine piece, and I marvelled that one whose hands had held the oar so long could make something so well. But in his life before, in Wessex, he must have had leisure to make many such things.

Sidroc had never trusted him, and I thought his dislike for the man grew with each day, and yet he kept him with us. I also could not trust the man, and after what he said to me last night did not like him, but somehow wanted him to stay. He was a link to Wessex, and the life I had been carried off from; but there was more. Sidroc had claimed me as his own, but would never act on it while the man be with us.

I heard a distant jingling and chiming of tiny bells, and thought one of the large wains pulled by the long-horned oxen neared us. But then I heard the clap of hooves. "Horses," I heard Sidroc say, and heard him move to the door. I came out from behind the screen to see both men in the road, and a number of folk on horseback ride by at an easy walk. The horses were small, and shaggily haired, with long whiskers on their muzzles and tufted fetlocks, and the broad deep chests that told of good wind. Some of them were spotted brown and white, but most of them were solid brown, not a chestnut, for there was no red in it, but more the shade of old oaken wood. There were men and women too upon them, Pomerani folk, with the yellow-white hair and red cheeks of the honey-women, and they laughed and waved to those they knew who came out into the morning light to greet them.

There were seven of them, and Sidroc marked them all well as they passed. They rode on to the heart of the trading post, and Sidroc came back to where I stood.

"The cloth-seller will help me trade with them," he said, and it was clear his gladness in seeing them was great.

"You will buy horses," I said.

"Only saddles and bridles," he answered. "The horses themselves will take too much of our silver."

Before I could ask more the Saxon returned, and I was left wondering.

Sidroc took the Saxon with him at mid-morning, and felt we were well enough known in the post to leave me safely alone. I pulled a bench to the open door and began to hem the skirt of the yellow gown. The men were gone some time, and I followed the path of the Sun with my eyes. Its light had begun to mellow, and was no longer the brilliant gold of Summer. As I worked I saw other sheds and stalls begin to pack, and an ox cart roll down the road to the woman from whom we got our cooking kit. She cried out to the old man who drove it, and they began to hoist up baskets and chests, so I knew she was leaving too.

When the Sun was overhead the men returned. Sidroc carried two saddles, and the Saxon, one. The saddles were strangely odd, for they were naught but an open wooden frame, with a small leathern sling for a seat. Long leathern girth straps dangled from them, and small iron stirrups.

"They did not want to part with them, but the cloth-seller bargained hard for me," Sidroc said. "I am glad your gown was so costly."

202

"I have never seen such saddles," I said, and indeed they were quite unlike the heavy leathern ones used by the Saxons and the Danes.

"These will be easy to shoulder, and we have sheepskins and blankets already," he answered. He had brought three, so perhaps he meant to horse the Saxon too.

"Even the bridles are light; their horses must have good mouths." He held up the single ringed bit of one of them.

"They are not much bigger than my pony Shagg," I said, recalling the cream-coloured horse I had first come to Four Stones with.

"Yes, but they are tough, these little horses. They will carry us a long way." He looked around. Down the road the old couple had nearly finished packing up their stall. "We will leave in the morning."

Sidroc would not leave the Saxon alone with me, so each time he left the stall he took the man with him. I crossed the road and bought more barley from the baker, and as many loaves as I thought we could carry. The root-woman was still in the trading-post, and I bought cabbages and onions and carrots and turnips, and a handful of salt which the seller twisted into a bit of oiled cloth for me. Sidroc returned with another pottery flask, for we would need to carry water. He also found a haunch of roast pig, which would last a long time without going green.

When we had all of this gathered he looked around at it all. I did not know where we were heading, or how soon we might find other provender, and I felt he did not either.

The Claiming

After a while he took both spears and went around to the back of the shed. There was a long and empty yard behind it, and he paced off some distance and left the spears on the ground. Then he went to the fire-pit and took a piece of charcoal, and drew an ashy square about the length of a man's arm upon the wood wall of the shed. He returned to the spears and threw first one and then the other at the target he had drawn. He did this over and over, throwing both the long Danish spear and the light Idrisid one from close and far.

I had never seen him at any weapon practice, and stood and watched him now. He threw from a stand-still, and from a run, and moved his hand along the length of the spears until he found the balance point of each. Then he tied a narrow leathern cord tightly around the shaft to mark it, that his fingers might find the spot at once and the needed throw gain greatest advantage.

When the first spear had hit with a dull thunk against the wall the Saxon had come around to see. He stood watching Sidroc with narrowed eyes for a while, and then returned to the front of the shed. Other folk too came out from their stalls or paused upon the road to see him. He threw with great force and the spears whistled as they hurtled through the air, and nearly all fell within the target. When he was done the wall was pocked with holes.

There was sweat upon his brow as he crossed over to me and smiled. "The leather-worker will curse me when the rain blows in next Summer," he said, and I had to smile back.

"I would like to go and say good-bye to the honey-women," I told him.

"I will walk with you," he said.

"It is only the next road; I will be safe enough."

He shook his head. "There are now men with horses here."

I could not think that one of the red-cheeked Pomerani men would try to steal me away, but shrugged my consent.

The Saxon was kneeling by his pack, rearranging its contents so that he could fit more in.

We walked away and I said, "You will leave him alone with all those goods, and yet not let me walk to the next road."

He nodded. "Yes, one is only goods, the other is treasure."

"Treasure, or battle-gain?" I asked, tho' the words sounded awe-ful falling from my lips.

I heard his sharp intake of breath, and knew I had wounded him.

"If you say that again, I will strike you," he muttered.

I felt shamed, and then angry. No man could have guarded or protected me so well as he, yet I felt a prized captive and no honour from it. I wanted to beg his pardon, and I wanted to rage against him, and on the pounded clay road of that trading post I could do neither.

Chapter the Thirteenth: Shattered Spear

WE set off shortly after dawn. It was hard to leave the trading post, with the comforts and the safety that it offered, and strike out overland with our packs for what we knew not. And now that we were away from others I felt the Saxon to be more dangerous. He wore the knife that Sidroc had given him, and it was no match for all the weaponry that Sidroc carried, but I noted well that Sidroc never let the man fall behind him as we walked. I too had a knife at my waist, the small sharp one from the Idrisid ship that Sidroc had given me, but its presence gave me but little comfort.

We turned East from the trading post and walked along the shore line all day. Most parts were rimmed with trees or shrubs near the shore, but where the coast had softened there was marsh, and we must go inland and around it. The walking was level and not difficult, for which I was grateful, for we each carried our packs, and the men too had the saddle frames. I had the bridles, which were not heavy, and my workbasket, and some of our food. We stopped when we tired, and found some small creeks running into the sea with water that we could drink.

In the late afternoon the breeze picked up and the water to our left showed white tips as it crested. I pulled my mantle about me, and the late Sun shed some warmth. We made our camp on a sandy shore above the high water mark. There was much driftwood and we lit a big fire, and boiled a browis of meal and turnips and strips of roast pig. The night sky was clear and the stars and wanderers huge within it. The sand was dry as powder and settled underneath me when I sunk onto my plush weaving, making for good sleeping.

In the morning we set out again along the coast, but it was marshier this time and so we must go inland for firmer ground. None of us spoke much. Shore birds and marsh birds called out and dipped above the waters as we startled them, and once we saw a big stag deer at the edge of a marsh. It was too far to reach with a spear throw, and after looking at us for a moment it turned and vanished into taller grass.

We made camp that night on the rocky shore and had harder sleeping, for the beach was a pebbly one. Our loaves were growing hard and we softened them in broth I boiled in the morning made with roast fowl. Not long after we started out we came to a river. It was shallow, and no ship or even boat could sail up it, and no house could be seen. But now I knew Sidroc had been looking for it, for instead of wading across we turned South and walked along its banks. We went all day, and the river grew narrow and deeper. We stopped to drink from it, and the water was sweet. The bank was firm, with knee-high yellowed grass to its edge, and trees a long way off.

We walked on, following the path of the river, which went South and East. We made our camp on its banks, and had much good water to cook with. I heated basins full so we might wash, and only wished I might really bathe; but there was no place to go where I could strip off my clothing and do so. The next day we again followed the river, and Sidroc climbed a little rise when we came near it so he could see ahead, but when he came down did not tell us what he saw.

The grasslands ranged wide on each side of the river, and the trees had thinned so much and were so far off that finding wood for our fire became harder. I was growing tired now, with so much walking, and began to lag behind. We stopped more often, and once when Sidroc was not looking the Saxon tried to take the food bag I carried from me, but I would not let him. My boots were thin and I was crampy, and glad when we made an early camp.

"We are going too fast for her," the Saxon said when we had finished eating. We were sitting close together by the small fire.

"I am all right," I protested, sorry that he had spoken.

"She is not; she is a lady unused to this hardship." He spoke to Sidroc, not to me, and Sidroc looked at both of us.

"I should have bought one horse," Sidroc said.

"Do not say that," I began, and then felt confused to be defending his actions. "I am sorry to be so slow. I will be better tomorrow," I promised.

"She makes excuses, but you should be begging her pardon," the Saxon went on. He was almost scolding Sidroc, and would spur him to anger if he did not stop.

"Please," I told him, not knowing what else to say.

"Whatever you are seeking is not worth making her suffer," said the Saxon.

Sidroc had earlier removed his sword from his belt, but his hand flew to his seax so swiftly that all I could do was throw my body against that of the Saxon. I knocked him backwards upon the grass and turned to look up at the blade flashing in Sidroc's hand.

"Stop," I choked out, and trembled in every limb as I lay there. Sidroc reached down and pulled me with violence away from the man.

"What does killing him prove?" I pleaded. Tears flew from my eyes and I could scarce form my words. "We do not know where you are taking us, or for what purpose."

It took him a long time to sheath his seax. When he finally did, he said to the man, "If you speak of her again, I will kill you."

We passed the night almost in silence, and I felt Sidroc's anger against both of us. In the morning we walked unceasingly through grasslands edging the river. The Sun was hot above us and the ripened grass through which we moved waved pale and dry in the light breeze.

Before noon I called out, "I need to stop a moment," and set down my pack and basket. Sidroc and the Saxon stopped as well, and I waded through the tall grass for a place to squat.

Flies buzzed through the air, and as I turned to rejoin the men a puff of wind brought a rank odour to my nose. I sniffed but thought little of it. Then I heard a snort, and a rustle of dry seed pods and stems shaking. I glanced behind me and there rose from the grass the head of an immense bull. A cloud of flies lifted with it, and it shook its great head and blinked at me with bleared eyes. Its horns were curved and of vast reach, the head fringed all about with thick tufts of shaggy fur of brownish black, and the head itself was the size of a sheep.

I opened my mouth, and then the beast rolled forward and my yell died in my throat. It stood, and as it did rose in height so that the black and leathery nose was above my head. Now I screamed, and looked with horror as the bull lifted its great bulk and stamped upon the ground with its front legs. It snorted again, louder now, and lowered its mighty rack of horns.

I ran, tripped in my gown and fell, ran more. I saw the face of Sidroc, and the Saxon, not growing nearer it seemed, though I ran with all my speed. The men stood apart and had lowered their packs, waiting for my return. Now Sidroc yelled, "Saxon!" and flung the Idrisid spear from his fist through the air to the man. The Saxon caught it, and as I fell again I saw Sidroc run towards me. He was yelling and waving his arms and held his spear above his shoulder. He ran not straight to me, but off to one side, and yelled, "Stay down!" and I flattened myself in the grass. The bull had marked me and I expected any instant to be caught beneath its churning hooves, but I was too locked in my fear to scream.

The bull thundered past me, snorting and tossing its massive head, and the ground shuddered with its weight as it hurtled by. I lifted myself and saw that the Saxon had moved in closer, and was taking his aim with the light throwing spear as the beast now bore down on Sidroc. The bull was within a few lengths of Sidroc when the Saxon let loose his spear. It struck the beast in its right side, and the bull snapped its head up and to the right; and at this instant Sidroc hurled his own heavy spear at the shaggy throat now revealed.

The bull's hindquarters swung around, and the great legs staggered and found ground again, and I watched from my knees in horror as it reached the spot where Sidroc stood. The spear that had sailed from his hand lay embedded in the neck of the beast, and as the bull twisted his head Sidroc was caught across the body by the shaft of it and flung into the air.

The bull dropped upon its front knees and bellowed, and the spear shaft snapped off like kindling wood as the thrashing head drove it against the hard ground. It began to stand again, and the Saxon ran, knife drawn, to its side and thrust the short blade through the thick mane over and over. The tail of the bull whipped around with its hind legs and lashed at the Saxon, and he fell and was caught a moment in the horns. But the creature dropped, and did not rise again. It snorted with sucking breaths as it struggled upon the ground.

Both men lay senseless. I reached the Saxon first, who lay on his back near the huge head of the thrashing beast. I slipped my hands under his arms and dragged him clear of the horns that shook the air each time the animal moved. One of my hands came away bloodied but I did not stop to find his hurt.

I ran to Sidroc. He had been tossed so that he lay on his side, and was partly doubled over. I knelt at his shoulder and turned him towards me. His eyes were closed. There was a fleck of blood on his lower lip, but none foamed through his teeth. I cradled his head in my hands and bent over him.

"Sidroc," I summoned. I did not think he breathed.

I called his name again and pressed my mouth over his. My panting breath filled his mouth, and of a sudden he started awake. His arm rose slowly and wrapped around my shoulder. My face was pressed to his and I knew my tears wet both our cheeks.

I moved my face to see if his eyes were open. They were still closed, but he breathed freely now, and the arm that held me did so with strength.

"Where are you hurt?" I whispered.

He could not yet speak and shook his head a single time. I drew back to look down the length of his body. No gash had opened on his head, and I could see blood nowhere upon him.

The heavy leathern tunic had shielded his body from some of the force of the spear shaft, but I feared he bled within, a bleeding no leech can cure.

His lips moved, and I bent low over him to hear his words.

"You are not hurt?" he asked me. His eyes were still closed, and he wore the pain he felt upon his brow.

"No, no," I assured him. "It left me to chase you."

"Did we kill it?" he wanted to know.

The great bull's grunting breaths filled the air behind us. "It is dying now," I said.

"The Saxon?"

"He is over there, hurt."

He lifted his lids and squinted them shut. "I...I cannot see you," he said.

The glimpse I had of his eyes told me how glazed they were.

I laid my hand across them and again pressed my face to his. "You will be all right," I promised, and my heart leapt to be able to tell him this. "This means you have a hurt to the head, which will clear. Keep them closed so the Sun does not blind them."

I still feared for his body. "Tell me if this pains you," I said, and pressed my hands with some force under his arms and along the sides of his chest. I worked my way a few hand spans down his chest, when he grimaced on his right side. I went more gently, but this was the only place I caused him pain. I looked again at his face.

"Is there blood in your mouth?" I asked him. He licked his lips and shook his head.

"Your cheek is not pale, and no blood flows in your mouth. I do not think you bleed inside."

He nodded his head, and his own hand went to his side. "It is just a rib," he said. "But my head feels like an egg which has shattered."

"You will be dizzy for a while," I told him, "and it will ache." We had no Simples, none at all, and no way to ease the pain.

I heard a groan behind me, and turned to see the Saxon pull himself up so he sat upon the ground. "The Saxon is bleeding," I told Sidroc. "I will be right back. Do not move, and keep your eyes closed."

The man was sitting up, and gazing down upon his left arm where it lay in his lap. It was so bloodied that the light blue of the Idrisid tunic sleeve was now dark red. I knelt at his side and he lifted his head and looked at me, but did not speak. The tunic sleeve was torn from the shoulder down to the wrist, and I took my knife from my waist and cut it off at the shoulder seam. I used it to wipe away some of the blood. On the inside of his arm a long thin cut ran in almost a straight line. It was as sharp and clean as a knife cut, and we both looked at the curved horns which thrust from the bull's head. One of them had a jagged, broken tip, and it must have been one of these edges that had caught the arm.

The Saxon rocked forward to his knees, as if he would try to stand. "Stay there," I ordered. One of our packs was not far away, and I ran to it and pulled forth a pottery flask, and grabbed at some linen. The man was still on his knees, holding his arm.

"Is he dead?" he asked, looking over to where Sidroc lay.

"No," I said at once, and felt alarm. "He is only stunned." I pushed him back so he sat. "Hold it out so I can wash it," I told him, and poured the water so it ran, a red sheet, to the grass below. I took his arm in my hands and looked at the wound. Blood flowed freely from it, but the vein in the crook of the elbow did not spurt.

"It missed the vein. I could sew it up in places, but I think the cut will heal just as well if I wrap it tightly."

He nodded, and I ripped up the linen I had brought into long strips. I wrapped them tightly the whole length of the arm to staunch the blood. When I had knotted it off he again tried to stand. "Do not move," I ordered him. I went for the pack and dragged it to him. "Lie back, with your arm upon this until the bleeding clots. If you stand too soon you might burst the vein."

In fact, I did not think this would happen; the cut was not deep. But I did not want him on his feet when Sidroc lay defenceless nearby. I felt grateful he lay back and did as I told him.

I went back to Sidroc. I doubled up a piece of linen and drenched it with water, and lay it upon his brow.

"The Saxon," he said again.

"He is going nowhere."

The faintest of smiles crossed his lips. "Yes, I heard."

He drew his legs up so they were bent at the knees, and did so without difficulty; so they had suffered no hurt. "Where is the spear?" he wanted to know.

"The Idrisid one? It is stuck in the bull."

"Can he reach it?"

I glanced over to the Saxon. "He is flat on his back."

"As I am."

He was troubled enough by all this that I took a breath and said, "I will get it."

"No," he said. "I have seen a man killed by a boar thought dead. This is ten times the size. Do not go near it."

He pulled the cloth from his eyes and began to sit up. "Help me stand," he said.

This was just foolishness, and I sat back on my heels. "No. You must rest."

"Obey me."

"I will not."

He uttered the next as an oath. "Then my blood is on your hands."

He struggled to find his feet, and tho' I hung my head could do nothing but help him rise. He groaned as he rose, and I kept my arms about him to be certain he would not fall. He stood, but his head dropped forward to his chest.

"Can you see all right?"

"I can see," he reassured me. He spoke through gritted teeth and I felt he barely kept his feet. He put his hand on the back of his neck. "But I feel like I have been clubbed."

Now that he stood he looked upon the immensity of the beast he had killed. We walked slowly to its bulk, and I thought he marvelled, as I did, at its size and girth. The Idrisid spear was sunk behind the bull's shoulder, near the front leg joint, and jutted to the sky at a slight angle.

The beast was quiet now, its mouth open, the great bluish tongue lolled out, the long legs rigidly straight. Sidroc drew his sword and approached. The girth of the animal was such that he could not reach the spear without planting his foot on the great shaggy belly. He did so, and there came a rushing snort from its nostrils, but the head did not move, nor the cloven hooves twitch.

Now that he had reclaimed the spear Sidroc walked round to the back of the beast. There where I had dragged him lay the Saxon. He sat up as we approached. Sidroc looked down upon him, and I thought he might speak some word of praise or thanks to the man, but he said nothing. He reached out his right hand to pull the man up. The Saxon took his hand, and Sidroc let no sign of the pain from his ribs or head cloud his face.

The three of us turned to look again at the beast. It was as something from the sagas that skilled scops sang of; huge beyond reckoning, making men puny in its shadow.

The Saxon gaped at it, and at last said, "I have never seen any bull so great."

Sidroc answered the man. "It is no common bull, but the one called aurochs. Once they ranged over vast grasslands, and in and out of forests, but now their numbers are so few that they are almost as dragons. I myself have never seen one before; there are none left in my homeland. Old men tell tales from their grand-sires' time of herds of them, but are not believed. Now I know it was not just a boast of the mead-bench."

We moved to the head. The warm air buzzed with flies as they circled, lighting on the leathery black nose and huge dark eyes. "It is an old bull, and this is rutting-time, but it is said they are always fierce." He looked a while longer and ended, "I am sorry we had to kill it."

217

Lying not far away was the shattered end of his spear shaft. He looked at this, and back at the beast, and said, "I am also sorry one hundred men did not see us kill it, for we will never be believed."

The Saxon gave a kick at the haunch. "At least it will feed us for weeks," he said.

Sidroc shook his head. "We will not butcher it," he said. "To do so will take time and strength, and there is no wood to smoke the meat. Old as it is it would not be good eating."

I thought too that this beast might be a sacred one, and Sidroc did not want to butcher it as a common ox but leave it as a sort of Offering. We gazed upon the beast, but I did not want to look long upon it. My belly was still lurching with fear, and I brought water so that we might all drink. I shook my hands in the air to feel them again.

Sidroc looked around and said, "We will go no further today," and I nodded in gratitude.

I knew both men were weak from the hurt they suffered, and I dragged our packs near the river bank and draped the saddle frames with sheepskins so they might sit and rest their backs against them. There were no trees nearby, but I made a small fire by gathering twigs from some shrubby growth, and had enough to boil some barley meal and shreds of pig.

After we had eaten I took my workbasket and sat down by the Saxon. The cloth I had wrapped his arm with was red with blood, and I wanted to re-wrap it with fresh linen.

Sidroc was lying with his eyes closed, his head against the saddle frame, but I saw he opened them when I moved. I knew he did not want me to speak to the man, and I simply

218

nodded to the Saxon as I went to work. The cut was indeed a clean one, and oozed little. The honey-sellers had given me a small pot of honey, and I opened it now. The day was warm enough for the honey to flow, and I dipped my fingers in it and smeared it across the wound. "The honey will keep it from going green," I told the Saxon, and he nodded.

As I began to wrap the arm he spoke to me, in a whisper. "You have been kind to me, Lady. I will remember you when I am back in Wessex."

I caught my breath, but said nothing.

"Soon he will release me, and I will find my way to the coast, and thence home."

I raised my eyes to him, but his were cast down, and I could not read his face. I finished my work and went away from him. I was fearful for him to be caught speaking to me, and fearful too perhaps at what I might hear.

I went to the river bank and filled our flasks and basin and washed up. We had no more of roast fowl or eggs, but still in our food bags was a sack of barley and some cabbages and the roast pig. We had, I thought, two days' worth, or mayhap three, no more. As I knelt there packing these things Sidroc stood and came to me. He moved in such a way that made it clear his head ached.

"We can fish here," he said, as if he read my thought. "I have hooks the iron-smith wrought for me, and with your silk we can make lines."

I rose to meet him. "That is very good," I said, grateful to hear he thought on these things.

His eyes went to the hulk of the aurochs behind us. "First I must dig my spear point out."

"Can you not do it later?" I wanted to know. He looked as though he should be doing nothing but sleeping, but this I did not say.

"The flesh will only swell and make it more difficult," he answered.

"Can I help?"

He looked at the Saxon upon the ground, and then at me. "Yes, it will take two, but you will get bloody."

"If we are staying here I have enough day left to wash my gown."

"Then come," he told me, and we walked to the aurochs. Now that it was dead, and my fright from it over, I could look upon it for the creature it was: one of majesty and power. Sidroc felt it too, and murmured, "The Fates are kind, that we gaze upon this, that few men have seen. I am glad I share this hour with you, shield-maiden."

He drove the Idrisid spear into the ground by the animal's chin. He prised the bulk of it back, and we caught a glimpse of the wooden shaft.

"See if you can pull it out," he said, as he strained at holding the head off the ground. I took the short piece in both my hands and pulled with strength, but it did not budge. A pool of blood had collected beneath it, and the brown fur was clotted with it, and the flies that now swarmed all about the beast and the rankness of it made me feel almost that I would retch.

"Then hold this spear," he said, and I stood and took hold of it. I could not bend it as far as he did, but by using my whole weight and backing into the beast's great neck was able to lift it enough. With his seax he hacked away at the base of his broken spear, and then drew it forth, bloodied and clumped with tufts of fur.

He stood by me with reddened hands, and I recalled his words, that these beasts were rare as dragons. "Have you then seen dragons too?" I wanted to know.

He looked at me with interest, and I went on in a low voice, "You have a blue one on your chest," and lowered my eyes.

"I myself have never seen one, but when I was a boy I met a man who had. He still carried the singe burns from it on his arms, where no hair would grow."

He looked into the sky. "I have always wanted to see one. But if an aurochs is this deadly, I think I will content myself with the one I wear."

We set off in the morning, and tho' both men were stiff and sore they shouldered their heavy packs without comment. A raven rose from the body of the aurochs as we left; the hide was so tough it found but little there to fill its beak, and I thought that soon some greater beast might slink from out the grasslands and tear at the huge bull.

I was glad for the rest we had had; just not to walk all day was something to be grateful for. I had washed some of our clothing, which had dried in the afternoon Sun, and we had caught two fish, good fat bream, with the lines Sidroc had fashioned and the worms I had dug, so had fresh food too.

The banks of the river had gradually grown higher, the water carving a deeper channel as we walked along side it. I saw that Sidroc marked this well, for he began to look about him, and I saw the Saxon watch him as well. Whatever he sought we must be close to.

In the afternoon we came to a stream, which flowed into the river. We turned our backs on the river here, and began to follow the stream. The grasslands fell behind us, and the ground began to grow shrubs and small trees, and gentle hills lay on both sides of the stream, which made Sidroc cautious. He scanned the growth for any danger that might lie in wait behind them, but we came across nothing but birds flying low and calling as they followed the course of the stream, and big hares that sat up on their rumps and watched us with twitching faces.

The hills closed in upon the stream in places, and past one of these we came upon a heavy wooden fence, with no gate. We were so surprised to see it we all stopped, so long had it been since we had seen any of man's work. It was built across the rocky bed of the stream, and ran into thickly shrubbed hills on either side.

"Is this it?" the Saxon made bold to ask.

"Yes," answered Sidroc, without looking at him. "We will find horses here."

I scanned all about us. If there was a fence, there must be men, and hounds too. I did not want to be chased by anything just then, and neither man was wholly hale.

We slipped through the wide openings of the gate timbers, and the grimace on Sidroc's face told me how sore his side was. We kept walking and the hills opened up, and we found ourselves in a small valley. Within was grassland upon which horses browsed, scores of them. They were the same small stocky beasts we had seen the red-cheeked Pomerani ride into the trading post, and were of white and brown colours, with a few duns. The Saxon gave a low whistle, and a few of them lifted their heads to us, but then went on with their grazing.

"Whistle again and you may find someone other than a horse notices," Sidroc warned, and moved us in along the shrubs to cover.

We scanned all along the edges of the valley, but there was no farm house or other building to be seen. It seemed impossible that horses could be had just for the taking like this, but Sidroc said, "The cloth merchant told me we would find one of the Summering places of the horses if we came this way. He was as good as the silver I gave him."

"They are just kept here, unguarded?" I asked.

"Yes, but we must move now. The trading post is breaking up and at any time the folk who own these horses will be coming for them."

"We will just take them?" I asked, stupidly.

Sidroc was looking at the horses, not me. "The merchant got some silver out of the deal," he answered. He gestured

223

the Saxon to join him, but for me to stay back. "They may be wild, not having been ridden all Summer," he said, and took the bridles from my pack.

He and the Saxon started walking slowly towards a group of four or five of the little animals here. They did not walk together, but off to each side as they approached, and Sidroc spoke low to them. But the little horses were wily, and pricked their sharp ears forward and then back, and skittered off with surprising speed. This went on for some time, tho' the men walked slowly and stopped often. We had no long lines of hempen rope, only a few short pieces, and the bridle reins themselves; and a horse that does not want to be caught in a large pasture is one that will stay loose for some time.

At last they returned with their empty bridles and sat down. I was pawing through a food pack to get to a water flask when one of our few cabbages rolled out. Sidroc looked at it.

"Stay here," he told us. He took the cabbage and one of the bridles and turned to the Saxon. "Do not speak to her," he said, and walked out into the pasture.

Off to one side was a felled tree, and he went to where the trunk lay. He sat down upon it, and began to slice away at the cabbage with his seax. He did this slowly and calmly, and if he also spoke to the horses I could not hear. Those near the tree had wheeled away when he approached, but now returned to their grazing.

The Saxon and I watched this in silence, and the man moved a little closer to me. "I am just like you, Lady," he began. "He can forbid me, but I will speak to you anyway. Soon I will be free, as you will be."

"Hush," I said.

"He cannot hear, and you are worth the risk. You have shown me kindness. Let me speak to you a little time. I want to help you."

There was a pleading note to his quiet voice, and I found myself saying, "You are a thegn?"

"Yes, Lady, one of Odda's favourites. You may have heard my name. Let me, who has been nameless for so long, tell you who I am."

"No," I said urgently. "I do not want to know." I jumped up, and in doing so Sidroc saw me. He looked at us as I moved away and stood by a clump of birch trees.

One of the horses, a mare who had her this year's foal with year, was more curious than the rest, and had moved slowly towards Sidroc. The way she stretched her neck told me she smelt the cabbage he was chopping, and she came steadily nearer, her little brown foal bumping her side as she came.

Sidroc did not hold the leaves in his hand, but just pushed a few along the tree trunk. Her nose reached out and she grabbed one of them with her whiskery lips, and pulled it back. She ate another, and a white horse came up beside her and nipped her on the shoulder. The mare drew back and the white horse extended his neck and took a cabbage leaf. Now Sidroc put one in his hand, and the horse took it, and he slowly stood and holding the bridle by the headstall placed his hand on the animal's neck. It poked away at the leaves he had left on the trunk, and then in an easy move he slipped the bridle on the horse and began to lead him away.

As he walked towards us his face was blank, and I came forward with what I hoped was a smile. He did not look at me, just drew sheepskins and blankets from our packs, and went about the work of saddling the white horse. He moved it a little away before he mounted, but it did not buck or even start. He spoke to it and nudged it forward with his heels, and rode it about in a small circle.

"Give me the other bridles," he said to me, and I did. He rode at a walk to the herd of horses, which raised their heads at him, but did not move off. From the back of the white horse he looked them all over closely, and found a brown one, larger than the rest, at which he stopped. He swung off the white horse and drew a bridle on this one. He rode back to us and gave me the reins of the brown horse to hold, and returned to the herd to select another.

The Saxon had moved to my elbow and made bold to extend his hand to me. "Lady, you wish to return to Wessex. I will take you there."

I turned my face away. "He would kill you if he heard you say that," I breathed to him. My eyes were fixed on where Sidroc rode amongst the horses.

"Yes, but it is only my life I put in danger; he would not harm you."

"Do not say any more," I told him.

"Who has he taken you from, Lady? I see that you grieve. Your husband, or your children? They are waiting for you at Kilton. Let me take you there."

Tears flooded my eyes, but I moved away from the man. Sidroc had chosen another brown horse and led it to us.

"We are going," he told us, and began to saddle the larger of the two brown horses. He passed the reins of the white one to me. "This one for you," he said.

The Saxon could not handle the saddle well with his bandaged arm, and Sidroc pushed him aside and saddled the other horse for him. He dug through the hide packs, drawing out things and re-packing them, and handed us each one.

We were soon back at the fence, and had to lead our horses up and around the scrub growth of the hill to get around it. Once on the other side Sidroc turned to face the Saxon.

"You have much to be grateful for. You are only alive because of her." He said this with such vehemence I started. He drew the small leathern purse from his belt and flung it upon the ground. "Here is your silver. Get on your horse and ride."

The Saxon never looked at me, just bent to retrieve his winnings. Sidroc still held the Idrisid spear.

"You said you would arm me," the Saxon complained.

"You have a knife. If you want more I will be glad to sink this spear into your back as you ride away. Now go."

The man uttered an oath under his breath and swung onto his horse. He kicked savagely at its flanks and the animal nearly reared as it charged off.

"Get on your horse," Sidroc ordered me.

I was afraid to move, fearful that he would let fly the spear at the Saxon's retreating back, but tho' he clutched it so his fingers paled, he did not.

We rode off at almost a canter, and saw before us the Saxon following the stream the way we had come. Sidroc turned his horse so it plashed through the shallow waters, and we crossed over and rode fast across the shrubby landscape until I was breathless. We finally stopped, and Sidroc swung down from his horse and nearly pulled me from mine.

"What lies did he pour into your ear?" he asked.

"Why are you the only one who knows what is good for me?" I demanded. "He is going home to Wessex, and asked me to travel with him."

"How can you be so foolish? If you had gone off with him he would have used you in every way, made you whore for him, and when he had had his fill of you would have sold you, or dragged what was left of you back to Wessex to seek ransom from Kilton."

"I am here, still," I shouted in my fury. "I did not even want to listen to him, but perhaps I should have. What do you have a right to expect? You tell me nothing, save you have claimed me for your own."

I tried to take breath, to calm myself, but the words tumbled forth just the same. "You kept me from being ravished, then took me from the Idrisid ship. You have fed and clothed me, and saved me from the great bull. But you will not help me get back to Wessex, and said you would even kill your own men to keep from being found. If I am your battle-gain, tell me."

His words were beautiful, and cruel.

"You are my wife, not my captive. I have not waited these ten years for you to do you any hurt. A man does not treat his wife thus. Not if she is a good woman, and you are the best."

I screamed out my answer. "What does that make Ælfwyn?"

He turned his head away, and then turned back. "I did not plan our capture. I could not know what each day would bring. I am living by my wits, every hour. It has been all I can do to keep us alive." He ran his hand through his hair. "As to what I expect, it is this: That when we are in danger you obey me, at once and without question. This one thing I demand of you."

He glared down at me, and I shuddered so in my fury I could scarce return his look.

He shook his head, and took a deep breath. "I am too angry to speak more to you, or be this close. Tell me that I can trust you not to run off with the horses."

Now I was enraged, and plucked at a clump of grass and tore it at the roots and flung it at him, as a sullen child would do.

Chapter the Fourteenth: You Cannot Do This

I felt sunk in misery. Sidroc went off a little time by himself, vanishing through the trees and leaving me alone with all our kit and the two horses. I wept some, and then straightened my clothes and wiped my face with water. The Sun was low in the sky when he came back and began moving about to make our camp for the night. I got up and helped him gather dry twigs and branches for our fire, and set to work starting it. Behind me he unsaddled our horses and carried over our packs. He spread the tanned hides we used as ground covers and lay his with sheepskins from the saddles. On mine he unrolled the beautiful plush weaving he carried for me each day. He did all this without speaking to me, and I too could find nothing to say.

I made up our meal, and we ate in near silence as the dusk grew. He had given the Saxon very little of our food, but what remained to us was only enough for a day or two. The air was grown chill and I drew my mantle closer about me as I leant nearer the fire.

"We will need food soon," I told him in a low voice. I was not going to ask him where he thought we might find some.

"I know," he returned in a low tone of his own. "If we ride almost North-East to the coast for a while we will come to a trading post that will be well stocked. The cloth-merchant told me of it, and so far his words have been true ones. It should not be more than two days, or even less, now that we are horsed."

The Claiming

I looked up at him, grateful to learn so much.

He went on. "The post is a large one; we will find all we need there."

I nodded, but did not trust myself to speak.

We had gathered much wood, and now he placed a few more branches onto the fire. "Are you chilled?" he asked, seeing how tightly I held myself in my mantle.

I shook my head, but he went on. "It is cold in these parts in Winter, with much snow. But I will buy you many furs, so you will never feel it."

He could not see the tears that streaked my face, and I made no sound. I thought of how hard he planned and worked for our safety, and of the choice things he had given me, and those he had promised; and could not stop my silent tears from falling. I knew he rode with a broken rib and a head that still ached, and never made complaint, and sat next me promising furs to keep me warm.

He leaned back against his saddle frame, and a long while passed as the night sky deepened. He began to hum a song to himself, and had a voice that was deep and pleasing.

After a while he sat forward, his hands clasped over his knees. The fire light flickered over his face as he spoke.

"The priest at Four Stones tells sagas, as you heard. One he told was about a man who loved a maid, and had to work seven years to win her for his wife. The seven years came and went, and by trickery he was forced to take the maid's sister instead of she he wanted. The man was told he must work another seven years for the one he loved."

I knew this story from the Holy Book, and how Jacob had fulfilled a doubled pledge to win Rachel.

"I made him tell it twice; I could not believe him. The maid was willing, and wanted to wed, but still the man accepted this. No man should do so, and the fact that the priest's God decreed all this made me angry. But the man agreed to it, and stayed, instead of running off with the one he wanted.

"But then I recalled when I saw you last at Kilton, when Guthrum made Peace with Ælfred. I rode to meet you in the fruit grove, and as I cantered there I thought, If I ride off with her now I will start another war."

He gave a low laugh. "And I was willing to do it; I had all my silver in my belt and was thinking even then where I would take you to."

My husband still lived then, and the daughter I had hoped to have had not yet been born. I pressed my hands to my face and spoke. There was no strength left in me and my voice was but a whisper.

"You have a wife, and children, and much treasure and many men you have left behind, and I have a son. You cannot do this, Sidroc."

"I give it all up."

"You cannot give up Ælfwyn, desert her like this. And leave her with my son to raise as well. She will be half mad with worry for you."

"She is not alone. Asberg rules until Hrald is of age; he will do as I would. She has her mother, and sisters, the priests

232

and those holy women. She is rich. She can marry again, or go to Oundle and live amongst her holy women as she once wished. As for the children and my treasure, it is no worse than if I were dead; better, for my killer cannot claim it and all is left to them. Missing them is a price I must pay."

I was shaking my head to keep out these words.

He looked out over the fire's glow. "And...she has never cared for me," he said, in eerie echo of Ælfwyn's own words. "I do not know if she wanted a man before Yrling, or..." He shrugged. "There are some on this Earth who never do. Ælfwyn may be one of them."

Now I turned to him. "She knew love, once. But it was snatched away from her when she was still a maid. It was Gyric she loved."

He looked at me and his lips parted.

The truth tumbled out from me. "He had travelled to Cirenceaster in the train of Ælfred when Æthelred was still King," I told him. "Ælfwyn and Gyric met, and knew at once they loved each other. But before he could sue for her hand he was captured, and then his eyes burnt out. Meanwhile Ælfwyn's father had sold her to Yrling as part of his Peace. This is what she had to live with all these years."

He was silent for a time. His eyes searched my face and he asked, "Will you tell me what happened then at Four Stones? When you ran away?"

"We were told there was a man of Wessex held as prisoner in the cellars, and almost at the same time that it was Gyric himself. She was resolved to make the Peace with Yrling work, but knew she must help Gyric to escape. I went to the cellars one night and saw how he had been maimed. He was going to die there, so I rode away with him."

"You did not know him?"

"Not then," I said in truth. "I had not ever seen or spoken to him."

He thought on this. "Why then did you run off with him?"

"He was going to die if I did not. Ælfwyn loved him. I knew him to be a good man. I could do nothing else."

He shook his head at this. "Into such danger. Like the shield-maiden you are."

Silence grew around us, and I clasped myself the harder, thinking on those days.

"I never knew this," he said slowly. "I thought you ran away because you loved him."

"No," I told him. "But Ælfwyn lost both Gyric and me, and then Yrling, who she was beginning to care for."

"I am sorry for her," he said. "Her God has not dealt kindly with her, but she says it is often thus."

A little while passed before I found words again. "I have a son," I said.

"He is a fine boy. Whether he stays at Four Stones or not, he will be a young man soon."

Now I sobbed.

"But I will give you another," he told me, which made me lift my face.

"Do you think your wanting me is so strong a force that all other things are meaningless before it?"

"I know it is strong enough to have kept me wanting you for these ten years, and for me to throw all else aside to claim you. Ten years is enough; I cannot wait any longer, nor do I have to. Freyja has brought us together at last."

"And me? What of my desire?"

"You told me years ago that if you had stayed at Four Stones you would have wed me."

I nodded my head, and explained softly, "When a man wants a woman very much, it is hard for the woman to keep refusing him. Especially if he be a good man."

He looked long upon me. "We are alike, shield-maiden; we are as one. Within you, you know this. At Four Stones you were very young, and the force of my wanting you frighted you. But I think a part of you wanted me too, even then." He turned his eyes to the glowing branches in the fire. "And I think that when you went to Kilton's bed, it was me you wanted."

I hid my face in my hands.

"I am sorry to make you cry so much," he told me. "Now we have horses and are truly free. If I have been rough with you today, I did it only to spare you from danger."

The Claiming

When I awoke at dawn I lifted my head and looked about me. Our fire had burnt out, and beyond its ring of stones I saw the short necks of our horses as they nibbled at the grass they browsed in. The sleeping form of a man lay a few arm-lengths from me, and our hide travel packs lay behind us. I lay there with raised head, blinking myself awake, recalling another life I had lived on the road with another man in another land.

But morning birds do not sing at the end of Summer as they do in Spring, and we were far from Lindisse or Wessex, in a land I knew not the name of; and I was no longer a maid of fifteen Summers. Yet so much was the same that as I went about the tasks of starting our fire, boiling broth from the roast pig, and shaking out my bedding, that these simple actions recalled me with force to that earlier girl I had been.

Sidroc had pushed one of our pottery flasks into the fire to warm the water within, and when we had eaten drew it forth and poured a little into our basin. He took a piece of linen and a small wood box from his kit, and as I watched I realised he was about to shave the beard he had worn for so many years. He always kept it closely clipped to the face, but now he took from the wooden box a razor with a bone handle along its spine. He glanced up at me and asked, "Will you hold your mirror for me?"

I brought it from my workbasket, small and round and silver and flat, so that it gave a true image of the beholder.

He wet his face well with the water, and then began to scrap away at his dark beard. I knelt in front of him holding the mirror, tracing his moves so he might see as well as possible. The beard fell in clumps upon the ground when he snapped the hand that held the razor. He did not cut himself, tho' he had no oil to ease the blade along.

He had grown it to help hide his scar from Ælfwyn's eyes, and now in finally freeing himself from it I thought it an act both subtle and grave.

When he had done he looked almost as he had the day I had met him, save for the few strands of grey on his left temple.

He did not speak to me about it, and I too was mute, but after he wiped his face our eyes met, and I knew I had read the true meaning of this action on our first day alone together.

We packed our things and made our start. Our horses were steady little beasts, docile and quiet, but when nudged with the heels would pick up and canter as if they took their own joy in it. But we mostly went at a walk, for we rode over grassland and twiggy growth, not smooth pounded roads. Our weather stayed dry and fair, as late Summer so often is, and made for good riding.

We rode most of the day, and when the Sun had begun to drop overhead we came upon a stream, and so stopped to rest both horses and ourselves. The wild grasses on either side were almost like wheat, so even and golden did they grow. It was beautiful to look at in its way, but it made me wary to gaze upon, thinking of the tall grass in which the great bull I had startled was sleeping.

Sidroc must have thought the same, for he said, "I did not need the Saxon after all to get the horses, but I am glad he was there when the aurochs charged."

In fact, it may have been that his life had been saved by the Saxon, but I was not going to say this, and only nodded my head.

He was holding the Idrisid spear in his hand, and looking at it closely as he spoke. Now he checked the Sun above us, and the horses standing in the shallow water, content at their drinking.

"Since there is much water, and we have ridden far today, we will stay here for the night," he told me. I was glad at this for there was still much daylight, and I could wash out some of our clothes and have them dry by the fire before dawn. We made our camp, and as we had been careful to carry firewood with us, could have enough even in this grassy place. Soon I had the saddle frames propped near the fire and draped with leggings and my other shift, and even my stockings, tho' I had to go barefoot as they were my only pair.

After I did this I sat cross-legged upon my plush weaving. It had quickly become a source of pleasure to me, for not only was it soft, and the green of most of it like my eyes, but the blue and red and gold patterns that ranged round its borders were unlike any I had seen. These were not the interlaced spirals and plaits I was used to, or simple stripes; these were shapes that in my mind's eye might be flower blooms, and birds taking wing, and trees rising against stars. When I sat upon it I would stroke it like a cat, and petted it too this way before I fell asleep each night upon it.

Sidroc sat across me on his sheepskins, cleaning his seax and sword. He had got a whetstone from the trading post, and now put a new edge on the seax, and picked out bits of dirt that had lodged in the carved hilts, and with a leathern buffer polished both blades.

The Claiming

I watched him as he worked on his sword. It was yet a different one from that he had carried when he came to Kilton, and I knew that whenever he found a better one he made it his own. This one was pattern-welded, like all the finest blades, marked on each side with the rune for the God Tyr; and so deeply etched that the twisted hammered bands of steel caught the light and seemed to flicker as he drew the buffer across it. The movement of his strong wrist was smooth and sure with long practice. I recalled the day at Four Stones when I had seen him polish an earlier sword, and he had told me that he would wait for me to want him.

Now the Sun was moving steadily to its home, shedding gold light on the tall grasses. It was quiet at the edge of the stream and my voice too was quiet.

"How many men have you killed?"

I had never asked this of any man, and surprised myself by doing so now.

He paused and said, "Three-and-forty."

It seemed a huge number, forty-three, but from the way he spoke I could not tell if he thought it few or many. But the fact that he gave a sum at all told me each one was recalled in his mind.

"Those are killed outright. There will be more, perhaps two score, who died later from the wounds I gave them."

"That is a lot," was all I could say. I felt my voice grow small.

"More than some men, not so many as others," he answered.

The Claiming

"Even if it were only forty-three, there are also forty-three mothers, and wives, and many children, behind that number."

"You cannot think of that," he answered at once. "When you are in battle you can think only of keeping your enemy from killing you. The quickest and best way is to kill him first." He looked across the surface of the flowing grass. "Those are the things you think about later, when you have drunk much ale, or late at night, when you waken in the dark.

"Some of them I will have to fight again, after I die," he reflected. He spoke of dwelling in the heaven of Asgard at the Halls of the Slain, where warriors fight all day for glory but all wounds heal at dusk. Then the men sit in fellowship at table and feast on rich food and drink strong mead, brought to them by beautiful women. "But most of those I have killed are Christian, so I will not face them again."

I thought of his own cousin Toki, who Sidroc had slain, and it seemed he read my thought, for he said, "Toki will be there. He was a good warrior, always ready to fight. But you and I will be in Freyja's Hall, and he will be called to Odin's, with those who know treachery, so he still cannot look at you."

Thinking of this recalled me to their boyhood days.

"When did you kill your first man?" I wanted to know.

"Late. I was already one-and-twenty, and had come to Lindisse with Yrling. Then there were a few I killed together, with Yrling."

I thought about his uncle, now ten years dead, felled by the hand of Godwin.

"You must miss him, at times," I said.

"He taught me much, Yrling, both what to do and what not to. I will welcome seeing him again," he said, and gestured to the sky with his finger. "And he will be glad to see you, too, shield-maiden. He knew one day you would be there as well. It is easier to die if you know your companions are waiting for you." He smiled at me. "But I do not want to die now, unless we both die, because I do not want to have to wait for you again."

I said nothing to this and he went on with a shake of his head. "I am older now than Yrling was when he was killed. I knew little in those days."

I thought about when I had first met Sidroc; he had then twenty-three Summers. "That is not the way you looked. When I first saw you in the yard at Four Stones..."

His eye was bright and eager now, and I told him the truth. "You were fearsome, even then. You were tall and strong, yes, but it was more. The way you walk and stand, the way other men look at you with narrowed eyes, all that was already there." I knew I was praising him, and his face shone with pleasure in hearing this.

"I am stronger now than ever before," he allowed, "but I have lost some of my speed." He smiled again. "You were a good judge of men, even then." He shook his head and laughed. "You were so young, and fierce, I had never seen a woman like you. You had boldness, and such beauty that I knew at once I wanted you for mine." He fixed me with his dark blue eyes. "And you did not turn from the scar on my face."

The Claiming

The night was fine and dry, so that but light dew lay upon us in the morning. We had no tent, or any other covering, and as I sat upon my plush weaving readying myself for the day I was grateful we had suffered so little rain.

In the bottom of my workbasket I had found a slender stick, the length of my hand, and of hard wood. It was of a dark reddish brown hue, and I could not guess why the Idrisid woman had kept such a thing together with the ivory comb, silver mirror, fine needles, and other treasures. Today I took out the stick and looked at it closely. It had a curious smell, now that I held it closely to my nose, and I touched my tongue to it. A pleasing spicy hotness remained there. Each morning I broke off twigs from trees or shrubs to rub my teeth clean with, and now I used the tip of the brown stick to do just that. It felt better in the mouth even than fresh birch twigs, which I could not always find as we went.

"I think we will come to the trading post today," Sidroc said after we had eaten our scant breakfast. We were packing our gear to make our start. "There we will find fresh food, ale, and much else that is good."

"I am eager for it," I said, but the way in which he had spoken made me wonder if he was.

"There will be many kinds of folk there, and we must always be wary," he went on. "Cut-purses, and beggars, and thieves, also men who lurk in such places looking for trouble." I was not going to remind him that we ourselves had just stolen three horses, and said nothing. Now he stopped what he was doing, which was kicking out the remains of our fire, and looked at me.

"Tell me that if we are in danger I can be certain you will obey me."

I felt anger flare that he would even ask such a thing. I swallowed it back and told him, "Before he was maimed Gyric and Ælfred used to fight shield-to-shield. They kept each other alive and killed many enemies this way. If I am not worth your trust you are not worth mine."

He heaved a sigh. "Then I tell you: You have my trust." He shook his head and gave a short laugh. "A man should not ask these things of a shield-maiden. They make their own choices on the battle plains."

We did not speak much for the first part of our ride. The day was a cool one, but the skies were fair, and there should have been pleasure in it to ride on our nimble horses through the golden grassland. I felt sorry that I had spoken to Sidroc thus, and greater anger at my helplessness as we rode further from the lives we had known. We would provision ourselves at the trading post, this was clear, but what lay in his mind beyond that I could not guess, and I feared to ask. Perhaps he had yet no firm plan; or perhaps if he told me of it I would somehow become a greater part of achieving it. All of this spun in my mind as we rode side by side, heading North again, to the coast.

"It is an empty land," I finally said, to show him I was not still angry.

He turned his head and scanned the grasses stretching as far as the eye could reach.

"I told the cloth-seller I wished to meet no one, and this is the way he sent us."

Just then a red vixen, followed by her two half-grown kits, crossed in front of us and vanished into taller grass. With their pointed muzzles and full tails they were so beautiful that I gave a laugh of delight.

"You have not had much to laugh about on this trip," said Sidroc. "I promise that each day you spend with me you will have some pleasure, and I hope, laughter too."

Chapter the Fifteenth: Tyr's Son

WE came to a road, well-rutted with use, and took it North. It crested a small rise in the grasslands, from which we saw the buildings of the trading post, and the blue of the Baltic beyond. Several piers extended into the water, and we counted four large ships, and many smaller ones. A man driving a horse-drawn wain passed us, and nodded as he did so. His horse was much like our own, and I looked after it. Our horses were unbranded, and bore no ear-marks, so if any disputed our right to them they had no real claim, but this I hoped we would not have to prove.

The trading post was indeed large, and filled with timber buildings. On the outskirts of it we rode past rows of narrow streets, such as that the honey-sellers had lived on, and saw at a glance tradesmen and women of all sorts lining their borders. There were coopers forming barrels, leather workers cutting shoes, and a man carving troughs. There were folk sitting out with wares to sell, and others who wandered the roads calling out in shrill voices to turn the eyes of passers-by to their wheeled carts. We saw a wash shed, which made me glad, for here men and women might find water ready hotted with which to bathe, and rinse out clothes.

Apart and to one side were men who worked with fire, and I saw Sidroc mark well a weapon-smith's shed. Next him were tool-makers and an iron-smith, and other men bent at work at glowing forges.

Before us, nearest to the water line, were larger buildings still, and the road nearing them more crowded. We came into

245

a sort of square, with large store-houses all about it, and many folk within. Here against the walls of some of the large store-houses were open stalls at which were piled baskets of food. Folk swarmed around them and my mouth watered at the smell of fresh bread and roast fowl.

We rode slowly and carefully in this crowd. There were men in wool leggings and tunics such as Sidroc wore, but none that might be mistaken for a Dane or a Saxon; they had about them a different look in their dress and weapons and boots. Some men wore flowing robes almost to the ground, and I opened my eyes wide at this; and started too when I saw some dressed almost as the Idrisids had been. These wore full and gathered leggings as the Idrisids had, but did not wrap their heads, nor wear sashes, and I saw they carried straight swords and not curved. Also they had skin that was fair and not amber-coloured. The women too were of all sorts; some with dark and flashing eyes and head wraps that hid every strand of hair, and others had the round heads and red-cheeks of the honey-sellers, which made me glad, as I knew these to be Pomerani and so good folk. But there were not so many women here as there had been at the smaller trading post.

Mixed within the square with these were many men with spears and swords, all who bore about their breasts a sash of dark red cloth from shoulder to waist. From the way they stood at the doors of the store houses and watched the passage of folk from the narrow roads into the square I saw they were the men of the lord of this place.

We got off our horses and began to buy food, both to fill our empty bellies and our hide food bags. Each stall had a metal scale at which the silver of the buyer was measured, its weight compared against a set of small iron balls of differing sizes, and tho' we could not speak to the sellers were understood by our gestures. Some who purchased goods paid in pieces of silver jewellery, or slender silver rods which were hacked down bit by bit. We had whole coins of silver, but each stall holder had a small axe with which to make half and quarter pieces, and by chopping off fragments of these we bargained for what we wanted. We bought roast fowl, still hot and sizzling on wood sticks, and small flat loaves of wonderful savour, and filled our flasks with what we hoped was good ale. Sidroc was packing all this up when I spotted another stall.

"Apples," I said. They had yellow skins flecked with brown spots and were large and firm. So we bought apples too.

We put all this into our packs and were about to mount and leave the square when a horn rang out. It grew more crowded, and I saw the tips of spears being carried in a row. Men called out, and a space in front of one of the store houses was cleared. The warriors with the spears came in front of it, dark red sashes across their chests. Behind them was a man dressed in long robes, who held in his hand a chain of iron, and behind him linked by their hands to this chain, came slaves.

There were three of them, men with light hair and beards. Two of them were no more than five and twenty, and the third a little older. They were stripped to the waist and had ragged leggings, and iron chains linked them as well from ankle to ankle.

Another man walked behind, and he led five slaves, two of which were women. Both of them were young, with dark brown hair that flowed from under short head wraps. Their gowns were of the simplest make, of undyed wool, the skirts unhemmed. The women did not wear chains but their hands were bound, and one was clasping them together as if in fear, or in prayer.

I shuddered to see them. The words of the Saxon rose in my ears, when he told me of my Fate at the hands of the Idrisids: You will be worth only what you will bring in the market as a flesh-slave.

Some who would be buyers pushed forward to get a better view, and Sidroc was able to make enough room about us so we could turn our horses and quit the place.

I had been about slaves all my life, in my kinsman's hall, where they were those he had captured; at the Priory, where they worked as freed men and women after the Prior had redeemed them; at Four Stones, where they had been cruelly mistreated by Yrling; and at Kilton. The slaves at Kilton were those who had been taken into slavery for wrong-doing, and were working to redeem themselves; or those who through misfortune had fallen into such poverty that they had asked Godwulf to become his slave and thus, dependent. In either case these folk, both men and women, were decently clothed and fed, and it was in Ælfred's law that no man might mistreat them. Work they did once their duties were done each night they could sell, and thus accrue enough to redeem themselves one day. Looking upon these in the trading post square I thought no such protection would extend to them, and no such hope.

Sidroc had taken us down one of the narrow roads, and we went a little way beyond the last tradesmen's sheds. The remains of someone's camp was there, with a wooden bench and a fire pit and a shattered pile of planks, and we dismounted.

"You should wrap up your hair," he said almost at once.

I still wore the short linen head wrap the honey-women had given me, and looked at him.

"It is so bright," he said, and I knew that after what we had seen he feared unwanted notice. "At least braid it up so it does not show so much."

My mantle had no hood, and I did not have linen enough to make a larger head wrap, but I plaited my hair in a single thick braid and tucked it under my mantle.

We ate, and all that we had tasted was good, but in thinking of what we had just seen it was hard to take pleasure in it. Some of the slaves had blank faces, some angry or insolent, but some wore the pain of grief upon their brows. One of the slave-women had looked into the crowd, and I thought, at me, with dark eyes that looked beseechingly for help.

"You have not seen slaves at sale before," he said.

I shook my head. When the Danes had first come and overrun the Kingdoms of Northumbria and Lindisse and Anglia they had taken many folk into slavery, and shipped them off to distant lands. I knew Yrling had been part of this, and probably Sidroc too.

"I could have been one of those women," I murmured.

"Only if I were dead," he answered.

"Then I would have had a double misery," I said, and looked up to see the sudden light in his eyes.

We went next to the weapon smith. On our journey we had passed no ash tree from which Sidroc could cut a straight bough and fashion a shaft for it. Now he held the iron spear point out to the man who had a store of ready cured shafts to fit to it. Hung on the back wall of the shed were two round wooden shields, and Sidroc pointed also to them. Both were iron rimmed, with leather-clad faces and an iron boss before the hand grip. Both showed wear, and as Sidroc took first one and then the other onto his left arm, I knew that he who had before wielded it must be dead. The one he chose had a black and white spiral painted on its face, and he hung it upon his saddle.

We went back into the square. It was late in the day and the place mainly clear. We led our horses to one of the storehouses, and Sidroc stepped within and gestured that I wait. I could see the glint of silver within and from the two men who guarded the door knew that jewellery must be bought and sold there. Sidroc was gone some little time but came back with nothing in his hands.

We bought more food, including a sack of oats and turnips and carrots, and a big piece of smoked pig. When Sidroc was putting his coinage back into his belt I saw his wrist.

"Your bracelet," I gasped. "It is gone."

He had never had it off for a moment and I stared at the bare wrist now.

"It is all right," he told me. "The silver-smith is taking out the dent in it. It will be ready in the morning."

He had worn it dented for many years without having it fixed, and I thought it strange that he have it smoothed now. I wondered if he thought to sell it, but that could not be, for he would rather part with his seax, I thought, than this silver disk he wore on the wrist which held the weapon.

"It must be perfect again when I give it to you," he said.

I turned away from him, not knowing what to say. We got on our horses and went to the camp we had had our meal at. Few folk were about at this hour and we moved our horses to the back of the site and stood near them.

I knew I must make some answer, and began.

"I do not have the right to accept your bracelet, and you do not have the right to give it me."

"You must accept it. It has always been yours. I have only been keeping it for you until I could once again place it on your wrist."

It was hard to answer, knowing all that the bracelet had meant to him, and recalling Ælfwyn's words about it.

"In your homeland I know men take two or even more wives. But when you wed Ælfwyn you knew she expected to be your only wife. I love her as a sister. You cannot do this to her."

251

His words were gentle. "Do you think she would grieve so much? She has known from before she wed Yrling that I wanted you. And her love for you must be as great as yours for her. She would want you to be happy." He looked around the camp site, as if for answers. "And I do not want you both. I want only you."

Now he lifted his hands in the air. "Also, she thinks we are dead."

"We are not dead," I answered back.

"I do not know what else to say to you." His voice was so pained that my heart clenched.

"And Ceric, my son?"

"If I could snap my fingers and bring him to you I would do so. But I cannot. You must trust that he will grow strong and be well at Four Stones, or that Kilton will come and take him away."

Ceric had found such happiness at Four Stones that I thought to lose Ælfwyn and Hrald and Ashild would only further his loss.

"All I can do is tell you the truth. I will not give you up."

We made our camp. We still had no tent and Sidroc wanted to buy hides or oiled cloth so we might make one, but the stalls selling such things were closed down for the night. We staked the horses and struck a fire, and ate the browis I boiled. Sidroc was at work carving the rune for Tyr into the back of his new shield, and then upon it, so that the two were made one, the rune Sigel, with which he was wont to mark his name. He carved it above the boss, so that each time he took the shield into his grip his eyes should fall upon this bindrune.

Dusk fell, and I tho' I said almost nothing, Sidroc sat across from me as if at ease in the silence.

I thought of his ease with me, and his certainty in what he was doing, and the greater certainty that stamped so many of his actions.

"You said that Freyja had marked me," I said at last. It was now almost dark, and he was poking more branches into our fire. "Tell me what you mean."

He wove another stick into the hungry flames. "That you are her daughter, just as I am Tyr's son," he said, and gestured to the shield that lay upon the ground. "She marked you to be like her, to follow in her ways, whether you want to or not. Thus she watches you, just as Tyr watches me."

"Do you feel - watched?"

He laughed, and sat back next me. Around his neck he had hung a leathern cord tied with a tuft of the great aurochs' mane, and he tugged at it now. "I know the Gods look at me. Sometimes only to laugh, and sometimes they fight over which of them will have their way with me; but yes, I know they see me."

I believed him; I could not do otherwise.

"How do you know you are Tyr's son?"

The Claiming

"I gave myself to him when I was young."

"Like a dedication to a saint, for the holy women," I thought aloud.

He considered this. "Yes; but I cannot know for sure. It was like...the pledges that your men give to their war-chiefs, that they will follow him and obey until death, vowing all the works of their weapons to his aid."

I nodded, thinking on this most solemn of pledges. "Why did you choose Tyr?"

"His arm. I wanted an arm like his, that never failed me in battle."

"Even tho' he let his arm be bitten off?"

I spoke here of the wolf, Fenrir, begotten of the Trickster God Loki, which grew so huge and fierce it threatened even the Gods. Odin had forged for it a magical binding, as fine as a single hair but stronger than the stoutest iron chain. Fenrir was wary of it, and despite the Gods' promises would only allow it to be placed about his neck if one of them, as a good faith offering, laid his hand between his jaws.

"That was his courage. He was the only one of the Gods willing to pay this penalty. He lost the arm, but the Gods gained the peace they sought. And you know...it was right he had to make the forfeit. He had vowed that there was no treachery, when he knew there was. So he knew what was coming, knew the justice of it, and still placed his hand in the wolf's mouth. It helped me learn, even when I was still young, that everything has its price."

I knew he had always been one to count the cost of his desires.

"And Freyja?" I went on. "Did you always revere her?"

He smiled, and shook his head. "When I was young she was like a perfect woman to me, nothing more. Beautiful, fierce, one who loved freely. It was after I saw you I began to make Offering to her. Especially after you ran away from me."

"I did not run from you," I said, but so quiet were my words he had to lean in to hear them. It was the dangers of Four Stones I had run from, to save the life of Gyric lest he perish there.

"Yes," he said quickly. "This I now know." He lifted his hand slightly. "It means much to me, to learn this."

We passed the night under the stars. The trading post did not feel so secure a place to sleep out in the open in, tho' we saw some of the red-sashed men walk up and down, as wardmen. It was not a night of deep rest for either of us.

In the morning I sat upon my plush weaving and combed out my hair and began plaiting it. I knew Sidroc disliked seeing me use the comb the Saxon had carved for me, but there was no real place for me to go, and I did it as quickly as I could. Even doing something such as combing my hair in front of him was hard for me, for this is something only done in private rooms before one's husband, but in our travels there were many such things we must do before each other.

He shaved his face every few days, and he saw me washing out my shifts, and saw me barefoot too.

I finished my hair and took the Idrisid comb from out my basket and brought it to him. "This has value," I said as I handed it to him. "We should trade for it."

He fingered the comb and shook his head. "No," he answered. "I want you to keep all that was in the workbasket; they are all fine things. Also it is the first plunder I took, and the first thing I could give you." He looked carefully at the small comb. "It is of ivory, and thus costly. The teeth are close, but will be good to comb the hair of a babe with."

There was nothing I could say to any of this, and I put the comb away.

When we were packed we rode into the square. It was still quite early, but the place was crowded with food and drink sellers and folk milling about. We got off our horses and went from stall to stall. At one we bought eggs and butter too, pale and glistening, scooped from a deep wooden tub, a treat which we had not had since we left Lindisse.

We went to the silver-smith and Sidroc emerged from the dark door, looking well pleased with the bracelet once again upon his wrist. He did not show it off, but I could see the smith had polished it highly so that it glinted in the light.

As we walked about the square I heard amongst all the babble of those about me something that made me stop of a sudden. I was so struck I stood still, and let my eyes rove over the crowd searching for who it might be.

A man, a Christian priest to judge by the large cross about his neck, was speaking my tongue, and in my own accents; for by the way he formed his words I knew he was of Mercia. I made my way to him and touched him on the arm.

"Good Father," I blurted out.

The priest turned to me.

"Lady," he said, and his eyes widened. He was a man of some size, well-built and well-made, tho' he be past the midpoint of life. Over his shoulder was hung a sword, and he looked as though he well knew how to use it. He had short cropped grey hair, and his eyes too were grey, and piercing.

"I am Ceridwen, daughter of Cerd, ealdorman of the shire Dee," I said of myself, for the first time in many years.

His mouth opened in surprise. "And I am Eardwulf, servant of God and our Holy Father in Rome." He reached his hand to me, and I took it in both of mine, and curtsied to him. His grasp was warm and strong, and when I raised my eyes to him saw he smiled on me. Then his eye flicked behind me and I knew he must look at Sidroc.

"How came you here?" we asked each other, almost at the same time.

He smiled and answered first. "I was with our good King Burgred when he fled to Rome. After he was called to his heavenly home, I stayed on in the service of our Holy Father. He has asked me to journey to these northern climes to survey how far God's word has reached, and determine how best to bring Christ's message to the heathen. I have sailed with my men in stages from Frankland, and have now been two years at the task. Just now I have leave of the lord of this place, the knez as he is called, to travel thus, and do so unmolested. But we have not always been so welcome."

257

He lifted his hand to indicate those who stood with him. They were three thegns of Mercia, young as me or younger, well-armed and well dressed. They looked upon me with interest, and dipped their heads.

"And you, Lady Ceridwen? I have seen no gentle-woman in many a month. How came such as you to be on these wild coasts?"

I paused, thinking on what I could say, but before I had to say it Sidroc stepped forward and a little in front of me.

Eardwulf eyed him and asked, "This is your body-guard?"

Sidroc answered, "I am the lady's husband." He did not offer a name, or say more.

Eardwulf looked around us, and asked, "Where...where is your retinue?"

"We were captured by Idrisids," is what Sidroc said in answer.

"The infidel," nodded Eardwulf. "You had God's favour to escape."

"Yes," agreed Sidroc, and a slight smile played at his lips. "We have already given thanks for that."

The priest nodded and again looked at us. "I have not seen you before, and have been here five days."

"We came only yesterday," Sidroc returned. He said no more, and the men eyed each other in silence. I moved forward and addressed Eardwulf.

"Did you know my father?" I wanted to learn.

He shook his head. "I did not, Lady, I would I had for your sake. But I heard tell of him."

I wondered what he might have heard of my heathen sire, dead so long.

"Cerd...he has been dead these twenty years," he reckoned.

"Twenty-three," I answered.

"You have them all numbered, like the good daughter you are," he praised.

The market-place was growing more crowded, and someone jostled us slightly from behind.

"I am stopping at the hall of one of the spice merchants," Eardwulf went on. "The lodging is good, you must join us."

"We cannot," said Sidroc quickly.

The priest would not be stayed, and tried again. "Then you must come and sup with us tonight. See the hall for yourself, Sir, and then judge if it be best for your lady."

"We will come, thank you," I said before Sidroc had a chance to refuse again.

"Good. It is the yellow painted hall at the end of the last pier. We will welcome you at dusk."

The men bowed to me and moved away. I stood still with amaze looking after them.

"I can scarce believe it," I said to Sidroc. "Men from Mercia, here."

He did not return my smile. "Why did you tell them we would come?" he asked, and tho' he tried to keep the sharpness from his tone, it was there. "We know nothing of them."

"He is a priest," I said in astonishment. "And from my home land, which I have not seen for years. Just to hear him speak like me gives me pleasure." Sidroc's face did not soften. "He is a priest," I said again. "He cannot harm us."

He led me a little ways away. "What will you tell him?" he demanded.

"Tell him?"

"Yes, of us, why we are here, where we are going."

"I...I...do not know yet." I cast around in my mind for these answers, most of which I did not know myself. "What will you tell him?"

"Nothing. Because I will not be there for him to question. Or that is what I would choose. Now you have said we will go, and I cannot send you alone. If we do not go at all, he may grow wary and send his men looking for us, and I do not want to leave the post yet."

I could see his concern grew the more he thought on it.

"He is only a priest," I repeated.

"Yes, one well-armed, and with three warriors at his back. Next time pick one more like Wilgot."

Chapter the Sixteenth: The Oath

LATER in the day we rode to the last pier to see the yellow hall of the spice merchant. The piers were teeming with folk, and chests and casks and huge barrels of goods were being carried on and off the big ships there. Sidroc looked long upon all this wealth, and at the handsomely dressed men who stood over it, numbering each parcel, and said, "Trading is not as quick as raiding, but one lives longer."

We reached the yellow hall and looked upon it. It was large, with its own palisade built round it, but the gates were swung open and we could see into the yard. Folk moved about within, but we saw nothing in the way of treasure. Two men dressed in long tunics and holding spears stepped forward out of the gates after a while, and tho' they spoke not to us, we nudged our horses along.

We went to the wash sheds, and took turns staying with our horses while each of us went in and bathed. I went first, and on the woman's side found large wash basins into which the women who kept the place ladled hot water, and plenty of cold water caught in rain barrels. I rinsed my body and hair, and rubbed both hard with the linen towelling we had, and shook out the red wool gown and for the first time drew it on. The gown was a little snug over my breasts, but the length was right. I had no brooch or necklace but the blue and gold thread work at the throat and hem were such that this loss was not great. I combed my hair until it dried a bit and wrapped it in my head wrap. I looked at myself in my mirror, and recalling what Sidroc had said about the women of the trading post in his home land, again took a tiny dab of the ruddy beeswax and touched it to my lower lip. I held also the vial of the precious rose oil to my throat, and let a drop rest in the hollow there. Thus arrayed I went forth to meet Sidroc, and my countrymen.

Sidroc was standing by our horses, slapping the reins of one of them idly into his palm. When he turned and saw me he stopped, and the smile that spread across his face made my own colour.

"You look very fine," he said, and kept smiling.

"Thank you," I said, and felt like a foolish maid trying to keep the flush from my cheek.

A woman walking nearby with a pail in her hands also saw me, and smiled too, and he said, "I should have gone first, so you would not be standing here like a queen alone."

"Put on your mantle," he said next, "so you are hidden a little. I will not be long."

He was not, and came out with his leathern tunic wiped free from dust, and with the glitter of his newly polished bracelet and the glint of his weapons at his waist proclaiming their worth.

We got on our horses and headed to the yellow hall. "Even if the meal is not a good one, it will all be worth it to see you look thus," he told me, and I was glad he was no longer troubled.

"It will be a fine meal," I promised him, "and I think the ale will be also; and just to speak with those from Mercia will be pleasure for me."

The Claiming

The palisade gates were shut tight, and we got down from our horses and knocked on the small door cut within the heavy gate. It opened, and I told the man who looked at us, "The Lady Ceridwen to dine with Eardwulf the priest."

I did not know if he understood me, but he turned his head and spoke to another, and then swung the big gate open for us. It swung closed so heavily behind us that we both turned. Men came forward and took our horses, and we were pointed to the door of the hall.

Just inside was a small chamber with two more men with spears. Ranged about on benches were a great deal of armaments, bows and quivers of arrows, spears and swords. I was about to speak to the men when a large door opened and Eardwulf came forward.

"Welcome," he told us both, and I curtsied to him. I was glad that I was finely arrayed, but the way he searched our faces gave me sudden concern.

His eyes rested on Sidroc. "Sir, I am unaccustomed to sup with strangers," Eardwulf said. "Pray tell me your name."

I did not know what Sidroc would say, and was grateful at his answer.

"I am Sidroc of South Lindisse."

The priest flinched, ever so slightly. "You were with Guthrum when he drove Burgred from his Kingdom."

Sidroc nodded. "There is peace now in that land, and we are far from there. Let there be peace between us tonight."

The priest studied him for a moment. "Your words are wise ones," Eardwulf agreed. He folded his hands together. "Our host is a wealthy man who allows no weapons at his table. I must ask you to leave your sword here, where it will be waiting for you."

He did not ask Sidroc to surrender his seax, nor me the small knife I wore, for these we would of course use for cutting our food. Sidroc unbuckled his belt and slid the sword scabbard from it, and laid it with the other weapons upon the bench. Eardwulf led us through the door to the main room of the hall.

I had never seen such a hall. It was of timber, but the walls were hung with lengths of broadly striped fabric, which trailed down upon the floor and draped over openings. Oil torches thrust from the walls, but their mellow light was not marred by smoke. Men and women sat upon benches at long tables, as in any other hall, but the bare wood of the tables themselves was hidden by long bolts of brightly hued cloth. The floors were of wood planks, and here and there upon them lay richly coloured plush weavings such as my own.

I opened my mouth in delight at them, and all else that lay before me, and Eardwulf smiled and said, "As I said, our host is a wealthy man."

I nodded my head and said, "The weavings - I have one like it," and the priest looked at me with keenness.

"A gift from the Idrisids," explained Sidroc, with a smile of his own.

"Then their generosity was great," answered Eardwulf, not understanding. "They are called carpets, and their value is such that whole wars are fought over shipments of them."

At the middle of the main table was seated a man in robes of brilliant yellow cloth, and as we neared him I saw by their sheen that they were of pure silk. He was squat and round-shouldered, with a flossy silver beard and a bald head, and Eardwulf gestured to us and spoke to him. He answered Eardwulf in a high pitched, flowing voice, and smiled and bowed his head to us, and I curtsied to our host.

We sat with Eardwulf and his thegns at one end of the high table. Some of the other folk in the hall were the same sorts we had seen about the trading post, that is, men and women from many lands; but most of the guests were men dressed in the way of the warriors we had seen all about the square.

Great salvers of food began to be brought, and a pretty serving girl filled our brass cups with ale. The food was of the finest sort, and much of it was sweet, which pleased Sidroc; and the rest of it savoury, which pleased me, and gave balance to the whole. There were tiny birds roasted whole and glazed in apple-juice, perhaps; and plates of shelled cooked eggs rolled in yellow seeds, and stews such as browis made with a kind of grain I did not know, and plates of honeyed dried pears and much more. The ale was strong and bitter and pleased me much, and I could see the same was true for Sidroc. But I saw too that he was careful to only sip and not to quaff; and so I took no more, fearful of being made giddy and thus less cautious.

Eardwulf sat at my left side, and Sidroc at my right, and the Mercian thegns on either. They were good-looking young men, and tho' one of them was tongue-tied the other two were not, and they spoke to me in the playful way that men use when they have not seen a woman of their kind for some time. In fact they had been for years in Rome with Eardwulf, and tho' a few folk of both Mercia and Wessex lived there one thegn told me with regret that nearly all the women thereof had taken the veil.

I asked them and Eardwulf much about Rome, both because I wished to hear of it, and also to keep them from asking questions of us. All told me that the buildings were of such magnificence, and the size of the place so great, that they could not describe it justly. Much of it was of stone, of a whiteness and pureness that dazzled the eye; and every road within was a Cæsar's road, cut of smooth rock fitted long ago; and the numbers that dwelt there were above counting. Ælfred had been there twice as a boy, and would recount with pleasure his memory of it, and it seemed all I had heard from him was true, and not a child's fancy.

Sidroc said little, and as I hoped Eardwulf did not question us closely. When the meal was drawing to a close Sidroc looked at Eardwulf and observed, "I have seen no gaming in the trading post."

"Gaming?" the priest echoed.

Sidroc nodded. "Where there are brew-sheds, there are often men playing at dice. But here I see none."

"Nor will you," was the response. "You have been here only two days, but must have seen the riches that pass through this trading post. The knez who rules over it, and indeed much of this southerly coast, will not permit it. When men game, some will lose, and then blood flows."

266

I could read the disappointment in Sidroc's face at this news, but he said no more on it.

By and by the food was taken away, and the ale cups filled once more, and a man came out from behind a drapery and sat upon one of the plush weavings. In his lap he held a strange harp, and he pressed it against his chest and began to pluck at the strings which went up a long stick of wood from the back of the harp. The sound was soft and pleasing, and his fingers thrummed upon the strings so that I wished the scop from Kilton might see and hear him.

Two tumblers dressed in striped leggings then bounded into the room, and did all manner of tricks and hand-walking and jumps, and filled the space with flailing legs and arms and leaps so high that we gasped and laughed.

As we were watching this Eardwulf leant near me and spoke so Sidroc might hear too.

"Lady, soon the evening will reach its end. Life is uncertain, and journeying dangerous. I invite you now to come with me and make confession."

I was so surprised that even if I had known what to say I do not think I could have said it swiftly enough. The priest had already taken my hand and was rising. The spice merchant nodded and smiled and returned his eyes to his tumblers, and none of the rest of the folk nearby took notice.

Sidroc stood as I did and his hand went to the sword that was not there. Tho' my heart began to pound I looked back at him and smiled and nodded as I was led away. My fear grew the greater as we passed through one of the draped doorways, for I saw the three Mercian thegns stand as well.

267

The Claiming

The priest walked me down a short passageway and into a tiny room. It may have served as chapel to the priest, for there was a cross upon the wall. He let go my hand and sat down upon a bench, and I too sat. He turned his face away from me, and crossed himself as if he truly meant to hear me confess, and I struggled with myself to think what to say.

But I did not have to speak, for still keeping his face from me he began to talk.

"Lady, I have seen much in this world, and heard more. Everything about you tells me you have been abducted. I do not know who this Dane is, but at a sign from me my men will overpower him. I have no authority in law to hold him after I seize him, but I can hand him over to the knez to deal with. I myself will never see Mercia again, but I can place you on the next ship sailing to Frankland."

My shock was so great that I jumped up. "Good Father," I started, and then faltered. "He has told you his name, Sidroc of Lindisse."

Eardwulf turned his grey eyes to me. "But he has not, I think, told me his right relation to you. This Dane is not your husband."

My face flamed and I could not lie it down. "He...is a friend to me," I stammered.

"He has misused you."

I was not certain of his meaning, but shook my head.

His eyes raked my face. "You have not been disgraced?"

"He has not laid hand upon me, if that is what you mean."

He snorted, and I felt my anger replace my fear. He studied me closely. "Then you are renegades." I opened my mouth in protest but he demanded of me, "Who is your husband?"

"An honourable man, now dead," I told him, as I fought my fear. "I swear to you, I am a widow."

He drew breath and leant back. "He has carried you off from a convent?"

This was a crime so great, and a sin so grievous, that I clapped my hand to my lips.

"No, no."

"What was your husband's name?"

I did not answer, and he went on, "Your silence is the badge of your shame. I can assume then that he was a Mercian lord, killed when Burgred lost his Kingdom, and this Dane laid claim to his hall and you as well." He looked at me sharply. "It does not explain what you are doing here."

"He told you the truth, we were both taken captive by Idrisids. We escaped when a ship of Danish raiders attacked it."

I said this with such firmness that he paused.

"I told you about my weaving," I went on, "the one you call carpet, and I also have other things of the Idrisids I can show you, as proof."

He spent some time considering this, and me. "Tell me where you are journeying, Lady. I cannot let a noble woman of my country wander about far from her home with a renegade."

His voice had softened, but as it did I felt my own anger rise.

"I am sorry, Father Eardwulf, but I do not have to tell you that. I am not in your keeping. Where I go is no concern of yours."

He scratched his brow and looked back at me. "Swear to me on our Saviour's blood that you are in no especial distress from this man, and that you travel with him freely."

I was quick with my answer, and what I said made his eyes widen and then narrow.

"That I cannot swear, for like my kinsmen before me I am heathen. But I will swear by their blood, and every drop in my veins, that I do travel freely with this man, and that my safety is dearer to him than his own."

He let out a long sigh, and clapped his hands upon his lap. "You are an obstinate, and likely sinful young woman, but your heathen arrogance makes me believe you."

"You are believing the truth, Father," I said, as earnestly as I could. "Please let us go our way now."

"I can do nothing else," he conceded. "I sought to help you, and see I cannot. But I grieve for you, Lady, and what you may be brought to."

This was kindly meant, even tho' it was not kindly said, and I could only nod my head.

He stood and led the way back to the hall. The tumblers had left, and some of the guests were making their way to where the spice merchant sat to give him thanks. Sidroc was sitting with the Mercian thegns on either side of him, and none of them were talking. When he saw us pass through the opening he rose, and I smiled and said as boldly as I could, "Thank you Father Eardwulf for such a pleasant meal."

I nodded at Sidroc and said, "We are going now."

We went and joined those who stood before the old spice merchant, and bowed to him, and he smiled and waved his hand at us, and then we were in the arms chamber and Sidroc once again had his sword. Our horses were brought and the heavy gates swung open for us to pass. The night was a cool one, but the chill I felt stemmed from a deeper source than that.

"Well?" he asked, as we rode through the darkened square.

I hardly knew where to start. "He was certain you had run off with me. He wanted to seize you, and put me on a ship to Frankland."

He blew out his breath in answer.

"I had to swear, on my kinsmen's blood, that I travelled with you freely."

"You swore that?"

271

"Yes." Now I looked straight ahead at my horse's mane. "I am...very sorry to have put us in such danger," I said.

He was not angry, and even laughed. "Your tongue put us into it, and got us out, too. You said we should fight shield-to-shield, and we are. I am proud of you, shield-maiden. You are a full partner to me."

We passed down quiet roads to our camp site, grateful to be free to go our way in the cool night. We went about staking the horses and setting up our bed rolls. I did not want to sleep in the red gown, it was too fine for such treatment, and Sidroc turned away while I pulled it off to sleep in the long-sleeved shift.

We did not strike a fire, but only lay under the clouded night sky. I thought he was already asleep when he spoke across the distance to me.

"A few years past, there was a girl at Four Stones. The daughter of one of my men. She was - something like you. She moved like you. Bright hair. I would look at her, and soon she saw me looking. She began to...put herself in my way. One day when I was out riding I found her waiting for me. She smiled at me. It would be so easy. I came closer to her.

"But it was by the Place of Offering. In the beech tree was the silver chain I had hung there in place of your sash. It hangs there still, where I put it for you. I looked again at the girl. She was not you, would never be you. I turned from her and rode away."

In the silence that followed I could not keep from asking, "What happened to her?"

272

"She took up with one of my men. They farm over by the valley of horses. When she sees me now, she scowls."

He had ended this story with a laugh, but I knew he was not smiling.

He rose and crossed the narrow gulf between us, and as he knelt at my side I drew my breath and held it. It was so dark I could not see his face well.

"Do not be fearful," he whispered.

"I do not fear you, Sidroc," I whispered back.

"Did you truly swear that you go with me of your own free will?"

"Yes, I truly swore it," I breathed.

He bent over me, and felt me tremble under the hand he laid upon my shoulder. He stopped himself then, and pulled back. "I will not take you," he told me. "You must give yourself to me."

I awoke under clouded skies which mirrored all I felt within me. After what I had sworn to the priest, and then told Sidroc, I felt my Fate a flown arrow, never to be recalled. Eardwulf's final words to me - I grieve for what you may be brought to - sounded over and over in my ears.

The dawn was dull with the threat of rain, and Sidroc was eager to get us that which we needed to build a tent. He spoke of this, and other things, as we made our morning's fire, and cooked and ate our meal. I found it hard to speak to him, or attend on what he said.

I sat upon my beautiful weaving and shook out my hair and began to comb it. I stopped and lay the wooden comb in my lap and looked across the barren camp yard.

"The Saxon was right," I said, and my throat clenched with coming tears. "I will never see Kilton, or any part of Wessex, again."

Sidroc reached to me and lifted the comb from my lap, snapped it in two and tossed it into the fire. I cried out as he did this, but he only said, "I will buy you a better comb."

I covered my face with my hands for a moment, but then lifted it to him. I asked, "How can I take pleasure in any thing, when my son is even now grieving my death?"

He stood up. He walked a little away, and then back, and looked down at me.

"Think what would happen if we were to go back now," he began, in a low voice. There was no anger on his brow or in his words. "It is not too late in the season, we could find ships to take us, in stages. We would face the same dangers all open sea travellers face: ship wreck and storms and raiders. But we could succeed. I myself do not think we would. I have sacrificed and prayed to Freyja so long for you that if I surrender you now, after she has at last given you to me, that her wrath against me for spurning her gift will be very great. We would not live to reach Angle-land, but die in ship wreck or amongst raiders, or if she is truly cruel she would force me to watch you being taken from me by other men.

"But perhaps I am wrong, and we reach Lindisse again. It is your son you want, so I must take you to Four Stones. They think us dead, have lit fires for us, sung their Masses, whatever they think right; and we return. There will be gladness, yes. But you and I will then be parted, for all must be as it was. But I think we will not even have that chance. After travelling so long together, who amongst them will believe, even if it is the truth, that we have not been man and woman to each other? Then think on this: when my men met the Saxon ship you were meant to take, Kilton's men were aboard as your escort. Some of them rode at once to tell him of our vanishing. Ælfwyn too will send word to Kilton. He claims you as his kinswoman and will ride to Four Stones to look for you. He is likely on his way there now. When we return, and he sees me, he will want to kill me. Even his laws allow him to try. He knows I have always wanted you. No woman's tears or pleading will turn him aside. He will challenge me and I will have to fight him. You say he cannot hold a shield, so we will be forced to fight with knives. Knives do not make a pretty way to die, but one of us will. If I kill him, I gain your anger, and that of Ælfred, which I do not want. If I die, all is worse for Ælfwyn as it was your kin who killed me. Either way we will never see the other in this life again."

I squeezed my eyes shut at the suddenness of this aweful truth; I had to. But it did not darken the terrible vision of Godwin's fury, and the two men locked in their death match. I saw too clearly Ælfwyn and I clinging to each other as they fought, and her, thrice-widowed, as it were, if Sidroc died, and all Kilton left lord-less if he lived.

He had been looking down at me all the time he recited this, and I was unable to take my eyes from his face. The calmness of his words had not wavered, and he spoke almost as if he were telling me something that had befallen many years ago, an old saga that ended badly. Listening to him, watching his face, I felt the truth in his words, and not only my desire for Ceric and the things I had lost.

He was not done.

"I know they grieve for us. But perhaps it is better for them to grieve, and then go on with their living. Perhaps some of them will have hope that we are alive somewhere, and well. I would rather have them keep that hope, or even grieve for us dead, than return and spatter my hall with Kilton's blood, or take his killing-thrust for dishonouring you when I have not."

Chapter the Seventeenth: Danes

WE had bought the oiled cloth and hempen line and other things we would need to string a tent, and now walked our horses along one of the narrow roads of the trading post. We paused and watched a stream of folk coming out of the big square. It was mid-day, and crowded.

"I think these are my brothers," said Sidroc.

He was looking at a group of men who had just emerged from the square and were walking in our direction. There were eight or nine of them. Those in front were young, and wore long hair and no beards, and even the oldest of them looked to have no more than thirty Summers. The heavy wool mantles over their tunics were fastened with big bronze pins, and each carried a spear and a sword-belt with both sword and knife.

"Come," said Sidroc, as he nudged his horse forward. He glanced back at me a moment to add, "Do not look at them."

I hated to be told such things. At Kilton I might look upon any man without fear or reproach, and the loss of this simple freedom irked me. But the men at Kilton were sworn to protect me, as a dependent of their Lord. Away from one's own hall or that of friends, a woman who looked too boldly at a man could invite trouble.

I took another look before I ducked my chin. Sidroc had reined up in front of them, and I knew they were looking each other over. Then Sidroc spoke, and one of the men answered. Sidroc spoke again, and the other Dane went on at some length. I could not guess where they might be from; their speech was harder for me to follow than that of Sidroc's men, and I could catch but a few words.

Both were now silent, and I heard a third voice. Sidroc answered, and the edge in his voice made me look up. One of the Danes was pointing at me, and Sidroc finished what he had to say. The Dane laughed and shrugged, and we stood our horses as the group passed on.

"What did they say?" I asked as we turned our horses.

"He wanted to know if you were for sale. I told him I would trade you for his life."

"That was not all you spoke about."

"No. Only the way we ended it. They just now sailed in, and will be here a few days."

"Are they traders, or...?"

"More raiding than trading, I think. Whatever comes their way. It is hard to get any war booty out of Angle-land or Frankland these days; it has all been claimed. But any ship that sails is fair game." We were walking before the piers now, and saw the ship that must have brought them. It was a slender-hulled fighting boat such as that which had attacked the Idrisids. A few men still moved aboard it, left as guards. Sidroc looked at it for some time.

"Where there are Danes, there are dice," he said.

"Gaming is unlawful," I reminded him.

"Also profitable."

278

I shook my head. "You cannot risk it, Sidroc. Eardwulf told us it was forbidden to game. You have seen how many warriors the lord of this place keeps."

"Right now I have few ways to win us silver or goods. I can steal or I can game. The third way is to pick a fight with a man, kill him, and seize his goods. You choose."

I did not want to make such a choice, but I would not be stayed. "They will be watching all the brew-sheds."

"Yes. But what is done aboard a trader's ship they can have no say over."

I am sure I wrinkled my nose as I looked at the ship. "We would go aboard and you would play them there?"

"I would go aboard. You I am keeping far away from them."

"Where will I be?"

"I do not know yet, but I will have an answer soon."

Amongst the folk at the piers was one of the Mercian thegns. He turned and came towards us. Two ships had lately arrived, that of the Danes, and a broad-beamed merchant ship. The young man saluted us and said, "The good Father will be again disappointed. We are waiting for a monk, who has been delayed from day to day. If he does not come soon the task Eardwulf seeks him for will go unfulfilled."

"What task is that?" I asked.

"The monk is a scribe."

279

"But surely Father writes his own letters, and all else that is needful."

"No longer, Lady, for tho' he reads perfectly, and in a loud voice, his eyes are now so strong that he can no longer handle a quill." The thegn shrugged. "I myself can write but my name, as can my fellows."

"Each day brings more ships," said Sidroc, and I felt he wished to end this talk.

"Yes," answered the thegn. "Because the good sea weather is nearly at an end. Soon the post will end its trading, and all depart for their Winter homes. And monk or not, we ourselves will depart in a few days."

We went back to our camp site and set about building the tent. Sidroc pounded stakes in the hard ground as I laced lengths of the oiled cloth together with cords I cut of leather. We lay over the spine of the strung tent a narrow piece of tanned hide so that no rain could run in. Our other tanned hides we used as ground cloths within. It was big enough inside to sit up in without Sidroc's head touching the top, and for both our bed rolls to fit with a little space between, but when we had both crawled in, it seemed small indeed.

I did not see how we could sleep so close to each other. Any space with a roof over it, even one of cloth, seems smaller than one under the sky; and just sitting so near Sidroc felt as if we were touching, when we were not. I crawled out almost at once and wondered if he felt this too.

If he did he said nothing of it. There was still much light in the sky and he now went about the camp site, picking up small stones. He brought a handful of them back to where I sat on the bench by the fire pit, and placed them wordlessly by my side. He came back with more, including two long stones. Now he moved to the fire and with a burnt stick traced a square in the wood of the bench, and sat down next me.

"We are going to play at bones," he told me, and began to sort out the round stones for counters. To these he added a single die. "You said you are good at it. Some men do not like dice, or if they lose too often they wish to switch games. So I need to play well at both."

He wished to learn what I knew, and in doing so was praising my skill before he had seen it.

"Good," I said, and could not hide my smile. I thought of all the times I had sat with Edgyth at Kilton and fingered the delicately carved pieces of bone we placed upon the coloured gaming board.

We began the play. He made the sort of errors that boldness makes, and that in my own play I no longer did.

"Do not risk so much on your first toss. Each play is doubled in value and if you lose on your second, you will have a hard time making it up."

He was not fast in adding sums, and I told him, "That is why it is important to drink little ale and no mead when you play bones. But look," and here I held my hand before him, "if there is a table or a bench you can put your other hand under, you can do this. If you tap your thumb once with your first finger, that means five. Tap twice, ten. Each tap of your thumb on any other finger is one." I quickly tapped out how to silently count to odd numbers and recall them.

When we came to the end of the game I had beaten him, and badly.

"How did you know what I was going to play?" he asked.

"That is simple. When your opponent spends much time thinking hard and looking at your counters, he is likely reckoning numbers backwards. That helped me guess what you would risk on that last play."

"That is what the Saxon did," he said.

"That is part of the reason he was a good player," I agreed. "But I still do not know how he never lost."

"That was just another lie," he said shortly, and I did not pursue it.

We played another game and he did better, but it was hard for him to work numbers backwards.

"Who taught you so well?" he wanted to know.

"The Lady Edgyth played with me, and taught me many tricks, the ones I am teaching you now. As for the sums, the Prior gave me those."

"I am glad he was good for something. And the lady has my thanks for giving you her skill. But for tonight I will stick to dice."

The Claiming

Sidroc stole away from our camp site well after dark. He went on foot, so both our horses stayed behind, and none who had grown accustomed to seeing us would think him gone. I was already in our tent, and he left both spears standing upright just outside it, with his shield resting against them. A light leathern cord ran from both spears to inside the tent, lest anyone should try to lift one in the night.

"Tell me you will not sleep, but stay wary when I am gone," he pressed. "Do not leave the tent unless you must. If anything troubles you, take a spear in your hand and scream. The ward-men that come about will hear you."

In truth, I did not want him to go. I would not be fearful to spend the night alone in the open, if I had good fire to keep wild beasts away, but to do so on the outskirts of the crowded trading post was different. More than this was my fear at his being caught gaming by the knez's men, or snared in some treachery by the Danes themselves. This last worried me least, for I thought few men more cunning than Sidroc, and if any man might know the tricks of the Danes it should be him; but as I lay there all these fears joined me in the small tent. I had no way to measure the time, for the sky above was clouded over if I chose to rise and look at it, which I did not. I lay upon my plush weaving in my shift, with a blanket over me, and looked out at our dwindling fire through the slit in the tent opening. By and by it began to drizzle, and the fire sputtered low and then out.

I thought of the comb Sidroc had broken and thrown into it that morning, and his words kept sounding in my ears. He had thought much on my yearning to return, and spoke so; but even more important was what he had left unspoken. His meaning was clear. Despite all he feared, he would return me to Angle-land, if I truly desired it. Tho' it mean disaster to him, or even both of us, he would face it. The thought of us surviving the journey, only to face the wrath of Godwin, made me shudder as I lay there.

I thought of what would happen at Kilton in my absence. By the laws of Ælfred, any man or woman who was missing five years could be proclaimed dead, and his or her will executed. In the will I had signed following Gyric's death I had left most of what I owned to be divided between Ceric and Edwin; two thirds to the first and one third to the second. Ceric would be rich, for almost all his father had left me would now be his; and Edwin as eventual heir to Godwin richer still. Both boys would be loved and well-guided by those at Kilton, and tho' I knew Ceric would be tearful to be taken from Four Stones by Godwin, he would still recall the joy he knew with Hrald and Ashild and their mother. These months he had spent in a Danish keep, with a jarl such as Sidroc, and the fast friend he had found in Hrald, would not be forgotten. He had come to know and care for those once thought to be his enemies.

I thought then of Edgyth, of her gentleness and wisdom, and how she who had spent so many years sorrowing for her lack of children should now have both my boys to raise; and as my eyes welled I knew they could not have a better mother.

Of Ælfwyn I could not be sure; and I spent a long time turning in my mind what she might think, and do. Despite all the fear and uncertainty she must be feeling, I knew that if we were somehow able to return and meet the Fate Sidroc felt awaited us, her lot would be far the worse. I knew Godwin would challenge him, and thinking of their death battle made my throat knot with rising tears.

The Claiming

Godwin dead meant Kilton lord-less, Edgyth and Edwin and Modwynn bereft, and mayhap even war, as Ælfred's anger would be great. If Sidroc fell - here I broke and wept, and lowered my wet face to the damp wool of my mantle. I wept for Ælfwyn, watching he who had been husband and father to her children be slain; and wept for me, that had brought him to such a pass; and wept most of all for Sidroc himself, who had loved me with an undivided heart for all these years.

Through my tears I spoke aloud Ælfwyn's name in the dark. Her goodness was such that she could speak of Sidroc's desiring of me without shaming me, or blaming him. With all my heart I wanted her well and content, and that those about her, family and holy folk, would close up ranks around her to give her the comfort and peace she deserved.

I heard some sound upon the road, and thought I saw one of the red-sashed ward-men pass. Hours had passed, made longer by the troubled thoughts tumbling in my head. I put my head down and yawned but my unease was such I knew I would not sleep even if I tried. Our horses were moving slowly about and pulling at the neck ropes we had staked in the ground, and I was grateful for the company it gave me to hear them nicker and snort.

At last I knew I dozed, for I jerked up at Sidroc's low whistle. The rain still fell and I could just make out his form crossing from the clay road. "Shield-maiden," he hissed, and when I called back he dropped on his knees and crawled in.

He was smiling, and I could smell the strong ale he had been drinking, but he did not speak.

"You won," I finally prompted, not understanding why men always needed to be asked.

He nodded. "I won, and then I lost, and then I won again, so it was time to leave."

He was dripping wet, and first I pulled a piece of linen from my pack and passed it to him. It was so dark in the tent that I could scarce see him, and I was glad he could not see me, for I was sure my face bore the trace of my tears.

He shrugged off his leathern tunic, and a small pile of metal clinked together and fell on his sheepskin. He drew from over his head the woollen tunic he wore that day, and rubbed himself with the towelling. Once or twice his arms hit the oiled cloth of the tent, and small drops which had formed there showered down on us.

I heard his fingers moving amongst the metal things before him.

"Where..?" he whispered, and his fingers reached across and found my face. "This chain is yours," he went on, and rocked forward and slipped something over my head.

My fingers went to it. I could not see it in the dim of the tent, but I could feel it was a braided chain, nearly as thick as my little finger.

"It is what kept me playing when I was losing. It is like the silver chain I hung in the tree at Four Stones for you, only larger and finer."

The thickness of it and the weaving of the links told me without seeing that it was of great value.

"How wonderful," I murmured, speaking carefully so my voice did not show all I felt.

"One day I will get you a necklace to rival Brisingamen," he promised, speaking of the fabled jewelled collar that Freyja wore. He laughed a little. "But you must swear never to repay its maker as she did."

To show her thanks to the four dwarfish smiths who had forged her necklace, she had granted each of them a night of her love. I did not know what to say to this, and felt his nearness more strongly than ever.

"There is more," he said, and reached out to me again. "Here is a bronze pin for your mantle."

He held it by the tip so I would not stick myself, and I touched it briefly and thought of the pins the Danes had worn on theirs.

He put it down again, and I heard more jingling. "Also there are six small pieces of silver, two silver finger rings, and some hack-silver."

"You did very well," I praised.

"I ended well, which is what counts."

"Yes," I agreed, and wondered if this meant they would play no more with him.

He did not speak again, and since I could not see him I could not read his face. I wondered if he was still sitting up. It felt late, and he had drunk much ale, and he must be weary. I pulled the blanket over me and lay still. Some rain still pattered outside, but we were dry within. I heard him move where he lay, and hoped he would rest soon. I was drifting into sleep when his words awakened me.

"I wish I were drunk," he said, to no one.

Chapter the Eighteenth: The Scribe

AT mid-day we walked our horses into the big square. The wet night had given way to a fair morning, and folk who sought food moved from stall to stall. A man's voice called out sharply, and we looked to see the group of Danes sitting at one of the brew-sheds. It was a larger group this time, and the way they looked at Sidroc told me they had all been aboard the ship with him the night before. A man in front with sandy hair and a red beard called out to him again, and Sidroc laughed back his response.

He turned to me and said, "Now he wants both you and his pin back," but he was not smiling at me as he said it. Still, we headed to the men, who gestured that we join them. They sat ranged around on benches before the open stall, and the brewster came forth and placed wooden cups of ale in our hands. I sat down by myself on a bench behind Sidroc.

He spent some time talking to the men, and by their jesting tone I thought that they did not hold a grudge for what they had lost to him. After a little while one of them got up and came over to me. He was more boy than man, no more than sixteen or seventeen Summers, I guessed, with stringy brown hair and a wisp of fuzz on his lip. He looked down at me and cleared his throat.

"I was two years to Anglia," he said, and the careful way in which he spoke told me of the effort it took to do so. He sat down next to me and smiled. His front teeth were very crooked.

289

"I have never seen that Kingdom," I returned, speaking slowly back to him.

He grinned and went on, "A long time and no speaking," and nodded as if proud of his attempt. His eye rested on my new neck chain, and I wondered if he had worn it last night.

Sidroc had turned his head to look at us. Now he swung around. He rose and stood in front of the young Dane and stared down at him. He placed his hand on his sword hilt and said slowly and loudly, "You can talk to me."

The young man shifted on the bench, and glanced at me before returning his eyes to Sidroc's hand resting on his sword.

"He is doing no harm," I said to Sidroc, and stood up to face him.

The moment I did so the Danes behind Sidroc began to hoot and whistle.

"Sit down," said Sidroc, between gritted teeth.

I knew if I did not sit down at once he would lose face before them. I sat down.

As I did the young Dane rose and went to join his fellows. Sidroc turned and the hooting stopped. In my anger I would not raise my eyes, but I heard them go on with their talk. At last Sidroc stood and we mounted our horses and headed out of the square. The men called in a jesting way after us. We rode behind the large store houses along the shore line until we were out past the line of piers.

Tho' he had been laughing and talking with the men I knew he was angered at me, and my own anger was such that I did not trust myself to speak.

"We are not in Wessex," he observed.

I bit my lip to help keep the sharpness from my answer. "Why did you threaten that boy? He was trying to show me courtesy, and merely wanted to speak. There was no danger."

"We are always in danger," he shot back. He paused and looked up at the sky before going on. "I am alone. I do not have two hundred men at my back, or even two."

I did not want to hear this, and almost shrieked at him. "Alone? Yes, you are alone. That is the way you want it! Far from your men and hall, and all help. That is why you have driven me this far, so that you can be alone."

I plunged my heels hard into the side of my horse, but Sidroc reached across and grabbed the cheekpiece of the bridle, and horse and I jolted to a stop. I nearly lost my seat, and struggled to take the reins again.

"You do not understand," he said. "The red-beard. The ship is his, and the whelp who came to speak to you is his sister's son. Thus there is a strong bond between them. The uncle must help him make his mark, in battle and in plunder. You are healthy and comely. Either of them might decide that they want you enough to lay claim to you. There are one-and-twenty of them. I cannot fight so many."

I had to listen to him, and loosed my grip on my reins.

He let go my bridle. "I know you are bold. It is part of what makes me want you. But I know the ways of these men as well as I do my own. They can help us, for they think I can help them. But if for one moment you give them cause, their woman-lust will make them kill me."

"How...how would you help them," I began, almost fearing to ask. "Would you...take up with them?"

"They have not asked me yet. I do not know. They have the ship."

"They are raiders," I said, with all the unease I felt.

"Sea-raiders, the sort we would have to face if we were to take ship ourselves. Still, if the Gods smile, the ship could be mine."

In order for this to happen, both the red-bearded man and his nephew would have to die in battle. I looked at him, not wanting to believe that this was something he would choose, to become once again a raider. His face and eyes were steady as they met mine.

Out on one of the piers a ship was landing, and a group of folk had gathered to meet it. I saw amongst them two of the Mercian thegns, standing a little space apart from the crowd, waiting with intent upon the wooden pier. My eyes were as restless as my thoughts, and I turned back to Sidroc.

"Where would I be?" I finally asked, not willing to ask anything else.

"That is a problem. They have no base. Red-beard has some trouble at home; he cannot go back just yet. I cannot take you on a sea-raid, even if I had none but my own men aboard."

I recalled the Danes who had been cut down as they tried to board the Idrisid ship. I shook my head, and had a hard time forming words. "You...you cannot do this to me. To put yourself in such danger." Tears were flowing down my cheeks before I could even try to stop them.

There was no harshness in his answer. "Then act like the wife I told them you were and do not defy me."

I reached out and took hold his wrist. "Please tell me you will not do this thing," I begged. I would not let go of him, and kept my grasp on his wrist. "I do not want you to do that, to raid again. And here, so far from home..." I looked across at the piers, every ship from another land.

He looked down to where my hand had closed over his silver bracelet. "I would not want you to be stranded," he conceded.

"It is not just that," I said, and drew back my hand. I did not believe he would make me say it like this, but it seemed I must. I tried to steady my voice. "I do not want you to be in that danger. I do not want any harm to fall to you."

"Why?" he asked softly.

"You...have been...my...true friend for these ten years," was all I could say.

He looked at me a long moment, but for answer only nodded.

The two thegns began to leave the pier; they were alone. I fastened my eyes upon them. Without another word to Sidroc I nudged my horse forward and went to meet them. He did not call out to me, and I did not hear the jingle of his bridle metal behind me, but I thought I felt the force of his eyes bore through my back as I moved away.

The thegns raised their hands in greeting to me, but I saw from their faces that their hopes were once again dashed.

"The monk you await, he was not aboard this ship," I asked, as I reined my horse in near them.

"No, Lady," answered one, turning partly to look back at it, "and this is the ship that was to have taken Father Eardwulf's letters on the morrow."

"I will serve as scribe to Father Eardwulf," I announced.

Their eyes widened, but one asked, "Truly, Lady?"

"Truly," I told them. "I have this art, and will copy out the letters for him."

"Then come," said one, and lay his hand upon the bridle and led horse and me away. I did not look back.

We went straightaway to the yellow hall of the spice merchant. I waited inside the outer room while the thegns went for Father Eardwulf. The priest came out to me alone, and wore his confusion on his face.

"My men have told me that brother Alphonse was not upon the ship, but that you, Lady, had come forward and claimed the scribal art as yours." His face did not believe it, and his eyebrows lifted over his grey eyes. He cleared his throat. "I think perhaps you have re-considered my offer, and are desirous of my protection."

I was swift with my answer. "I will copy out your letters for you, Father Eardwulf. I was Priory raised, and the black

294

monks gave me this art. You tried to do me a service, one I did not want, and now I return to do you one I know you greatly desire. But you must understand that I in no way wish your protection, and you must vow to let me leave as freely as I came."

I knew he was not a man used to hearing women demand he vow anything, and he stood speechless. He raised his hands, in wonderment perhaps; but said, "My letter is in Latin."

"I can write the Holy Tongue of Rome," I countered. "Only vow to me, upon your Saviour's blood, that you will let me freely leave."

"I will vow, of course I vow," he said, and pulled open the door to the hall.

Within the aged spice merchant stood with a buyer of his goods, for before the two men, ranged about upon the tables, were tiny chests and caskets, open and displaying their contents. When the priest and I walked in, the odour from these things was like the fragrance of every dusted cake or cup of Yule-spiced ale I had ever smelt. The merchant bowed to us, and I curtsied to the old man, and the buyer, who was an amber-skinned man with a huge gold finger ring, bowed too. As we passed through the hall the contents of one of the little chests caught my eye, and I stopped. "Those sticks," I said aloud to the priest, and he paused and looked down at them.

"Cinnamon," he told me. "They are not truly twigs, but the dried bark of a shrub. The best leeches grind it and use it in their healing potions. I am taking two pieces to our Holy Father in Rome, along with a supply of frankincense."

It was then a costly spice, and a valued help in healing, and I was not about to tell the priest I had such a stick with which I cleaned my teeth each morning. The old merchant had seen me stop before the cinnamon, and he grinned and bowed again. He said something to the priest.

"Our host recalls you, and asks that you stay and take a cup of wine with him when we are through."

I looked back at the old man, and then at Eardwulf. "O, I could not," I said at once.

"I will take it with you," the priest assured me. "He means you no harm."

I looked again at the toothless old man, and at his great store of treasure arrayed before us, and nodded.

Eardwulf took me through the hall and to the little room with the cross upon the wall. There was a small table set up, and a stool at which the priest had been working, for a few things were scattered about. Two oil cressets hung from the rafters above, and a third sat upon the table, so the light was good. He lifted the top of a shallow chest and took from it four pieces of parchment, ready trimmed, and all of the same size. One bore the letter, in a small and curling hand, and the others were blank.

I took hold of a piece. "I have never seen such parchment," I told him, for in truth it was of a thickness and fineness of grain that made it seem almost soft.

"It is vellum, from calfskin, and not parchment from lambs," he told me.

The Claiming

I had never written on vellum, and knew it to be so dear that in Angle-land only such things as the Holy Book were copied out on it; and I wondered to myself if it would take ink as well as parchment did, and if I would spoil this fine ground with clumsy handling. I knew he watched me closely, and I only nodded.

"The letter, you will see, is in Latin," he said again, as if in warning.

"If you have a quire trimming I will show you my hand," I said in return.

He gestured to the shallow chest. Within was a supply of quills, a scraper, a flat measure for lining, pins, and all else I would need. The quills were of the best sort, feathers from the wings of a large goose, and when I touched them I saw they were fresh and not brittle. At the bottom of the chest was a handful of vellum scraps for testing inks, and some cut quills stained dark with prior use.

"Here is ink," he said, and pointed to a pot upon the table. "I mixed it just this morning, in my hope Alphonse would be here now."

I took my knife from my waist and set to work trimming a fresh quill. The blade was sharp and I made my five cuts, dipped it into the pot, and set its point down upon a vellum scrap. "In Principio" I wrote, the first Latin I had ever learnt, and now about the only I could still trace.

I turned the scrap to him, and through his eyebrows lifted, he nodded.

"Shall I copy your letter, Father?" I asked quietly.

He pressed his lips together, but answered, "It would be a kindness to me, Lady. Three, just as the original, if you please."

He left me then, for which I was grateful, and I set to work. I studied the letter. I could read almost none of it, but the letters which form the Holy Roman Tongue are mostly the same of those I wrote in my own speech, and if I were careful and copied it closely there should be no error.

I lined the first sheet with the measure, taking as my guide the letter. I dipped my quill and began.

It took me a long time, and my back ached and my eyes began to smart before I had begun the last of the three. But I had spaced the lines fairly well, and only in one place had I skipped a word, which I had to then write above the line; and in no place did I drop ink or smear my work, so to my pride I did not need the scraper. When I had finished the last I took some little time looking at all four, so that I knew each I had copied was complete and whole. My hand was not as small as the scribe's who had written the first, but the letters as I formed them were round and bold, and stood out cleanly and clearly upon the creamy vellum.

I went to the door and going out in the passage found Eardwulf in another small room. I curtsied to him and said, "I am done, Father."

When he came to examine my work I saw how poorly his eyes served him for such matters, for he must keep the vellum upon the table and stand well back from it to be able to read. But read he did, for I saw his lips move as he scanned the letters I had copied, and tho' he took a long time reading each one, his face told me he was well pleased.

He looked then at me in such a way that told me he found it a sad use of skill in a heathenish woman; but this he did not say. What he did say was, "The service you have rendered to me is a large one. You will want silver, which I will provide."

"It is not your silver I want, Father," I began, and he looked at me with all the sharpness his grey eyes possessed. "What I wish is your knowledge."

"My knowledge?"

"Yes. When we met you said you had spent already two years along these coasts, travelling about. Thus you must have learnt about the people and places of these parts."

"In this you are correct," he answered.

"Since my escape from the Idrisids I am not even certain where I am, save the shores of the sea known as Baltic. I am seeking a place where those who do not wish to be troubled can settle. A place with good farming lands, and with enough folk so that silver can be earned through trade. Not too cold," I added, wondering if that were possible in these climes.

He stroked his chin. "I see," he said. "You find these parts to your liking, and would remain here."

I could not in truth agree with this, and bit my lip. "It would be difficult to return to Angle-land," I said.

"And most hazardous," he added, and I could not know if he meant the hazards of the journey or what we might face once at home. I only nodded my answer.

He pressed the points of his fingers together and looked at me. "Bring a large scrap of vellum and a quill and ink and come with me."

After a time we went out to the hall. The wares of the spice merchant were put away, and his serving men were readying the room for the coming meal. The old man sat in his yellow silk robes at the high table, and waved us over.

Eardwulf and I sat down with him, and were each given a small bronze cup of pungent wine. It smelt like all the spices the old man sold, and I found its potent warmth delicious. In my empty belly I felt it almost at once, and tho' I felt weak and welcomed its spreading heat, took care not to accept a second cup.

Eardwulf could speak to him, in a halting sort of way, and the spice merchant was partly deaf, so the priest spoke loudly and rarely. When I had finished my wine the merchant called to a serving man, who came forth with a small piece of cloth. He laid it on the table and the old man smiled and motioned that I open it. Within was a stick of the precious cinnamon.

"It is his gift to you for gracing his table," Eardwulf explained. "He knows, too you have rendered me a service, and he begins to be interested in the True Word, and so is well-disposed to me." He listened to the old man and then spoke to me with a smile. "He says to sell it to a Frank. It will bring enough to dower the two daughters he sees you bearing."

This was a rich gift, and I knew the colour rose to my cheek for the giving of it, and to hear the old man's words.

"Please tell him how grateful I am, first to give me a fine dinner and now this gift of his treasure."

The priest walked me out. It was nearing dusk, and I did not know what I would face outside the closed gates. "I have not truly thanked you, Lady," said Eardwulf, and he seemed nearly to smile. "But I am glad we have met, and I must wish you well on your journeying."

I bobbed my head to him. "And I thank you Father, and wish you too good journeying."

So we took our leave. I took my horse's reins in my hand and the gate was swung wide, and I walked outside.

Sidroc was sitting by the wharf across from the hall in the gathering dusk. He sat on a bench, his eyes fixed upon the gate as it opened. One hand held the reins of his horse. He stood up when he saw me, and I came straight to him.

I walked to him and stopped just before him, and without a word his free arm slowly rose and he lay it across my back. He pressed me to his chest, and held me without moving, and I thought, without breathing, with that one arm.

"You have come back," he said in my ear. "I would wait here until you did."

I looked up at him, and the warmth of the wine wrapped me within as his arm wrapped me without.

"I did not like to see you go off with those thegns," he murmured.

"I needed something from the priest," I murmured back.

He did not ask me what it was, but lowered his arm and released me. I opened my hand to show the cinnamon piece I held. "The spice merchant gave me this. He said it will bring enough silver to dower the two daughters I will have."

Now he smiled at me, and helped me on my horse.

On the short ride to our camp site he asked no questions, tho' I felt his unease in his silence. We built our fire.

"I cannot think of what the priest would have that you wanted," he said, after we had eaten. His careful tone told me he had been thinking on it. "You did not stay with him to take ship to Frankland, so it was not that."

"I do not want to get on any ship, ever again," I answered, in truth. "Especially to go to such a place as Frankland, unknown to me." I raised my eyes to him. "What I wanted from the priest was his knowledge."

I pulled my pack to me, and drew out the vellum quire trimming. The scrap was a large one, and on it I had traced as much of the chart that Father Eardwulf had showed me that would fit. I came around to sit by Sidroc's side, and held it near the fire's glow.

"This is the small trading post of the Pomerani, where we first landed," I told him, and pointed to the mark I had made upon the long curving shore of the South Baltic. "This, the river we passed on our way to get the horses. This mark is where we are now. Beyond us, to the North-East, is a smaller post, which will be almost shut down now. But here, further up the coast, is a great river, called Vistula, and beyond that is a settlement of the tribe called Prus, which houses folk

Summer and Winter. Merchants trade there, and live there too; and there is good farmland and grass for sheep and cattle."

He looked at me as if he almost did not believe what I said.

"There are two problems," I went on, steadily. "The first is that I must get on a ship to reach the town of the Prus, for Eardwulf said a wild folk roam the shoreline East of here, and that only the largest troop of horsemen can go safely through those parts."

A long moment passed, and he was still looking at me in wonder. "What is the second problem," he finally asked.

"The Winters are very harsh there," I admitted.

"For which I will buy you many furs," he reminded me at once. "But...that is all? If we sail there, and I keep you warm, you will go and live with me in that place, and be my wife?"

I did not know if he was about to embrace me, or to take my hands, or what he might do; and I could not look at him as he awaited my answer.

The tightness in my throat pinched my words. "It is well-guarded, like this trading post," I said instead, "and not a place for raiders. The laws are strict. It is a place for farming, or to try to trade at, sell some goods..."

"As long as there is silver to be made, I will make it," he returned. "I need a small stake to start with, then I could trade salt, or amber, or furs, or even falcons. We will have all we want."

The Claiming

I said nothing to this and was looking down into our fire.

"If we can find ship, we will start for it tomorrow," he finished.

Chapter the Nineteenth: Out of the Fog

WE were not the only ones with thoughts of leaving. The trading season was coming to a close, and for days past, as at the smaller post, we had seen stall owners and trades people load up their wares and tools and pile ox carts to the brim. Some of these headed down the clay road and out into the grasslands, but most were driven the short distance to the piers, where packed ships returned folk to their Winter homes. Sidroc left our camp site early in the morning, before we had broth or bread, and took with him the vellum chart I had traced. When he returned it was almost noon, but he looked well pleased.

"We can sell the horses in the square tomorrow. They will not be the only ones there, but we should get a good price for them, as some folk are taking the road and not the water."

I handed him a cup of broth and some bread and butter. "And...the ship?" I made myself ask.

"Red-beard will take us. He has never been that far, but he will trust that the Prus will be worth the effort."

My concern must have shown on my face, for Sidroc said, "At least I can speak to him, and he is willing to take us swiftly. The other ships are likely full, and may make many stops."

The fewer days I was aboard, the better, so I was not going to say anything to that.

"How much silver does he want to take us?" I made bold to ask.

"His ship is too small to take the horses. He knows I have to sell them, so he wants the equal of what I get for one of them."

This did not sound too unfair to me, as they had cost us nothing to begin with. "And you...trust him?" I had to know.

"No," he grinned. "But he wants to win against me at dice, and if he kills me he cannot do so."

We spent much of the afternoon sorting through our things, and choosing that which we would try to sell on the morrow. Our sturdy little horses had been heavy laden, and soon all we owned we must be able to once again carry ourselves. The knez had declared that any person could sell goods for one day without paying fees to him, and to lighten our load we determined what we would offer. The saddles and bridles we would need to sell with the horses, we thought, for those who wanted them would want these as well. The tent was too large to carry, and we could make another should we need it. We had as well some hides and one iron pot and other oddments which we rarely used, and these we set aside. Sidroc had no mantle, nor cloak of any kind, and each evening grew a little colder. He went with me to a cloth-merchant's stall and we traded the pot for a good length of heavy dark wool.

"Now I will have to win another pin," he jested, as we settled back at our camp.

I smiled at him, aware that all day I had not matched his high spirits. My workbasket was open before me, and I

306

threaded up one of the thin steel needles and began to hem the wool.

It did not take long, and the light was just failing when I snapped off the last thread and made him stand to see how it would fall over his shoulder. I put my new pin on it, as my own mantle could be fastened with the ties I had cut on the Idrisid ship. Other than stitching up his torn legging this was the first sewing I had done for him, and felt the homeliness of this task with some keenness.

We gathered wood for our fire, but did not yet strike it, and just sat before the tent in the gathering dusk. He was stretched out on some hides, his back against his saddle. His eyes were half lowered and fixed.

He was so quiet I had to ask. "What do you think of?"

He lifted his eyes to me. "Of you, in your red gown. And of taking the gown off you, and seeing you lying naked on your weaving."

I lowered my face quickly, but he went on.

"Of my hands, on your breasts and belly. Of how you will feel moving beneath me."

I knew his eyes were upon me, and he added, "Do not be shamed. Thinking on this has given me much delight. Also torment."

I had to look at him now, tho' I could not speak.

"For years I would awaken at night and want you next me," he went on. "Now when I awaken you are truly there, and I do not touch you."

I felt I could almost not bear the strength of this desire, and the strength that held him back from acting on it.

"You have had but one kiss from me," I began.

"Two," he cut in. "When the aurochs threw me, you kissed me awake."

"I did that to see if you lived," I answered.

"I lived," he returned, and his smile made the colour rise to my cheek.

"Two, then," I allowed. "But...you have wanted me for so long, thought so much on it. I am fearful that...I would not be all you hoped."

He thought about this. "Since we were captured I have seen you tired, filthy, and sea-sick. You have seen me bound, and knocked flat. At times we have raged at the other. But deep roots are not hurt by frost. I want you now more than ever I have."

His eyes were as steady as his voice. "You do not have to answer any of this, just as last night you did not answer when I asked if you would be my wife once we reached the land of the Prus. When you are ready, you will find a way to answer me."

Sidroc would not let me stand with him as he sold the horses and other things in the square, lest those who gathered round him thought I was to be traded, too. I fed apples to the horses as my parting gift, and stood by the fruit seller as he joined those with surplus by the wall of the great store house. The red-bearded Dane stood by him, to make certain, I felt sure, he received full value for the price of the better animal. Neither man got as much as he hoped, for with so many leaving by sea there were more horse-sellers than buyers; but the tent we made brought more than Sidroc had hoped, so this made up for some of it.

We packed a final time and made ready to go to the pier. I had made no friend amongst the women of this place, as I had the honey-women in the smaller trading post, and hoped that the folk of the Prus would be those with which I could one day feel at home. Thinking on all of this clutched at my heart, and added to the dread I felt at getting on another ship.

We had two large hide packs, and I had my workbasket, and my mantle which I wore; and Sidroc had both spears and his heavy shield, which he slung over his back with a leathern tie. He bade me keep my new necklace of braided silver hidden, and so I kept it inside my gown. We made our way to the crowded piers, and I saw the Mercian thegns and Father Eardwulf upon one already, piling their goods to take ship for some new port I did not know. After a while they saw me too, and we raised our hands to each other in Fare-well. Sidroc looked at me as I did this, and I felt he thought about the night I had walked off with those thegns, and given him fear that I would leave him, and not come back.

The Danes were all busy upon the ship, loading water barrels and ale casks and baskets of food and chests of those goods they had bought aboard. Like most men at this sort of work, they laughed and jested as they went about it, and chaffed each other in their gladness to be once again on their way; and when they saw Sidroc they called out and hooted.

But they did not look at me, and I wondered if Sidroc had made it known between them they were not to see me. Only Red-beard's nephew looked at me, and smiled with his crooked teeth, and I nodded my head and looked down at once.

Sidroc took everything from me, and went on first, and I walked across the planks with hands unfettered. He swung me down onto the deck. The ship was yet narrower than that of the Danes who had fought the Idrisids, and made even more crowded by a boat which lay beneath the great mast. It was small, the sort that would fit four or five men, no more, and had a short mast that could be raised to sail it with. Around this, and on every bit of free deck space, was lashed the goods as they came aboard.

Red-beard was already aboard, and soon all lading complete. At least this ship had fewer men than that of the other, but even so I was grateful we would be crammed in with them only two days. What was even better was that we would be coasting, and stop and spend nights ashore.

We moved our things to the bow, and men took their places at the oars, and on one side dipped them into the water, and pushed us away. The ship moved quickly in the still and shallow water, and the trading post grew small behind us. The day was not a bright one, and but little warmth could be felt from the weak Sun. I wrapped myself tightly against the freshening breeze and watched the green coast slip by, and tried to calm both my belly and my nerves.

I did not grow sick, and began by and by to feel more ease. Sidroc had been at the steering-beam talking to Red-beard, and now came forward with two loaves. I was grateful I

310

could eat, and after a while I stood up and looked across at the grey-blue waters.

"How will you teach me to swim?" I asked him. To me, swimming was something that one could either do, or not; as a duck could and a hen-fowl not. Gyric and Godwin had swam since boyhood, as if they had been born able to do it.

He laughed. "I will not teach you in the sea, it is too cold. Next Summer, when the water is warmest, I will take you to a lake, and teach you just as my own father taught me. I will hold you up in the water, and you will move your arms and legs until you can stay up yourself."

I thought of how my gown had bound around my legs and dragged me down. "In my shift?"

"The less you are wearing, the better," he smiled.

As dusk began to fall we headed closer into shore. The coast was sandy and Red-beard's men shipped their oars and using just the sail drove the ship upon the beach until it stopped. Men dropped into knee-deep water and waded ashore, and used the little boat to ferry me and our kit for the night to dry land.

Red-beard did not wish to build a fire, and attract the unwanted attentions of any who might be wandering the shores, but we had good blankets and did not suffer much chill. We ate, and I felt sleepy almost at once and went and lay down where we had spread our bed rolls. But Sidroc spent a long time talking with the men, and I guessed his wariness of them would make him the last to lie down.

There was a great deal of mist in the morning, with a fog rising from the water thick enough that it took me a moment to find the ship as it lay beached. I did not know how we could sail in such fog. Red-beard and one of his men stood at the water line, and we saw him hold something small in his fingers and lift it to the misty sky. Sidroc walked over to them, and in a short time back to me.

"He has a Sun-stone," he told me, as we readied our kit. "It will catch the gleam of the Sun in its eye, and so show him the way." I had never heard of this; it seemed a wondrous art, but Sidroc knew of them from past voyages.

We were on our way almost at once, and tho' the rising Sun burnt off some of the fog, it was hard to truly see the coast as we skimmed by. There was so little wind that the Danes rowed the whole time, but not hard.

At mid-day Sidroc was sitting near me in the bow. The sail had been lifted but no wind filled it, and wisps of swirling mist hovered above the water. Of a sudden we heard a shout, and a blazing point of light arced its way through the still air and buried itself in the damp sail cloth. It was an arrow, and its point was aflame.

It was followed by another, which like the first struck the sail and sputtered out, and a third, which fell upon the wood planks of the deck. The Danes were yelling as they shipped their oars, and we heard war-hoops and whistles not their own. Sidroc leapt up and pulled the flaming arrow from the deck and cast it overboard. I had dropped on my hands and knees, and watched him as he peered over the side of the ship at the coming enemy.

He flattened himself almost at once at my side.

"No," he said, and groaned. "No."

A racing thrill shot through me, that somehow these were men from Four Stones, but whether it was fear or hope I felt in that instant I could not say.

"The Trickster is really laughing at me," he said, and dropped open his hands. "This is Ulf, my brother who took the Idrisid ship, coursing for more game."

I took this in. "Who will you fight for?" I asked, in a panic that we were to be once again beset. I found my legs and began to stand, and caught one glimpse of the crowded ship gaining on our stern before he pulled me back down again.

"There is no choice. For the side that will win."

Red-beard's men were bellowing as they scrambled to arm themselves, grabbing spears, pulling on what protective gear they owned. Only Red-beard himself had a helmet.

Sidroc was on his knees now, and grabbed hold of a walrus hide line that lay coiled in the prow. "I have not seen him fight, but I think Red-beard no match for Ulf's men."

Once again he would be upon one ship, fighting against and amongst its warriors, as he tried to aid the onslaught of the other. "Lift your arms," he said.

I did so, speechlessly, and he tied the end of the line firmly about my middle.

"I can only say this once. I will cover you with our packs, and then I must go and fight. Try to stay behind this cover. Whatever happens, do not fight. Whatever side that wins will want you alive, and unharmed. But if you swing with spear or knife, you become the enemy, and will be hacked down. Ulf's

313

men will try to swarm this ship. If the fighting gets too hot about you, jump into the water, and hold fast to the line. It will get you out of the fighting, but the sea is cold. You will have to kick your legs to warm them, lest the cold saps all your strength and you sleep and drown before you can be hauled up."

A few men had run to lay hold of the boat upon the deck, and Sidroc stood up and joined them as they hoisted it over the side to clear the deck for fighting. Water splashed me as it hit the sea surface. Sidroc had the bow rope in his hands, and took a moment to pull the boat alongside and fasten the line to an oarlock. "If you can pull yourself into the boat, good. But never let go of the line I have tied you to."

He dropped on his knees and crammed me into the prow space, and began piling the packs before me. The ship was bearing down upon us now; I could tell from the yells of the men aboard our own, and from the way Sidroc straightened and looked at it. Their taunting cries grew louder. He grabbed his shield, and fitted his arm through it, took hold of the grip. He had no helmet and no ring shirt, and I was still not able to speak. I thrust my hand out and closed it about his ankle, the only thing I could touch.

He looked down at me, and then swept his eye over the men on the deck against whom he would soon turn.

"I will not die," he vowed to himself. "Not like this."

Then he moved down the deck to where Red-beard's men were massing. He stayed a little behind them and was careful not to let any of them near his back, and I saw he waited for the moment to call out to Ulf in signal. Ulf's ship was close enough now for spears to be flung from one to the

314

next, and men on both sides were howling oaths and clattering their swords against the iron of their shield rims. In the uttermost stern of the ship I saw Red-beard, with his young nephew at his side, baring his teeth as he swore at his attackers.

As horrible as land combat could be, battle at sea seemed much the worse to me, for there was no place of safety once your ship had been caught. The fighting must be fierce and fast in such tight quarters, and the merciless waves waited beneath to swallow any who fell.

I could tell from the closeness of its mast that Ulf's ship was nearing, and I braced myself for the impact. I thought of our ship being rammed, and sinking, and me being dragged to the dark bottom by the walrus hide line, and readied my knife so I could reach it and cut myself free if I need to; for I would rather drown splashing on the surface than be pulled speedily down by Ran's cold fingers.

The two ships struck, bounced back, struck again. I watched Sidroc stagger to his knees, stand, and yell through the air as he swung his sword at Red-beard's men nearest him. The first fell almost at once, slashed in the side so the blood flew up in bright droplets against the still unfurled sail. The second gaped open-mouthed as he turned his spear from Ulf's ship to fend off Sidroc's blow, and then dropped to his knees as Sidroc's blade found home.

Sidroc kept yelling, and now men from Ulf's ship were leaping across, and Red-beard's men were fighting them as they came. Now a few of Red-beard's men broke off, turning back to corner Sidroc, and he was forced down the deck nearer me.

There were three of them, and they came at him with such fierceness that he leapt backwards from the force of their blows. One had a spear, and the other two swords, and all had shields. They tried to get behind him, but he used the narrow deck to his advantage, and at one unguarded moment thrust his shield arm so violently at the spearman that he was caught off balance and fell into the shallow oar well. The man's scream filled my ears as Sidroc swooped down and raked his sword across the man's back. The other two gave ground at this, and Sidroc with his greater height was able to drive them near the mast. One backed into its girth, and for a moment hesitated, and in that moment was killed as Sidroc flung his blade under his slightly opened shield. Ulf's men were surging everywhere now, and had reached where Sidroc fought.

He had never stopped yelling the whole time, and it was the utter fury in his face as he hacked and slashed that made him fearsome. He seemed driven to kill beyond his hard training and long years of combat; and I knew he only lived because he fought every battle thus.

I did not scream as I watched this all, but crouched dumb, peering out with frozen eyes. Men closed around Sidroc, and he was lost to view; and thrown spears shuddered as they sunk their points into the deck planks before me. A few arrows smouldered nearby, the oil-soaked rags tied to their shafts sputtering low flame.

A knot of men were driven back to the bow, thrusting spears and swinging swords at each other. One was flung backwards and fell upon the packs covering me, and as he rolled off a spear followed him and sunk its point through a hide sack before me. The force of the thrown spear was such that the pack was slammed into my chest and the wind almost knocked from me. Its thrower jumped forward and ripped his knife into the man that still lay upon the deck, and the man's howling scream was followed by the hot gore that spurted from him. His blood shot across the bow and struck me in the face. As the killer began to straighten a third man leapt upon his back, and sliced through his throat so deeply with his sword that the head fell back, half severed from the neck. Blood pumped as a geyser into the damp air, the hot smell of it like metal in my mouth. It sprayed down upon the deck, red rain in the lifting fog, and without knowing how, I was on my feet and slipping through it. A man's arm lay there, blood still running from its stumped end, the green tunic of the sleeve gone crimson; and my booted foot touched it as I lurched forward. My fingernails dug into the smooth wood of the ship rail, and I cast myself over the side and into the waters below.

I glimpsed the little boat as I fell, and feared I might strike it, and saw bodies of slain men where they floated. Then I was jerked hard by the line I wore, as my legs tangled in it; and the sea closed over my head.

I was not screaming as I fell, so my mouth did not fill, and I popped to the surface and thrashed to loosen the line about my legs. I shook it free and began reaching hand over hand until I had pulled it taut and my head was above water.

The sea was so cold that I could scarce draw breath, and but for the pounding of my heart and churning of my belly I think I would have swooned in its icy grip. Ulf's ship had been made fast by lines to that of Red-beard's, but its dragon prow rested by the other's mast. I did not think any man marked my leap; from my vantage I could see but little upon either ship. Few could know and only one care that I had leapt. The small boat was not far from me, and I tried to thrash my way to it, but could not without loosening my line so much that I could no longer hold my head from the water. I could hear battle cries coming from above, and the screams of men as steel met flesh. One of them toppled backwards and dropped into the water, and the shield that floated from his now-still hand drifted near me. I kicked towards it, straining to reach it, and it came within my grasp. I took it in both hands and heaved myself a little upon it.

My teeth were chattering so that I thought they might break. My legs felt as if burnt, so cold were they; and I worked hard to move them as Sidroc had told me. I tried to call out, to part my lips and scream, but no sound came forth from my strangled throat. My fingers slipped from the cold iron rim of the shield and I clutched them so that they cramped. I thought of Sidroc, fighting upon that gore-soaked deck that he might live. I fought against my terror at what I had seen, and my terror of the waters carrying me down, and of the creeping cold already making numb my body; and I too struggled to live. The pale Sun stood overhead in a grey sky, and I closed my eyes and feared it the last thing I would see.

I drew breath. Something heavy lay against me, covering every part of me. It was not water; my face was dry. From under closed lids I could sense the sky above. One of my hands felt wet, and very warm. The other was against my thigh.

I opened my eyes. I saw the dark brown of Sidroc's hair near my shoulder. My left hand was pressed to his face and he was licking the back of it with his tongue. The grey sky was above us, and from the motion beneath I knew we were afloat.

He lifted his head and saw my opened eyes. He drew back the weight of his body from mine, and bent over me. He placed his mouth on mine.

"You cut your hand," he whispered, when he finished kissing me. He wrapped it with a scrap of cloth and tucked it under the sheepskins covering me. I felt the skin of my waist, and moved my hand. I was naked.

I lifted my head and saw the yellow gown I had been wearing and my green mantle spread out over the edge of the little boat. We were adrift in it.

"You were so cold," he murmured. "I had to get you dry."

I struggled to reach for him, and pulled my arms from the coverings. I laid my arms around his neck, and sobbed.

I held him with all the strength I had left in me, and cried so that as I kissed his face I trembled with the force of my flowing tears. He lived and was whole, and I alive and safe, and I clung to him with all the joy I felt in finding us so. His arms came up around my naked back, and he pressed me to him into his stillness.

When at last my tears stopped he kissed me again. He put his hand on my face and pressed his lips over mine. My hands slipped into his hair and I clung to him, and tasted him as fully as he did me.

When he drew back he was smiling at me. I saw my bloodied fingertips where they had rested in his hair.

"You are hurt," I managed to say.

My hand went back to his scalp and he winced when I touched the clumped hair.

"I got hit by something," he said. "The flat of a sword, or the rim of a shield, I think."

I tried to sit up, and as I did the sheepskins slipped down my breasts. He turned and pulled my hide pack within reach, and I knew the dark splashes upon it to be dried blood. I opened the flap and found my other shift and pulled it on. I knelt and put my hand on his shoulder, and turned his head so that I could see above his right ear.

"I need my shears," I told him, and reached for the workbasket I saw by his pack. I cut away the bloodied hair and found the gash. "It no longer flows," I said, grateful for this, for we had no earthgall nor any other herb to staunch the blood. "Does it pain you much?"

He shook his head. I dipped a square of linen over the side and daubed at the wound.

"I will not stitch it," I said. "If I had wine, I would do so, but with nothing to dull the pain it would hurt too much."

He nodded. "It will be all right. I did not even think it bled." A smile again crossed his lips. "You are a fine leech," he praised.

"Lady Modwynn knew much, and Edgyth even more," I told him.

"In fact, you do almost everything well," he went on. "We will work on the swimming."

I had to smile and sat back on my heels. My eyes began to fill with tears again as I looked at him.

"What happened?"

"Ulf won. I took this little boat as my share of the plunder."

I looked around at the water that surrounded us. "Were...were they all killed, Red-beard's men?"

"No. Not all, and Red-beard lives."

"Was the young one killed, his nephew?"

"Yes."

"Did...you kill him?"

"No. But I would have, if he was in my way. He was trying to prove himself, and was foolish."

I nodded, and thinking of the wrathful fury of his sword-work made it hard to form my words. "I never saw you fight before," I started. "You..."

"Yes," he answered. "That is why I live, and why my men took up with me."

I wanted to grasp his hands and hold them to me and tell him I never wished to see him fight again, but knew that if I did so I would once again weep. It was his skill that had kept him alive all these years, that and his cunning; and he used it freely to keep both of us from harm.

I was glad he spoke again, as I could not. He turned his head back across the water, to the ships now far out of sight.

The Claiming

"At first I cursed Loki the Trickster for making it Ulf, but then I saw that it was Freyja who sent him. It made it easy for me to know who to throw in with. She has always been watching over you, shield-maiden."

I only nodded, and as I did I think tears shook their way down my cheeks. His brow was smudged with blood and soot, and the arm of his tunic was ripped. His whole face looked pale and strained and I saw he was bone-tired.

"I must sleep now," he said, and put his arms forward to lower himself upon the sheepskins around us.

I plucked at the pile of blankets and skins I had been under, and drew them up around him. He winced as his head rested back, and he turned it slightly. I wrapped my arms about his neck and lay my head on his chest, and his arm folded around me. He fell into sleep so quickly that he did not hear me whisper to him.

Chapter the Twentieth: The Bourn

WE could not have slept long; the sky was unchanged when I felt him stir and I opened my eyes. I lifted my head. Sidroc was looking straight into the grey sky covering us. His arm was still about me.

His voice was hushed. "I dreamt you spoke to me. You said that which made me put my bracelet upon your wrist: That you were mine."

"You did not dream it," I whispered.

"Say it," he told me.

"I will be your wife, Sidroc."

In answer he pressed me to him with such strength that a gasp escaped my lips. At that moment the boat was slapped with a wave so that a little water splashed upon us. We sat upright.

The green-grey sea was flecked with small white crests that spread around us in advancing and retreating furrows. Sidroc let go his grasp on me and stared hard at the sky about us. It too was showing white, as scudding rain clouds billowed in the distance.

"We must be on our way," he told me, and set about ranging through a pile of things stacked near the small mast. "We could not have drifted far, but the sooner we start for shore the sooner we land."

"Where will we go?" I asked.

"The settlement of the Prus. We are only a day's sail, now." He gestured at the packs heaped in the bow. "I have food and water, and even a flask of ale. And I have this," he added, and took something small from his belt. He held up the Sun-stone. It was not much to look at, like a small crystal of dull yellow, but I knew that much that held magic did not look so. "I can find the Prus shore with it."

"Would Ulf not take us?" I asked, looking about at the rippling grey waters. Even with the Sun-stone and his skill, the boat was small for such a journey, I thought.

"He...is not welcome there," Sidroc said.

"O." I thought about all the things this could mean. "Did he say anything of it? The sort of place it is?"

"He said we should be careful."

This did not sound promising, but I said, "We are always careful."

He nodded and turned again to the short mast. I sat back on my heels and scanned the swelling waters. If I had not lived at Kilton and watched the sea from its fastness I would not believe that a still and sullen sky could shift so quickly, nor the sea change from flat grey to frothing foam before one's eyes. Our boat was small, and my throat narrowed to think of how it could survive if a storm of any force overtook us.

Sidroc had been rigging out the square sail, but now stopped and looked down at our possessions. "We must secure all we have," he told me, and took up one of the tanned hides we had been lying upon. He set it on the single bench and began to slice long narrow pieces of it. A wave bumped again at the boat, casting a bucket worth's of water at us. "Get the basin, and have it ready," he told me, and I dug it from the kit in our food-bag. I knew we might need to bail and tried to chase back my fear, but my stomach was lurching not only from fright but from the rise and fall of the boat as it rode the unsteady sea.

I took one of our pieces of linen and tied my work-basket closed, lest any of its precious contents be lost should it overturn. I rolled up sheepskins and stuffed them into our hide packs, and Sidroc and I lashed all these together in an ungainly mass. There were not many places in the small boat to secure things to, but we made all fast.

The bow-line was coiled in the bow, the same that Sidroc had secured to Red-beard's ship after he and the other Danes had lifted the boat over the side. He took it and tied it about me. "Even if it grows rough and you are thrown from the boat, you will not be lost," he told me.

I could not think about that, and only asked him, "And you? What if you are thrown?"

He shook his head. "If it gets bad I will lash myself to the mast."

Of a sudden the boat tipped as we were slapped by another wave, and he grabbed the basin and scooped at the water that now ran in the keel-channel. Rain began to fall, surprising me as the great rain-clouds were still far from us.

"It is no use to raise the sail now, lest we capsize," he said, and I ducked down on my knees at the base of the mast and tried to help him furl it firmly. It was of thick linen, tightly woven and stitched with more linen panels laid crosswise, and damp as it was took more strength than I had in my hands to roll neatly.

There was no steering-beam, the boat was too small for that, but there were four stout oars and Sidroc took one and worked at fixing it as a rudder. We would be swamped if he could not aim the bow against the oncoming waves, and I handed him many narrow strips of hide which he braided and twisted into one of the oarlocks to make a long and flexible tether for the oar.

I watched his strong hands do all this and tried to take comfort in his quick calmness. The sea rose and fell beneath us and my stomach lurched with each drop. I was biting my lip to keep the bile in my throat from rising and choking me. Even kneeling in the bottom of the boat it was hard to keep my balance, and I found myself swaying against the mast or the edge of the single bench. The rain beat down steadily, falling in straight narrow streams, and my head wrap, mantle, and hair were soon wet through. I took the basin and forced myself to work at scooping up the water that now I sat in. Each time the boat fell another wave slapped its tip inside, and the rain water and sea water mingled as I tried to fill the basin and toss it overboard. Sometimes the boat moved in a way that my throw missed and the whole contents splashed back into the bottom. I felt Sidroc grab the basin from me, and heard him say something, but I turned my head and was sick and his words were lost to me.

Since I had left Swanawic I had suffered sea-sick, and I had felt in peril of my life. Now I felt them both, and together, and was in more misery than I thought I could bear. It was made the greater by the sense that the settlement of the Prus was so near, and by Sidroc's belief that the Gods had truly been guiding us. Now all of it, the promise of near safety and the protection of the Gods, was swept away by the waves that tormented the little boat. I lay huddled in the bottom of the boat, retching into cold water that encircled me. Both hands were clinging to the base of the wooden mast, and I sobbed out Freyja's name, and begged Tyr to help us. I could not accept that they had brought us so far, and brought me to Sidroc's love, only to let us be destroyed now.

I know it grew dark, and that the rain lessened as the wind grew. Tho' I gripped the mast with all my might I was thrown from side to side against the bottom of the straked hull as the sea made sport with us. I tried to call to Sidroc, but above the whistling shrieks of the wind I do not think he heard me. I heard him tho', for at times the oaths poured from his lips as he battled to keep us upright and afloat.

It was day, and I was shivering. My fingers were still clenched about the mast base, and were cramped with cold. I pushed myself up out of the water I was lying in, and sat on my heels. Sidroc was asleep, lying over the shipped oar he had used as rudder. The sea was nearly flat. The brooding sky was grey, but no rain fell from it, and the wind ruffled his hair where it was beginning to dry. Our packs sat in the bow, the hides gleaming dully with wet.

I pulled off my head wrap, wiped my face with it and took a breath, trying to steady myself. I plucked at the line knotted about my waist but could not unloose it with my stiff fingers. I turned to our packs and found that which held our food. The leathern cords were stretched tight and I could not undo the knots, and barely could snap them with my knife. Our water flasks were earthen, well wrapped with straw, and I had further wrapped each in cloth when the storm started. I reached for the first. The linen towelling was soaked through and the flask it held cleaved in two. I pulled another flask and it was whole, and gratefully wet my lips. Holding it with care I crept to Sidroc.

I was loath to wake him; he had fought with the oar for hours and needed rest. But the steady wind pushed us ever onward, and I could not tell if each hour took us further or closer to our goal. I knelt before him, laid my hand on his shoulder and spoke his name. I could scarce awaken him, and the blear of his eyes told me how little he had slept. He took a single gulp of water and I asked him how he fared.

He dragged his sleeve across his face and looked around us. "I feel my broken rib, and my head throbs where I got hit. My shoulders are aching. But we are not sitting with Ran in her cold hall, so I am well." He just touched his hand to my face, and I smiled up at him.

All of our things were wet through, but none had been lost over-board. The greatest loss was of the broken water flask, but one remained, and another that held ale. We ate soaked bread and damp smoked fish, and did so with relish, and allowed ourselves a sip from the ale flask. The Gods had sent us another test, but had not forsaken us, and I gave thanks indeed that they watched us.

I could not guess what hour of the day it might be, whether forenoon or afternoon. The sky above us was perfectly flat and grey, and Sidroc stared up into it. He pulled the Sun-stone from out his belt and held it before him. He spent some little time squinting at it as he turned it round the sky above us, and at last returned it to his belt.

"There must be at least a glimmer of Sun for it to catch," he explained.

I looked around at the seemingly endless grey sea we drifted on, and the even more endless sky above us.

He glanced at the sail, stilled furled by the little mast. "I cannot raise it until I know where the Sun is, and thus East," he said, almost as to himself.

If it stayed grey we would drift the rest of the day. I tried to take comfort in the thought that it might clear at night, and then the stars be seen; but if at Kilton it could stay grey for days on end, it might be so here in the Baltic too. We had little food and even less water.

I did not speak my fear and Sidroc too was quiet. We scooped all the water from the keel-channel, and spread out some of our things to dry, for the breeze was light but steady. A long time seemed to pass, though the light was unchanging.

Of a sudden something swooped low near the boat, and passed over our heads. Large white wings oared gracefully through the dull sky. Sidroc moved to the mast at once, raising the sail. "We are going to follow that bird," he told me.

It flew with intent in a straight line across the clouded sky, and Sidroc marked well the bird as it grew ever smaller. I held fast to the side of the boat and strained to see its goal. I saw nothing but the vastness of the grey waters, but knew it must head for the land I trusted lay ahead. In truth I was gladdened to see any other living creature.

The sail filled and the wind held steady, and we went on for hours. Sidroc was behind the sail, and I before it in the bow, and our eyes searched the distant line where grey sea met grey sky. As the day began to dim the clouds lightened, and a stronger light showed where the Sun was heading down. That light lay before us; we were not headed East towards the coast that held the settlement of the Prus, but West.

I was turning back to crawl to Sidroc when he called out, "Land." He had half-risen from the bench, and his dark eyes were fixed above the hand he held outstretched before him.

I stopped and strained my eyes to catch what he had seen, and there it was, a long low smudge against the edge of the sky.

Sidroc kept the sail fixed towards it. The sky darkened, and as it did began to clear, so that a few of the brightest stars could be seen. I lay near our packs in the bow, drowsing and waking. A worn and waning quarter Moon rose. At last he let drop the sail and slept himself.

Dawn gave us dry air and the promise of a fair day. We ate half of our remaining smoked fish, and shared a crumbled loaf between us. As the Sun rose we gazed out across the ruddy water at the land now so much nearer. It did not look to have great hills, and some of it which was darker might be forest; but what caught my eye was that it had a beginning and an end. The land we neared was either a large island or the long tip of some greater land that thrust itself into the Baltic, and we could not know which it might be.

Another white-winged bird passed us as it made for the place. I smiled at the sight of it, and turned back to Sidroc.

But he was not thinking of our guide, but unlashing his spears and setting them ready to his hand. I saw him scanning the waters and was grateful no mist could obscure any ship about to beset us. We knew naught of this land, whether this place be one in which we would be welcome or not. Yet we needed water, food, and shelter, and sailed steadily forward. We hardly spoke, just kept our eyes fastened upon the nearing land.

We could see trees now, and broad swathes of some whitish stuff, sand or stone, and made out coves against the deeper backdrop of the land. The morning was clear and warm, and the sky deepened into a rich blue. No cooking-fire gave out smoke, and no timber hall or cottar's hut met our eyes.

I moved to the back of the boat. I did not ask the question which I knew he could not answer. Instead I just sat upon the bench while he trimmed the linen sail. We were approaching the land near one of its ends, where swathes of white seemed to fall away into sea water. As we grew nearer we could pick out great pillars of creamy stone rising from the beaches towards the sky. They stood quite alone, as if some giant race had built huge dolmans or cairns to mark the graves of their beloved dead. But these were not columns of stone rising straight, but twisted into shapes like unto gnarled ancient trees. I marvelled at them, and turned back to see Sidroc staring at them with fixed eyes.

"Raukar," he said. Of a sudden he began to laugh. "This is Gotland."

"What place is that?"

"An island in the Baltic far to the East of my home. My father told tale of it; he came once when he was young, trading for salt, and did not want to come home. Only the coast of Gotland has these limestone towers. In their speech they are called raukar. I never forgot his telling of it. There is a great trading post here, where numbers of folk live year round, and every kind of choice thing can be had. The Earth yields much and all the folk are rich."

This seemed almost too wonderful for truth, and a far better place than the settlement of the Prus.

"What king do they have?"

"None; they are their own people."

Now I liked this place even more, for no king meant no wars to fight for him.

Sidroc was scanning the empty beaches as we skirted the shore. "It will take a while for me to gather enough for a stake, but then I will buy some goods and start to trade." His weapon belt lay on our packs, and now his eye fell on it and rested on the wealth there. He gazed long on the bright hilt of his seax. "I will sell my seax," he said. "It will bring much silver."

I knew what it cost for a man like him to utter these words, that he would part in this way with a trusted weapon.

I watched him as he held the sail line fast in his hand. "I have gold," I told him.

His face showed his amaze.

The Claiming

"In my mantle." I gathered a fistful of the hem and held it out to him. "I had it in my jewel casket but Burginde scolded me for carrying so much treasure in one place, and stitched it up for me. When the Idrisid woman ripped the furs from the front she did not find it."

He stared mutely at the corner of cloth I held up in my hand. "You could not tell me before..."

My throat had tightened and I made steady my voice. I told him the truth.

"I feared you would use it to drive me yet further away." My last tear about his claiming of me ran from my eye, and I wiped it away.

He just looked at me, and then nodded.

I stood up and lifted the whole mantle to him, but he did not take it. "Now I give it to you, freely. You...can think of it as...my bridal-goods."

He reached for me, mantle and all, and held me to him, and kissed the top of my head.

"How much is there?"

"Twenty pieces, new minted."

"Twenty!"

"Yes, all new minted; they have not been nipped or filed."

Now he lifted his arms to the sky, and his face, too. "Freyja!" he cried. "I will Offer seven sows in thanks-giving for this day!"

His words spilled forth as he turned to me. "We will never take ship again. I will trade in costly goods and you will have the best of them. I will teach you to swim in warm waters. There is much snow here, but not harshness to the Winter, and you will have furs all about you when the snow comes. You will have fine linens on your bed, and the two daughters the old spice man prophesied, and sons too."

He laughed again, and I with him.

The Sun was lowering in the blue sky as we rounded the sandy tip of the island. We began to see farms set upon the grassy highlands, and flocks of sheep too. The trading post was on the East, and Sidroc did not know how far we might have to sail to find it, but if it grew dark we could beach the boat and go on next day. We sailed round a point and saw two ships heading straight into land. We passed a cove, and then of a sudden came upon the trading-post.

There were a score of ships run up upon the pebbly beach, and many small boats too. There were tall fish racks where flayed fish lay drying in the late Summer light, and pens where curly-horned sheep waited to be taken on board ship or into the countryside. A main road ran along the shore-line, and buildings great and small ranged about it, and several roads of pounded clay led up a gently rising hill. The buildings all had steep roofs and were of timber, but some had ends which were built of stone, which together I had never seen before. Although it was late in the day a few groups of men and women were walking along the roads, driving carts, or standing upon the shore near the ships.

Sidroc dropped the sail and ran the little boat up onto the beach. We climbed out, and when my feet hit the firmness of the wet pebbles my knees trembled with weakness and with gratitude too for solid ground beneath me. I stumbled to a large rock and sat there while Sidroc gathered our packs. A few people looked at us with interest, and a little girl playing on the beach with her brothers regarded me shyly, but no one troubled or challenged us.

We shouldered our packs. On the main road several buildings stood clustered in a sort of square, and one of them was a brew-house. The awnings were partially down, but we stepped inside. Off to one side sat a group of folk taking their meal at a rough trestle. One of them, an older woman, rose to meet us. She was an ample woman, and the jangle of keys hanging from her sash and wealth of bead necklaces around her plump neck told of her success as a brewster. Sidroc pulled silver from his belt and spoke to her.

Her tongue was not quite his own, and I could understand nothing save their first greeting, but after speaking to her for a time she gestured us to sit. I sunk upon a bench and we were brought deep cups of ale and pottery bowls of browis and a wooden platter of wheaten loaves. I did not know if I could eat, but after the first bit of bread I began to feel stronger, and realised how hungry I was. Sidroc ate as if famished, and had more of everything. We drank all the ale and sat next each other on the bench, saying little. I felt the ale and the food and the safety of the place and could not speak of any of it, but knew an ease unto pleasure at it all.

The brewster came back to where we sat and Sidroc questioned her, and they spoke at length.

He turned to me. "She owns a house at the end of this road. It is empty and we can stay there for the Winter, perhaps longer. There are some outbuildings, and a well so good it is full now, at Summer's end. In a few days she will be able to spare us a serving man and woman if we want them."

He spoke more to her, and then we were lifting our packs and setting out into the twilit day. Fewer folk were about now, and the Sun was raking its long red fingers into the darkening water. We turned and walked up the hard clay road. There were small houses on both sides, and then a few crofts of work-men, and then the road rose and we climbed with it. It ended at a house. It had a high steep roof, and timber walls, and the two narrow ends of it were of stone, as some of those we had seen below. We turned into the yard and looked back over the trading post and sea beyond. The Sun was dropping fast, and the water pushed its dying rays to us like shimmering silk. We stood together and gazed on this, and my whole heart went out to this steep-roofed house and the place wherein it sat.

"There is room for a garden here," was all I could say.

Sidroc nodded, and reached out his hand to me, and I took it. This would be home to me, as he had always been home to me, set fast in my very core. Through the joys and loss and sorrow I had met since first I stood before him as a maid of fifteen Summers it had been so. We were alike, and now would live as one.

Sidroc put the key the brewster had given him into the iron box-lock, and pushed open the door. I could just make out the fire pit in the middle of the floor, and that there were alcoves, and a window, and a wall with a door that led to another room.

The Claiming

He set to work with flint and iron, kindling the charcoal that remained in the fire pit. I took my pack and stepped into the other room.

When I returned Sidroc was kneeling by the fire. He had just unrolled my plush weaving, and he turned his head to look at me when I came in. I stood before him in the red gown.

He rose. His left hand went to his right wrist, and he unfastened his silver disk bracelet from it for the last time. He took my left hand and fixed the cord of the bracelet around my wrist. Its warmth encircled me.

"This has always been yours, shield-maiden," he told me. "Years ago I swore to you that in one land or another, one day you would sit at my side. White-armed Freyja never forsook you, nor did I. My vow to you is in every thing I have done to bring us alive and well to this place, and every day of the long years I wanted you."

My answer was in my kiss.

Ceridwen, wife of Sidroc of Gotland

Calendar of Feast Days mentioned in the Circle Saga

Candlemas - 2 February

St Gregory - 12 March

High Summer - 24 June

St Peter and Paul - 29 June

Hlafmesse (Lammas) - 1 August

St Mary - 15 August

St Matthew - 21 September

All Saints - 1 November

Martinmas (St Martin's) - 11 November

Yuletide - 25 December to Twelfthnight - 6 January

Anglo-Saxon Place Names, with Modern Equivalents

Æscesdun = Ashdown

Æthelinga = Athelney

Basingas = Basing

Caeginesham = Keynsham

Cippenham = Chippenham

Cirenceaster = Cirencester

Defenas = Devon

Englafeld = Englefield

Ethandun = Edington

Exanceaster = Exeter

Glastunburh = Glastonbury

Hamtunscir = Hampshire

Hreopedun = Repton

Jorvik (Danish name for Eoforwic) = York

Legaceaster = Chester

Limenemutha = Lymington in Hampshire

Lindisse = Lindsey

Lundenwic = London

Meredune = Marton

Sceaftesburh = Shaftesbury

Snotingaham = Nottingham

Sumorsaet = Somerset

Swanawic = Swanage

Wedmor = Wedmore

Witanceaster (where the Witan, the King's advisors, met) =
    Winchester

Frankland = France

Haithabu = Hedeby

Land of the Svear = Sweden

Glossary of Terms

browis: a cereal-based stew, often made with fowl or pork

ceorl: ("churl") a freeman ranking directly below a thegn, able to bear arms, own property, and improve his rank

cottar: free agricultural worker, in later eras, a peasant

cresset: stone, bronze, or iron lamp fitted with a wick that burnt oil

ealdorman: a nobleman with jurisdiction over given lands; the rank was generally appointed by the King and not necessarily inherited from generation to generation. The modern derivative *alderman* in no way conveys the esteem and power of the Anglo-Saxon term.

frumenty: cereal-based main dish pudding, boiled with milk. A version flavoured with currents, raisins and spices was ritually served on Martinmas (November 11th) to ploughmen.

seax: the angle-bladed dagger which gave its name to the Saxons; all freemen carried one.

scop: ("shope") a poet, saga-teller, or bard, responsible not only for entertainment but seen as a collective cultural historian. A talented scop would be greatly valued by his lord and receive land, gold and silver jewellery, costly clothing and other riches as his reward.

thegn: ("thane") a freeborn warrior-retainer of a lord; thegns were housed, fed and armed in exchange for complete fidelity to their sworn lord. Booty won in battle by a thegn was generally offered to their lord, and in return the lord was expected to bestow handsome gifts of arms, horses, arm-rings, and so on to his best champions.

trev: a settlement of a few huts, smaller than a village

tun: a large cask or barrel used for ale

wergild: Literally, man-gold; the amount of money each man's life was valued at. The Laws of Æthelbert, a 7th century King of Kent, for example, valued the life of a nobleman at 300 shillings (equivalent to 300 oxen), and a ceorl was valued at 100 shillings. By Ælfred's time (reigned 871-899) a nobleman was held at 1200 shillings and a ceorl at 200.

Witan: Literally, wise men; a council of ealdorman, other high-ranking lords, and bishops; their responsibilities included choosing the King from amongst their numbers.

withy: a willow or willow wand; withy-man: a figure woven from such wands

Additional notes to The Claiming

The retelling of the Wedding at Cana told by the priest Wilgot in Chapter the Third is taken from the *Heliand*, the Saxon gospel, written by an unknown author in the first half of the 9th century. The *Heliand* presents the New Testament in the form of a saga, with Christ as a powerful chief.

The Viking Sun-stone mentioned in Chapters the Nineteenth and Twentieth is a piece of calcite crystal.

About the Author

Octavia Randolph has long been fascinated with the development, dominance, and decline of the Anglo-Saxon peoples. The path of her research has included disciplines as varied as the study of Anglo-Saxon and Norse runes, and learning to spin with a drop spindle. Her interests have led to extensive on-site research in England, Denmark, Sweden, and Gotland. In addition to the Circle Saga, she is the author of the novella *The Tale of Melkorka*, taken from the Icelandic Sagas; the novella *Ride*, a retelling of the story of Lady Godiva, first published in Narrative Magazine; and *Light, Descending*, a biographical novel about the great John Ruskin. She has been awarded Artistic Fellowships at the Ingmar Bergman Estate on Fårö, Gotland; MacDowell Colony; Ledig House International; and Byrdcliffe.

She answers all fan mail and loves to stay in touch with her readers. Join her mailing list and read more on Anglo-Saxon and Viking life at www.octavia.net.